BRE LUCAS-ROBERTS

THE REAL ESTATE OF
LUCY BELLTOWN

For information regarding permission, please write to:
info@barringerpublishing.com
Barringer Publishing, Naples, Florida
www.barringerpublishing.com

Design and layout by Linda S. Duider
Cape Coral, Florida

ISBN: 978-1-954396-81-4
Library of Congress Cataloging-in-Publication Data

Printed in U.S.A.

Dedication

To Conor, my first and only love, whose simple question,
"Is there anything you've always wanted to do?"
set this journey in motion.

I dwell in possibility.

– Emily Dickinson

Contents

BRE LUCAS-ROBERTS

CHAPTER ONE

Lucy's Dilemma

Lucy felt the gritty sand rub under her feet as she stepped across the rough, weathered boards, flanking the porch. She knew she could sweep it away, but it would come right back. After eighty years, she was used to it and welcomed it.

She arched her back, placing her hands on her hips and stretched. She lowered herself into her weathered rocker, letting it hold her as she rested her elbows on the chair's frame. The duct tape was peeling where she had wrapped it to hold the wicker in place. Most people would have thrown the chair to the curb, but not Lucy. Lucy leaned her head back and stared up at the overhang. The paint was peeling away in big patches, leaving the brown wood paneling exposed. This time, she would have to ask for help. The boards wouldn't paint themselves and climbing a ladder was out of the question. She hated to admit that the house needed a lot of repairs, and it annoyed her that she couldn't keep up with the ever-growing list of to-dos.

She sighed loudly, *if only things had gone as planned*, she thought. She felt it in her bones. It was time for the house to switch hands.

It passed to her when her daddy became ill, and it would have belonged to her brother if he had made it past his thirtieth birthday. But as many did during the war years, he gave his life to his country and was buried alongside the other heroes. Lucy's mama kept his old fishing rod leaning against the fireplace mantle, and Lucy had it there to this day. A quiet reminder of their shared love of fishing.

She coughed into the fold of her elbow, feeling the rise and fall in her chest. Her daddy had built this home, hammered every nail himself and selected each board with care. The house was built with love and determination. He was building a legacy, for generations to come, and it was his hope that a Belltown should always reside under its roof. It wasn't just a house; it was a depository of stories. The echo of tales of the lives lived within its walls—the parties they used to host, fresh crab and clams served on silver platters outside on picnic blankets, fishing expeditions, and the storms they survived—each one preserved within the very walls.

Though time had weathered the house's appearance, it belonged to her, and she held that close like a badge of honor. As a child, she could stand on the steps, and during high tide, throw a rock and it would land with a plunk, into the salty sea. She was that close. Without being washed away, Lucy's house was about as close as a house could be to the shoreline.

In comparison to the sprawling mansions rising around her, filled with imported tiles, Tiffany glass, and boasting twelve or more bedrooms, Lucy's house stood as a humble testament to a simpler time. Despite its modest appearance, it held a treasure no other Naples home could claim—fifty coveted acres of beachfront, a sprawling corner lot at the very tip of Gordon Pass inlet. Despite the regular flow of realtors knocking on her door, with a gleam in their eyes, Lucy was no fool; she knew exactly what that "prime real estate" was worth. More than money, legacy mattered most.

She looked out, squinting her eyes. The endless view never disappointed.

Lately, she found herself pining away her time on her back porch, her favorite spot. The ocean was kind to her and didn't require much in return. She crossed her ankles, her eyes falling to the worn steps that descended to the beach. Yesterday, she almost had a spill, as the bottom board had finally come lose. She'd been surprised they'd lasted this long; half a century of salt and sand could wear down anything. She smiled, thinking of her father, hammering nails into the boards, his strong hands building something to last. However, nothing lasts forever. Like many things to do with Old Blue, the steps needed replacing.

She did not want to think about that now and closed her eyes, allowing the sun to warm her skin. The waves sounded soft and smooth, like the echoes of her childhood. Lucy could tell anyone the tides, in the blink of an eye. She knew them, as she would a composition played on her piano. The rhythm of the sea was enshrined in her heart and trained to her ear. The sea a soundtrack to her life. This was her home.

Her father's dream, a Belltown always living under Old Blue's roof, was fading quickly. She had to act. Like champagne bubbles rising to the surface at a rapid rate, so did her regrets. Unlike her close bond with her father, her relationship with her daughter was broken. She clenched and unclenched her gnarled hands, feeling the tightness of age.

Lucy heard her best friend, Sandy, before she saw her. Although a petite woman, she had heavy feet. She would have made a terrible thief. Sandy came around the corner in a burst of hot pink. She was wearing her all-time favorite flamingo dress.

"Yoo-hoo," she waved her hand in the air as she caught sight of Lucy on the porch.

"Well, you're up early," Lucy said back as she stood ready to greet her friend.

Sandy took each step, one at a time, holding onto the loose railing.

"Ah, here we are." Sandy embraced Lucy then finding an empty chair gingerly sat down, letting her lime green handbag land with a thud next to her.

"Tough morning?" Lucy remarked and looked at Sandy.

Sandy sighed, "Just the same old bull from the city. Sam Swanson called me this morning at 7:00 a.m., can you believe the gall of that man? He thinks he runs this town."

The city of Naples was cracking down on building permits. With so many new homes going up and going up fast, they were running around like chickens with their heads cut off, squawking "no" at everyone just to keep a sense of order.

"All I want is to turn my walk-in closet into my bathroom, is that too much to ask? An old lady wants to walk five steps to the toilet not twenty-five." Sandy shook her head in annoyance.

"Did you tell him that? You know, those exact words," commented Lucy.

"Of course not, that's too personal!"

Lucy smirked. "Well, it might have helped. Maybe, he would have felt bad for you and your bladder and signed off on the paperwork."

They sat and listened to the sound of the waves. Comfortable in each other's presence, it helped that they had been best friends since first grade. Folks assumed they were sisters, and they were never quick to correct it.

Lucy broke the silence, "Well, you're looking very pink today."

"Thank you," Sandy nodded her head in recognition, sensing the sarcasm. "I like my colors, and it wouldn't hurt for you to wear something other than those old things from time to time." Lucy had so many lovely dresses in her closet, but she had barely touched them let alone wear them since Bill died.

"I am sensible and practical," Lucy said, looking at Sandy with accusing eyes. "I don't need fineries to make me happy." Sandy didn't need to know that Lucy had already mended her linen pants in five separate places, and they had once belonged to her mother.

"Well, you could at least throw those away," Sandy eyed Lucy's tattered pants, raising her brow.

"Waste not, want not, Sandy."

"Oh phooey, you are still as stubborn as the day I met you. And, speaking of 'waste not, want not;' I'm wasting away in this heat. Do you have any iced tea, honey?"

"I have some cooling in the fridge, a fresh batch I made an hour ago."

Lucy went inside, letting the screen door snap shut behind her. She wiped the few beads of sweat from her brow. The house felt cool and shaded. Despite the climbing heat, the ocean breeze kept it exactly right. The large, live oaks towered over Old Blue, giving it a covering on hot days. Right after purchasing the fifty acres, Lucy's daddy spent time, collecting live oak seeds. He then sprouted them, carefully monitoring their growth. As they gained their limbs, he planted each one, by hand, all around his property.

Howard Belltown, her daddy, a legend with his green thumb, transformed their land into a paradise that drew exotic birds and admiring gardeners. Lucy, placing cups on a tray, looked out the kitchen window. Who would care for the trees after her? She couldn't bear the thought of them being cut down.

Lucy filled the two amber-colored glasses to the top and stirred a spoonful of sugar into each. As she carried the tray back outside, the ice clinked and popped, already beginning to melt. Lucy pushed the screen door with her hip, setting the tray before Sandy. Her tummy growled—she must have forgotten to have breakfast.

"I didn't know you had a dog," Sandy joked, hearing the same rumbling sound.

"I'm a little hungry, it seems," Lucy laughed.

"Can I offer you a ham sandwich?" Lucy didn't wait for Sandy's answer. She turned to go back inside. "It's never too early for ham on sourdough."

"Okay, but let me help you." Sandy set down her glass and stood.

"I'm not old and decrepit; I can make a ham sandwich." Thwack, the screen door closed behind Lucy.

"I'll take mine with no mustard, please." Sandy shouted through the screen and a disappearing Lucy.

Lucy busied herself with the sandwiches, throwing them together in a moment. She placed a pickle wedge and a handful of potato chips on each flowered plate. She walked back outside, "here you go," she handed Sandy her plate, "no mustard indeed. When did you stop taking mustard?"

With chips already in her mouth, Sandy mumbled, "today."

Sitting down, Lucy shook her head. She unfolded a checkered napkin, laying it over her thighs.

"I'll never tire of this view, Lucy." The chair creaked under Sandy as she rocked. Sandy pulled little wedges of her sandwich apart, squeezing them between her finger and thumb as she plopped each morsel into her mouth.

"Eye candy, that's what daddy used to call it." Lucy said pointing toward the expanse. "Especially at sunset." What lay before them was a sight no human could capture with paints and a brush. It was what her daddy always said, "That is God's daily bread to you, Lucy, it will fill you up."

Her daddy had a lot of one-liners. Lucy sunk her teeth into her sandwich. "Hmmm," she chewed, leaving little streaks of mayo and mustard in the creases of her mouth. "There's nothing like comfort food to ease the ailments of age." Ham on sourdough, a staple in Lucy's life. A signature Belltown feast.

Sandy nodded and sipped her tea. She watched Lucy.

"How are you feeling today?"

"Oh, same old, same old." Lucy's voice was too upbeat. "You know me, Sandy, life is too good to find fault with it."

Life had dealt Lucy some tough blows. Life had not played by the rules, and several times had nearly knocked Lucy down for good. Sandy's hands lay gently in her lap. She faced forward. Ceased rocking. Her lips creased into a tight line.

"So, when are you going to admit it's not okay, Lucy?" A hint of frustration in Sandy's voice made Lucy squirm. Although Lucy tried to avoid the recent squall, every storm's wake demands a choice: confrontation or escape.

Lucy set her plate on the wicker table beside her and watched a seagull swoop into the ocean and arise a victor—a silver fish dangling from its beak. Sandy turned toward Lucy. Lucy felt her hazel eyes drilling into the side of her head. She fidgeted with her gold wedding band, twisting it around and around on her finger. She licked her lips and wiped her mouth with her napkin.

"Well, are you going to answer me," Sandy said loudly, "or just sit there like a spud in a mud hole?"

"Listen, Sandy," Lucy said, her voice firm. "Pity parties have never been my style. You should be thanking your lucky stars that I'm not some cranky old bird, sitting here all day, bored and cursing at anyone who dares come near. And contrary to widely held belief, I'm not about to plant myself in a chair and wither away, without a fight. You know me better than that. I've never been one to sit still, and I'm not starting now." She shifted in her chair, straightening her back. Conversations like this drained her.

"Some things never change," Sandy answered as she placed her hands on her face and rubbed her eyes. "Stubborn as always and forever shall be."

Lucy felt like she had to defend herself. She stood up and faced Sandy. Her small slender hands found her hips.

"You listen to me." Her heart began to race. Sandy just shook her head as Lucy found her voice.

"I'm a Belltown. My daddy taught me to till the soil, the ground that no one wanted to touch. The dirt filled with briars and thorns, weeds, and rocks. That's all this land was when we bought it. And look at it now. I won't give up."

"You know I'm not talking about the house," Sandy said as she set her plate on the table next to her. The leftover sandwich had gone soggy as it absorbed the pickle juice.

"Neither am I." Lucy's voice caught.

Lucy walked to the railing and leaned against it, letting her elbows rest on the firm wood.

Sandy rose and stood next to Lucy. She whispered, "Tell me how to walk with you in this, Lucy."

Lucy patted Sandy's hand.

"I wish I knew, Sandy."

"You gonna finish that?" Lucy turned and pointed to Sandy's sandwich.

Sandy shook her head no. "It's all yours!"

Lucy picked it up and took a big bite.

"Oh, how my daddy loved his ham on sourdough." She laughed. "I made him a whole plate of them weeks before he passed. He sat right where I'm sitting now." Lucy finished chewing.

"Daddy had the same disease that lives in me."

Sandy found her rocker and turned it to face Lucy, listening intently.

"Daddy never smoked a day in his life; can you believe that?"

"And, neither have you," Sandy added. Lung cancer. Some increased the risk with their daily habits; others were simply unlucky. It was a cruel lottery, like a child blindly pinning the tail on a donkey.

"Daddy gave me his dream, this big, old house when he passed, and I guess that wasn't the only thing he gave me." Genetics. A blessing and a curse.

Lucy wiped her fingers on her napkin. The plate was now empty.

"One afternoon, he was so sick, Sandy. He did not leave his bed all day. That evening, mama and I lifted him up and helped him get to the porch. We wrapped him in his favorite quilt, and we sat with him, the three of us, watching the surf. I asked him, 'How are you coping, Daddy?' You know what he said to me?"

"Tell me again," Sandy nodded, letting her body relax.

Lucy smiled. "He said, 'The pain runs deep in my body, and its voice is loud, but I don't let the pain tell me how I'm going to live.' He embraced each day, and he never complained. He gave his best right up until the end."

"He was one of the good ones." Sandy nodded.

"That he was." Lucy heard the catch in her voice. Decades later, she still missed her daddy—the salt of the earth. She wished she had been more like him. He was a man that could take a trouble and turn it in many directions until it led to a solution. Tender, yet tough as the steel nails he hammered into every board of Old Blue. He was quick to forgive a wrong. Always willing to help a person in need. "And boy, did he laugh—a lot." Lucy remembered, chuckling. "If I could even be half the human he was, I believe I would have lived a full life."

Lucy looked down at her lap and brushed away the few sandwich crumbs, she watched them fall to the ground.

Lucy heard the blaring ring of the phone through the open door. Her body jerked. "I better get that; it might be my doctor." She rose from her chair and hurried inside, hoping she could catch it before they hung up.

"Hello?"

Dr. Sams cleared his throat. "Ah, Lucy, I'm glad you're home."

She listened patiently as he went through his list of formalities. "How are you today?"

She wished he would just bypass niceties and come out with it!

"Well, you know why I'm calling."

She shook her head and rolled her eyes. She felt like a small child. Of course, she knew why he was calling.

"I'm sorry to tell you this."

From the sound of his voice, she already knew where this conversation was going. She listened but half of what he was saying was going in one ear and out the other. She grabbed the pencil and pad that she kept close to the phone and tried to write down the big words he was using. He listed stats and numbers, things she did not fully understand. He listed percentages, life expectancy and level of acuity as though it was to be her summer camp pack list. He had said enough. She set the pencil down. She was dying, and there was nothing more they could do for her but make her as comfortable as possible. She listened as he prattled on. She eventually sat on the stool and leaned her head against the wall. *How often does he have to give bad news*, she wondered. It no longer helped for her to know that the medication had proved resistant or chemo would only add a few more months to her life. She was dying and no one or no miracle drug could stop that.

"Again Lucy, this is not the outcome I had wished. You fought hard."

"Thank you, Dr. Sams, and really, I know you did everything you could." She felt like saying five cuss words really fast and loud but thankfully she missed her chance, as he had already hung up. He was a good man. But that didn't change the fact that Lucy was angry. Angry and sad. Dr. Sams would have been an innocent punch, her anger was not at him, it was at herself. Lucy faced the unbelievable truth: the disease would cut her life short. A life she was certain still held so much more. A cold anger settled on her, directed at her own failing strength.

Lucy walked back toward the porch slowly. She ran her hand along the wall as she went. Hoping the house would absorb some of the weight she carried. Outside, Sandy was leaning back on the chair, with her eyes closed. Lucy steps were slow and silent. The porch announced her arrival, groaning beneath her steps. Sandy looked up. Lucy stood motionless, holding the screen door. Out of nowhere, the wind blew. A gust swept through the porch, lifting stray leaves into a dance. As fast as they went up, they fell again. At least now, Lucy had answers, no more emotional roller coaster. She felt frozen in place. The distant sound of Sandy's voice thawed her.

Sandy stood and walked over to Lucy.

"I take it wasn't good news."

"How can you tell?" Lucy smiled.

"You couldn't hide that crush on Bobby Sears in eighth grade from me, and you're not hiding this now."

Lucy looked at Sandy, her eyes moist with tears. "It's my eyes, isn't it?"

Sandy nodded, ". . . they've always been a dead giveaway, my friend.

Lucy needed the humor, like she needed oxygen. It helped when she was afraid.

The warm salt air stuck to her tears. They dried in place. She could hear the waves and gulls in the distance. The sound was sharp, like she was standing in their midst.

"He said less than a year."

Sandy gasped. Then regained her composure. Lucy faced out toward the yard, her hands on her hips. She could not bear to see Sandy upset.

"We gave it our best shot didn't we," Lucy looked at Sandy with a wistful smile.

"You won't be alone, you know."

"I just wish Bill were here," Lucy said softly.

"He's not, but you know we are." Sandy reached her hand out to Lucy's shoulder. Sandy and Jim had always been steady fixtures in her life through all the ups and downs.

Lucy suddenly felt her full eighty years. She found her chair and sat down.

"Damn." Lucy pounded her fist in her lap.

Sandy knelt next to Lucy, resting her cool hand on her wrinkled arm.

"I suppose we all wish we could fall asleep then wake up gone, like a wisp of air. God knows that is my wish." Lucy looked at Sandy who was trying to inject lightheartedness into a tense situation.

"You know you've always been good at that." Lucy quipped.

"What?" Sandy asked, a hint of amusement in her voice.

"Taking serious situations and adding some wit. Most people would look at you cross eyed, but I love you for it Sandy."

Sandy squeezed Lucy's arm and stood up. She walked over to the railing and leaned against it, looking at Lucy in her rocker.

Sandy was uneasy, she fiddled with her gold watch, "You know she needs to know."

Lucy lifted her brows, "And, what makes you think she is going to change her mind after all of these years?"

"Well, things are different now."

"She hates this place." Lucy shook her head rapidly. Lucy saw not just the end of her own life, but the end of an era. The house, a silent witness to generations, would fall silent with her.

"You need to at least try and make some repairs, Lucy."

Lucy felt her body tense. "You have no idea how much work it takes to keep up a place like this all alone. I'm doing the best I can."

Sandy sighed, "I'm not talking about the house."

"Well, I am." She cocked her head to the side. Welcoming the course change in the conversation.

"And don't you get any fancy ideas about contacting her yourself. I will tell her when I am ready."

Like many of Lucy's oldest friends in Naples, Lucy too was depending on her only living daughter to keep the family home from being torn down. Lucy knew Grace despised this old house, but it was her only hope. Lucy would not go down without a fight. Old Blue would not be handed off like a handshake to a stranger. Like her father before her, she would give all she had to preserve her family's legacy.

Lucy knew Sandy was right. But she hated to admit it.

"Just promise me you will tell her." Sandy stuck her chin in the air ending the conversation and went and picked up the lunch plates. Lucy would make no such promise. Sandy went inside. Lucy turned around, her eyes landing on the beach glass wind chime Grace had made in eighth grade. Over the years, Lucy had to superglue or restring it, to keep it intact. The day Grace had given it to her, she had proudly held it up, the sunshine catching each smooth piece of glass.

"Look Mama, our collections, from our walks, all of our little gifts from the sea!"

"Well, isn't that clever," Lucy had remarked, as Grace gently handed it to her.

"I thought you would like it!" Grace beamed.

Like Lucy, Grace loved beachcombing and finding little treasures.

"Well, I love it, and I'm going to have dad hang it up as soon as he gets home," Lucy wrapped her arm around Grace's waist, pulling her close. She kissed the top of her head.

"Gifts from the sea," she said slowly, liking the sound of that phrase.

She held Grace out in front of her, a warm smile on her face.

"You are my gift from the sea, Grace Marie."

Lucy's memory waned, as she stood and walked to the chime, hanging from the eve. She fingered the remaining weathered pieces, feeling the smoothness of the edges, worn down over time. She was afraid of what Grace would say, yet she knew she owed this to her daddy, to the house, and to herself to have the conversation she had avoided for so long. A breeze blew the glass pieces and they clinked against one another. Maybe, just maybe, things could be different; one could aways hope.

Chapter Two

Anna's Decision

Anna set the letter facedown on the dashboard of the truck. She knew if she kept it there, she wouldn't lose it. She was prone to misplacing things, but the letter was as good as gold, and she would make sure it arrived to it's destination. In fact, it was the reason she had loaded up her dad's old truck and was driving east. She had been tempted to open it, but something held her back, a gentle gut response, that it wasn't hers to open. And now, here she was behind the wheel of a beat-up pick-up, embarking on an adventure.

She adjusted the side mirrors and the rear-view mirror as she checked the gas gauge one more time. Her dad's truck had been known to lean too comfortably on the full side when the truck was close to empty. She noticed the truck was already stuffy. Gus, her dog was panting, adding another five degrees to the warm vehicle.

She leaned over him and manually rolled down his window. Each rotation of the handle slowly allowed delicious pine-scented air to fill the car. Grateful, Gus licked her face and shoved his head out, sniffing. Anna sat in the driveway not quite ready to leave. She reached for the letter. She held it, turning it to the front and then back again, inspecting it for the hundredth time. She knew that if she found the smallest tear, she would take that as a sign that she should open it. It was sealed and buttoned up tight. She reminded herself, yet again, that it was not hers to read. If everything she had been told over a lifetime was true, why was there a letter in her mom's handwriting addressed to this person? Her mom's story was no longer intact. She stared at the address again, running her finger over it. If anything, this letter only added more holes and gaps.

She knew the creamy white envelope would continue to remain a temptation, so she sighed and stuffed it into the middle console, next to her dad's collection of sunglasses and maps. "Out of sight, out of mind," she said looking over at Gus.

The day she found the letter in the drawer of her mom's nightstand was the day she started planning this trip. That was over four weeks ago. It was time to let her brother know what she was up to. Anna dialed the long international number, knowing she would be waking him up.

"Hello?" Sam said in a sleepy voice.

"Sam!"

"Anna . . . is everything okay?" he said, suddenly alert.

She knew that living in a remote location such as Antarctica, Sam only received necessary calls.

"I'm fine, how are you?"

"Okay, good. You know I'm well; I was just sleeping." He said with a chuckle.

"Sorry, yes, about that, sorry for waking you, but I found a letter in mom's drawer."

"What type of letter?"

"Well, it appears as though mom didn't tell us the whole truth."

"Are you still going through her things?"

"I've cleared out the big stuff; it is more paperwork and old pictures I'm sorting now."

"Thanks for doing that, Anna, sorry I can't be there. The ice caps wouldn't let me take off another month."

Anna laughed, thinking of her brother, the ocean explorer. In many ways, he was a younger version of their mom.

The phone line started to buzz, and Anna knew it meant their time was ending. The old satellite phones were not dependable for chit-chat.

"Anyway, I know you need to go, I will reach out soon, when I find out more. I am driving to Florida, Sam."

"You're, going where?" The line broke.

"Florida, I sent you a letter! I love you." Click.

She had mailed a letter to Sam earlier in the week, detailing her trip. She told him she would forward her new address once she reached her destination. Most of all, she tried to reassure him that she was okay and not to worry. She and Sam were orphans now, all they had were each other.

She started the truck and let it idle. Black smoke from the exhaust pipe moved from the back to the front then slowly drifted into the trees. Although the truck had been sitting for a while, it still had some life left in it. "Well, here we go, Pacific to Atlantic." She tapped the steering wheel with her fingers, remembering an old Christmas song with lyrics about the traffic being terrific.

She put the truck into reverse and backed up. Her dad's Ford pickup was packed to the gills with everything she owned; she planned to stay in Naples until she found who she was looking for.

She looked longingly in the rearview mirror at her house. The only home she had known, tucked into the white pines, covered in shade. Her insides churned; she had to do this. She and Sam had agreed it was time to sell the house. He was happy with his life, and she would carve out a new one in Florida, at least for now. She wondered if she was off her rocker as she and Gus drove down the gravel road. When she reached Florida, there would be no one waiting for her. She had not secured a place to live. Was she chasing a puff of smoke? One letter. That's it. It was why she had to go.

She passed cabins as she left the trees and drove into the clearing. The Adams family, the Tanners, and Shoemakers helped her clean up the house, donate items, and sell others. Neighbors who had been like family to her.

She looked over at Gus, "Take it in, buddy, this may be the last time you smell pine for a while," but Gus had already curled up in his seat and was fast asleep. Within an hour, they left the California forest and reached the freeway. She looked for the signs directing her toward Nevada. The weather changed as they hit the border between California and Nevada; Gus's panting added to the car's internal temperature.

"I know it's hot. Sorry, buddy. You're wearing a giant fur jacket." He turned several circles and shook. Stray, cream hairs flew into the air and Anna blew them away. They both needed a break. She pulled the truck over at a Texaco and hooked Gus to his leash for a potty break while the truck filled up with gas. She heard the click and put the cap back on. "Hop in, I'll be back in a second." Her dog groaned. "I promise." She left the windows rolled down and grabbed things from the back seat. She needed to change into warm weather clothes.

The bell chimed overhead as she stepped into the air conditioning. "Bathrooms?" she asked the man behind the counter; he didn't look up, just pointed toward the back.

She changed into a pair of jean shorts and a T-shirt, and peeked out the window at Gus, who was wagging his tail at the woman in the next stall, filling her minivan with gas. Anna grabbed a Styrofoam cup and a bag of ice from the humming cooler and placed them on the counter.

"How much for these?"

The man looked up from his crossword, "A buck, twenty-five for the ice, the cup is free."

"Thanks, I'll take them both."

The man smiled, "Hot out there, huh?"

Anna paid him, "It's for the dog."

She pointed out the window; now Gus' head was hanging over the door and drool was spilling down the door collecting in a small puddle on the ground.

"He's not used to this weather," she shrugged.

"Say, what kind of dog is that anyway?"

"He is a Great Pyrenees,"

"Well, I hope some of that coat sheds soon or that guy is going to turn into mush," the man said sympathetically. Anna nodded. She hoped so too.

"Where are you headed?"

She counted the money, putting it on the counter, "Naples, Florida."

He whistled, eyes getting wide, "That sure is some drive; you have family there?"

"No, I mean yes, well, kind of." She didn't like answering questions from a stranger.

"Thanks," she grabbed her cup and ice and started to go.

"Just a minute, young lady." The man moved around the counter to the front, walking toward a far shelf; he pulled down a Styrofoam cooler. He walked over to the ice machine and put two bags inside. He motioned toward the door; she pushed it open for him while he carried it toward her truck; you'll need lots of ice for a trip like that." She pulled a few bills from her wallet to hand to him. He brushed them away.

"It's on the house; drive safe now." He set the cooler on the ground next to Gus' door.

Surprised, Anna stammered out a hearty, "Thanks!"

She opened the door, "Stay, no—we're not getting out."

She adjusted the cooler to fit on the floor just beneath the dog. She tore open one of the bags and used her hands to scoop out the ice. She poured it into Gus' water bowl. His ears perked up as she set it in front of him, "Let's see if this helps."

Climbing behind the wheel, she turned the key; the truck roared to life. As they left the station, a faded, blue road sign told them the next gas stop would be two hundred miles away. They were entering the desolate desert.

"Well, buddy, it looks like dry and drier."

As Anna drove on, the sun beat down, turning the road into a furnace. It was like driving on top of a stovetop. Out the window, the slight breeze created tiny swirls of dust that formed into little twisters. The landscape was vacant. No one around to care for it. Yet, it seemed content this way. Gus slept in the seat next to her. She hadn't seen many cars on the road today. People knew better than to drive in the hottest part of the day. She felt her body relaxing. Her sweaty palms were glued to the same ten and two position on the steering wheel. The big toe on her left foot felt numb. She was sleepy.

"I need to wake up!" She shook her head and breathed out. She reached over toward the cooler, using her left hand to hold the steering wheel and the other to shove the Styrofoam lid off. She reached for ice. Putting pieces in her mouth and the other chunks in a cup for later, she felt them melt on her hot tongue. Flavorless but refreshing.

Leaning back, the wind blowing in through her window she could smell the familiar scent of pine and linseed. It's what her dad always smelled like when she would bury her face in his shoulder. She still had his faded flannel shirts. In fact, one was next to her on the seat, waiting for a cool evening. She fingered it, rubbing the curve of one of the buttons, as she drove on. Her dad—she was just like him. He gave her a hammer when she was five and let her build a table for her dolls. She followed him around with a mini-tool belt asking which instrument he used for what. Tim Gentry kept his hands busy building furniture or other odds and ends from fallen trees that friends hauled to their driveway. Woodworking was his side gig. Construction or homebuilder, as Anna liked to refer to him, was what fed his family.

Sam, on the other hand, loved anything to do with the ocean. Even if they lived hours away, he devoured every book he could find. He loved the sea almost as much as their mom. Their mom knew the names of shells, fish, and creatures lurking in the deep and sea plants. Anna loved that about her mom, and it had left a lasting impression on Sam. Which is why he now lived on an iceberg, studying the frozen ocean.

She and Sam had gone through more than two kids should go through in a lifetime. But like her mom said the night their world turned upside down, "We will get through this. I don't understand all of the reasons, right now, but this is part of our story." Anna drifted back to that day, just as she did often. But time made the step back less hard.

Eight-year-old Anna clung to the calloused hand of her dad as they walked into the house.

"Honey, we're home," Tim said.

Anna smelled dinner. She hoped her mom had made lasagna. She loved lasagna.

"Hey, you two," her mom said as her dad let go of Anna and bear hugged her mom.

Anna noted, "We didn't find any of the special wood dad was looking for."

She watched her dad walk to where Sam was sitting at the dining room table, head bent over a book with a pencil in hand, as he took notes. He rubbed his hair. Sam didn't look up, he just kept scribbling away.

"Someone has a birthday tomorrow," dad said.

Sam's body jolted and he looked up at Tim. "Me!" he raised his hand.

"Have you decided what you want for your special dinner?" Mom asked.

His pencil pressed to his lips, he thought, "Well, since we're having meatloaf tonight," he turned toward Anna and winked, "how about lasagna?" Sam knew it was Anna's favorite. She nodded excitedly, as she locked eyes with her big brother.

Mom smiled, "okay, but is that what you want?"

Sam nodded, "yep!"

The phone rang and dad answered. Anna heard the concern in his voice. He hung up and ran to the coat rack, shoving his arms in the sleeves of his coat. "There's been an accident! Rod's truck went off the ledge, I'm going to go help." He rummaged through the drawer in the laundry room where they kept odds and ends.

"Honey, do you know where my headlamp is?" It was starting to get dark outside. Anna knew her dad was tough and would be the right man for the job.

Anna's Mom opened the cabinet and pulled a basket down, retrieving the missing light.

"Thanks!"

"Dad, is everyone going to be, okay?" Anna was concerned. She grew up playing with Rod's two daughters, the Gentry's closest neighbors.

"I don't know, Anna." He placed his hand on top of her head as he walked past her.

He walked over to Anna's mom and put his hands on her shoulders, Anna overheard his whisper, "Walt Washburn's the one who called, it doesn't look good. They've already called the ambulance but it's still thirty minutes out. The mud was so slick. Walt said that when Rod's truck slid, the ledge crumbled under him and the truck plunged about thirty feet. We may need to climb down and hoist him up with a rope."

"Tim, be careful." She whispered into his neck. Concern in her eyes.

He pulled his wife close. "I can't just leave him there." He kissed her forehead tenderly.

"Dinner smells great;" he said. "Will you save me a plate?" He tried to reassure her.

She laughed. "I will."

Anna's dad was invincible. In Anna's eyes, he could do it all. Even so, she felt trepidation, even a sense of doom.

"Wait!" she yelled as he opened the door to go.

She ran to him and wrapped her arms around his waist. Sam looked up and Tim waved him over. He hugged them both to himself. "I'll be back before you even know I'm gone." He kissed the tops of their heads. As he walked out the door he turned around and gave them his signature smile, "stick together and remember to help your mom!"

Then he was gone.

Anna watched her mom look out the window as her dad drove off.

"Okay, Sam, you set the table, and Anna, go wash up."

After dinner, Anna helped with the dishes. "Should I put dad's plate in the fridge?"

"Yeah, that's a good idea." Her mom kept walking over to the window to look out. It was late. Anna rinsed the last bowl, setting it in the drying rack. Wiping her hands on the towel, she heard the familiar crunch of the gravel. Relieved, because dad was finally home, she went to find Sam and Mom.

"Hey, dad's home," she yelled down the hallway.

"Okay, I'll be there in a sec." Sam yelled back.

When she turned around Mom had mysteriously appeared and was standing with the door open, framed within it. Everything happened so fast, Anna didn't have time to react.

Time stopped. Mom screamed. A breeze came in through the open door; the moon was full. Moments stuck in place. Anna heard bits and pieces from Walt who stood facing her mom.

"He reached Rod, but he was already dead." Walt's voice choked with the words. He took a deep breath. "I told him to leave the body, but he wouldn't. As I was pulling them up the side of the cliff, with the winch, the ropes broke." Walt's entire body shook as he relived the scene once again.

"The ambulance showed up, it took all of us together to get the guys up."

Sam walked out and stood beside Anna.

"What's going on?" He looked at his mom then back at Anna. Anna's face froze in place, as if she had seen a ghost.

"Where is he, Walt?" She yelled. "Where is Tim now?"

"They've got him in town, I'm so sorry. It should have been me."

Anna still wasn't sure she understood.

Sam shook his head, confused. "Mom, what happened to dad?"

When Grace turned toward them, Anna saw the look on her face. Dead. Her dad was dead.

Anna felt Gus' wet nose on her arm. It brought her back to the present. "Hey, boy."

A sports car whizzed by her, on the left. They were nearing a city, possibly close to the Arizona border. She gazed in her rearview mirror; Her gaze settled on the simple pine box nestled amongst her belongings in the backseat.

"Hey, mom." she whispered.

She glanced at the road again, feeling silly for talking to a box. Somehow, it was comforting. Her mom's ashes were in that box, making the long journey east.

Anna was taking her mom home.

She took the next exit, hoping to find a place with coffee. Her plan was to drive on, even as the sun was setting. They pulled into a diner advertising coffee and written underneath the coffee sign was, "Open 24 Hours, 7 Days a Week." She turned the truck into the nearest spot and parked. She knew the night air would be cooler and she could nap tomorrow somewhere in a shady store parking lot. Sam would kill her if he knew she was driving at night alone, *but what Sam doesn't know won't hurt him,* she thought. "Let's go!" She tugged on Gus' leash.

He jumped out and followed her to the one grassy spot. Anna would not let anyone, or anything derail her plan. Her heart was set on it.

Chapter Three

Broken Heart

Lucy stepped out of bed and did the first task of her day. Taking each corner of her sheets, she pulled them up and tucked them in under her pillow. It wasn't a hard job with only half of the bed rumpled from sleep. She hated making the bed, it was a tiresome task. Yet, it reminded her of Bill. She ran her hand across the sheet, removing the few wrinkles before tucking the sides under.

"Just the way you like it," she said turning toward the dresser where Bill's framed picture sat. "Good morning, sweetheart," she touched Bill's smiling face for the briefest moment, as she moved toward the bathroom.

A wry smile touched Lucy's lips as she looked at her reflection, ". . . every wrinkle in place, and I still have all my teeth." As she grew older and her body changed, it was pointless to be critical. Humor, she discovered, was the key. Laughing at herself made the journey more joyful. She dampened her washcloth, wiping her face, her blue eyes glistened in the morning light. She ran her comb through her short, white hair. The humidity kept her natural curl in place. She pulled the few loose strands out of the comb and tossed them in the trash. She brushed her teeth and tapped her toothbrush on the sink when she finished. No need for makeup, the sun gave her all the color she needed. She fastened her mother's diamond studs and surveyed her closet. Lucy was about as hassle-free as a good, overnight French toast recipe. The white, sleeveless, pineapple dress with the dangly tassels, stood out—perfect. She needed something light and cheerful today.

Each morning began the same. She walked downstairs, her hand automatically reaching for the cool curve of the left-side banister. The routine continued: the burst of fresh orange juice, the short walk to the back porch for the newspaper. Back inside, her simple breakfast of toast and eggs with a mug of coffee in the sunroom, the familiar sight of the sea a peaceful backdrop.

As she opened the paper she thought of a million other things she would rather do than pick up the phone and call Grace today. She took slow sips, lingering over the local news. Naples was a sleepy small town. No crime to speak of and aside from all the new construction, there wasn't a whole lot of action. She looked up at the clock. "Well, Grace is probably awake now." It was nearly 10:00 a.m. and the West Coast would just be getting up. Lucy remembered when Grace was little she was always up with the sun, she wondered if she was still the same. She stood and went to the kitchen to do the dishes. All three of them. A cup, plate, and mug. The clock ticked on the wall. *What else could she do to avoid the inevitable?* She wondered. She wiped the counter, straightened her mail pile, swept the back steps, and watered the few indoor plants she kept on her kitchen windowsill. She took the dish rag and re-wiped the counter.

"Ah, get a grip, Lucy," she threw the rag into the sink. "You can do this." Why was she so afraid of Grace?

Glass of water in hand, she walked to Bill's worn blue chair, the familiar scent of pine and honey still clinging to it. She sat down and set the cup on the side table, next to the phone. With her hands perched on her knees, she leaned forward. She stared at her toes. She took a deep breath then sat back up.

"Well, here it goes."

She reached for the phone holding her hand just above it. Frozen. She had images of Grace answering it. Would she hang up on Lucy? Would Lucy seize up and have nothing to say? What would Grace say after all this time? Lucy's mouth was dry. She took two large gulps of water. Knowing she'd never get answers without calling Grace, she lifted the phone. The dial tone echoed in her ear. By the looks of it, one would think she was holding a ticking bomb.

"This is silly; I can't believe I am scared of her." She looked up at the ceiling. "Pull yourself together, Lucy."

She knew Old Blue was at stake and she would do anything to save it. Even face one of her biggest fears. Lucy had her plaid-colored address book opened on her lap. She had Grace's phone number, scribbled next to it was the name Mike but Lucy couldn't remember why. The address was a California one and as far as she knew, nothing had changed. She looked closely at the area code; it was slightly smudged. Lucy guessed it to be a five rather than an eight. Her handwriting was different now than when she first wrote it over twenty years ago. Lucy let her gaze rest on the writing. When Grace had finally settled down and married, she had sent a postcard with her new details. At the time, Lucy was elated with the news of her marriage and new home; however, she knew Grace was not offering an open invitation for regular correspondence. It was understood that Grace had sent it out of a sense of duty. Lucy still had the postcard tucked into the back of her address book. And, every year after that first contact, she received, like clockwork an annual update. Hoping it was a step in the right direction, Lucy faithfully waited for Grace to come home, not for good, but at least for a visit. But she never did.

She dialed the number, then paused and realized she had forgotten Grace's husband's name. She quickly scanned the page to see if she had made a note somewhere. Then remembered he had passed. In fact, it had been over a decade ago. Her brain felt fuzzy and her palms sweaty. The phone buzzed in her ear. It rang once more, and then she heard, "Hello." Her stomach twisted like a knot. It was a man's voice. It was not Grace.

"Hello, I'm looking for Grace . . . Grace Gentry."

The line was quiet. Lucy wondered if she had dialed the wrong area code.

He cleared his throat, "May I ask who is calling?"

"Why, yes, this is her mother; my name is Lucy Wright." Silence. Lucy didn't know if the phone had gone dead or if the man had hung up on her.

"Pardon me, sir?" her anxiety slowly escalating.

"Just a moment, please." She heard the phone land on a table of some sort. *He must be getting Grace,* Lucy thought. She waited, looking up at the bank of windows in front of her, most of the windowsills had been filled in with beach glass.

When Grace was little, she loved collecting it. She would find all the colors: sea foam green, dark blue, and brown. At sunset, when the light flooded the room, the broken glass would come alive, creating a mosaic of color on the floor and walls. Every piece was there, just as Grace had left it, albeit now dusty and needing a good dish soap washing. She heard the line pick up again, "Hello, Mrs.?"

"Yes, hi, please call me Lucy."

"Lucy," he paused, and she heard a chair squeak as he must have sat down.

"First, I want to say that I was unaware Grace's parents were still alive, or we would have contacted you."

"Well, her father has passed, but I'm alive and kicking." *At least for a little longer*, she thought. "And who might I be talking to?"

"I was one of Grace and Tim's best friends; my name is Mike."

"Nice to meet you, Mike," Lucy was confused. Then she remembered when Grace had mailed her address, she had given this phone number; it was the number to her neighbor's house, the Gentry's hadn't gotten a phone line installed yet. And, sadly, this was Lucy's first time calling. "Mike," she said, "perhaps I could leave my number? You could pass it along to Grace. It's quite urgent that she call." *If she doesn't have a phone by now, she needs to get with the times*, Lucy thought. Then, a better idea struck. "Yes! A letter!" she declared. "Mike, could you confirm her mailing address?" She glanced down at what she had written down. "It's 1765 Newberg . . ." Mike cut her off. "I don't think you understand." His voice faltered. Lucy, taken aback by the comment, cleared her throat and paused. *Was this a slight?* Had Grace poisoned him against her, painting her as a terrible mother? This was precisely why she'd hesitated to call. This messy dredging up of the past was the last thing she wanted. She would end this call immediately. This was a terrible idea. Flustered, she slammed her address book closed.

"Perhaps," she said, her voice tight, "when you see Grace, you could relay a message." She inhaled quickly, trying to calm herself. *What message?* Her hand clenched the phone. *That she needs her desperately? That we're losing the house? That I'm dying?* "Please inform my daughter," she stated, her voice firm, "that I will be sending a letter immediately."

"Ma'am, please wait. I take it you don't know." A shift in his voice.

Lucy paused concerned by his sudden emotion. His chair squeaking as he repositioned himself.

"What don't I know?" she asked him.

Twenty years of Grace's life, that's what, she thought.

"There was an accident."

Lucy's body stiffened.

"I am deeply sorry . . ." His voice trailed off.

"Excuse me, what are you saying?"

"We lost Grace, ma'am. It was over a year ago."

Lost her? What did that even mean? Was he saying she was dead? Lucy's confusion deepened.

"She was found dead on scene."

Lucy's bare toes curled on the woven rug beneath her; her brow furrowed as the room spun, and the word dead, fell like a blow.

Her lungs began to tighten; they wouldn't let her breathe. She wrapped her free arm around her middle. She had to get oxygen.

"Ma'am, are you there?"

Phone to her ear, she fought for control, each breath a ragged attempt for air. A whistling intake, a held moment, a shaky release. The phone's hum filled the void. Mike waited, patiently. The flood threatened, but she pushed it back, whispering what he already knew, into the receiver, "I'm . . . her mother."

Instantly, Lucy felt the impact of this moment. She had made a full circle. A completion that no mother should ever have to embrace, her child's beginning and her child's end. Her memory jumps back momentarily; she sees her new baby wrapped in a soft, white swaddle, the nurse smiling as she hands Lucy the bundle, "It's a healthy, baby girl," the joy, the mystery, the weight of glory, all mingled into one majestic moment.

The man's voice, like hooks, drags her back to the present.

"Lucy?"

Like a distant echo reverberating off a cliff, Lucy hears him,

"Is there anything I can do?" She pushes his voice out, crawling back into her memory. There she is again, Grace, on a sunlit beach. Sand dollars cradled in her hands, one broken, one whole. Grace smiles. Her lips form the shape of a crescent moon.

"Look, Mama," she says, pointing at the broken one, "when they're broken, we find the treasure inside."

Lucy sees it, as Grace holds the tiniest little fragment between her thumb and finger.

"It's an angel, Mama."

"Ma'am?" The deep, unwelcome voice shattered her fragile memory. She wanted to scream. This was her worst nightmare unfolding.

She knew she needed to get off the phone before she burst. The silence between them is now awkward.

"I am her Mama." She heard herself say again. Maybe this is what a mental breakdown felt like. Rising from her chair, she watched a dark storm cloud form across the sea, closing in rapidly. Within moments, the wind picked up and suddenly a bang of thunder rattled her windows. *How fast the weather changes in these parts*, she thought.

He cleared his throat, "Ma'am, perhaps you should call your grandchildren?"

Her grandchildren. The ones she had never met.

What would she say, "no?" *Where does one begin when everything begins to crash down around them?"* she wondered. She had been here before, why couldn't she compose herself. *Remember—what did you do last time?* She'd played the part of calm before. Maybe, just maybe, she could pull it off again.

"Sam, yes, my grandson," she mumbled out. "Yes, perhaps I will."

She knew about him from the yearly update Grace sent to her. She coveted any news, even if it read like a formal newsletter. She knew Sam was a scientist.

Outside the waves crashed into the sand. The force of the water pushing the tiny, crushed rocks down, then just as fast pulling them out into the depths of the sea.

She looked longingly toward the sea, wishing those same waves would capture her and bury her in their depths. The first tear formed. It felt heavy. She blinked and let it fall.

The rain came. The little pitter-patter made a rhythm on her roof. Years of Florida storms had taught her: rain meant the storm was building.

After what seemed like minutes, she heard herself say, "Thank you, Mike"

"Ma'am, if you need anything, please don't hesitate to call."

She nodded, "I will, thank you."

She laid the phone in the cradle and slid to the floor. She would not escape this. But she hoped she would survive it.

After sitting too long on the floor, with her back against the couch, Lucy's body felt numb and if she was honest so did her heart. A hollow shell. The phone had been ringing off the hook, eventually it went silent and a few minutes later, she heard Sandy letting herself in. Lucy knew eventually she would come.

"Yoo-hoo, it's me," Sandy bellowed from the other room. Closing the door behind her.

"I'll be just a moment, I've brought us some cookies from Roger's Bakery."

Lucy stared blankly at the photo album sitting in her lap. She wanted to remember what Grace looked like when she laughed. She heard Sandy rattling around in the kitchen. Minutes later, Sandy tiptoed in with a tea tray. Lucy looked up and saw steam coming out of each cup. The rain had let up, but the air had a small chill. Hot tea would be nice. Sandy sat beside her commenting,

"Looks like it didn't go well?" Sandy knew today was the day Lucy had committed to calling Grace.

Lucy slowly closed the album and waited. She wondered where to begin. She shook her head from side to side. Sandy added cream to a white cup emblazoned with "cat lady," on it. The handle was the shape of a cat's tail. Lucy had never owned a cat in her life, but somehow this cup made her smile when she saw it at the thrift store, so she bought it. Sandy handed it to her. Lucy took it between both hands, and took a sip. Ceylon cardamon tea. It tasted good.

"There is no heir for the house, Sandy." Why beat around the bush. As the words left her mouth, she thought she might be sick.

Sandy finished stirring in a spoonful of honey and sat down. "Okay, so Grace said no?"

"In her own way, yes."

"Do you want to tell me about it?"

Lucy set her cup and saucer on the floor next to her. She squeezed her hands together, forming her hands into a prayer. She looked up at the ceiling. "Sandy, Grace was in a car accident." Sandy almost dropped her teacup.

"She is gone." Lucy said matter-of-factly.

"What do you mean gone?" Sandy said, setting her cup down on the small butler's table, her hands shaking uncontrollably. Lucy could barely form the words, "She died Sandy, in the accident, she's gone . . ." Lucy whispered, a fresh wave of emotion causing new tears to form. Sandy moved next to Lucy on the floor.

Lucy recounted her conversation with Mike, sharing the details relayed to her. Sandy listened intently. A sharp ache pulsed through Lucy's joints; a signal she needed to stretch her legs.

"A year," she murmured, "a year since she died. You'd think I'd have known."

Regret intensified with each passing moment, the guilt, suffocating. Lucy shifted onto her knees and pushed herself upright.

"Come on," she said, extending her hand to Sandy. Sandy grasped it, using her other arm to steady herself on the chair. Sandy had deeply loved Grace, a niece in all but blood. Lucy knew Sandy shared her grief.

Lucy turned to Sandy; her voice urgent. "I don't have much time, Sandy. I have to do something to save this house." Sandy stood frozen; disbelief written all over her face. "You just learned your only child is dead, and you're worried about the house?"

Lucy knew her words sounded callous. "There's nothing more I can do for Grace now, Sandy. You know that." She felt the house, and her control over it, slipping away. And she felt Sandy's silent condemnation.

Lucy spun around and faced Sandy. "What would you like me to do?" she spat out, now wishing she had held her tongue. "You have not lived in my shoes, Sandy." Frantic, Lucy began to pace the floor.

"I am out of options." Lucy held up her hand and listed her losses. "My husband is gone. My daughter is gone. I'll be damned if I sit by and watch the last thing that belongs to me, be torn into tiny pieces and plowed over."

Sandy tried to understand. She shook her head and wiped her eyes with a tissue she took from her pocket. "I just can't push things aside as easily as you, Lucy." Sandy blew her nose into the Kleenex. "You need to talk about this, Lucy."

"What good is talking going to do me," Lucy was furious, and it showed, the slits in her eyes burrowed into Sandy's back. "She's gone!" Calling Grace had been Lucy's 'Hail Mary,' her final play, and it had failed.

Lucy's pain was so raw, she feared it. The only way forward was to avoid it and to build a fortress around it, keeping anyone who tried to breach it, at arm's length. It's what she did when Bill died, and it is what she would do again. Evade, elude, move on. It was her shield against grief, a desperate attempt to avoid drowning in sorrow.

"I'm sorry." She said to Sandy, softening as she watched her friend sit down and finish her now lukewarm tea. "I know this is hard for you too."

"Jim and I will help with whatever you need."

It humbled Lucy. She had yelled at Sandy. Still, Sandy stuck by her, a loyal friend.

"I would like that."

She let herself fall onto the couch next to Sandy. She looked at her oldest friend, a lifetime shared, "I'm afraid, it's just that if I start to feel Grace's passing," Lucy hesitated, her voice choking. "I know, honey. You don't need to say anymore," Sandy grabbed her hand and held it. "I know."

The two sat there a few moments more. Lucy had lost her chance to make things right with her daughter, so now, she had to salvage what remained.

"Now tell me, what is the plan?" Sandy patted Lucy's hand before letting it go. Lucy had only thought of it moments before.

"Randall Gordon wants this place like fire wants fuel." Her heartbeat sped up. "He will stop at nothing to get it, you watch."

Lucy felt a fresh strength. "But, if he gets it, you and I both know, he will tear it down, board-by-board and put up some gaudy condos." Sandy nodded.

"Lucy, you need to pick your battles. Randall Gordon will throw everything he has into this. You know he's cutthroat and ruthless."

Lucy smiled, a flicker of something dangerous in her eyes. "He's a stubborn old devil. But Sandy, I've got nothing left to lose." She chuckled. "It's almost comical. I'm fading out, and I'm going out fighting."

"So, if you can't have it, you're going to make sure he can't?" Sandy asked, raising her eyebrows.

"Exactly."

"That sounds like revenge, Lucy."

"Revenge?" Lucy scoffed. "No, darling. This is my grand finale."

The Gordons were known for being cutthroat. They would buy a house and as soon as the paperwork went through, they tore it down. Some called them Romans, they didn't care who stood in their way, and if someone tried, all the better as far as they were concerned. They loved a good fight because they always won.

But not this time. Lucy would refuse their offer when it came through. She would weed out the investors and wait for the nice family that saw the bright potential of Old Blue, someone that embraced it as a home.

Sandy stood, her weariness obvious. Lucy watched her, feeling a pang of envy. Sandy would go home to Jim. They would surely sit and hold one another as they mourned Grace. Something Lucy would do alone when it was time. For now, she would channel her sadness into action.

"Tomorrow, I call the realtor!" Lucy said with triumph.

Sandy shook her head and rolled her eyes. "Like I haven't seen this all before," she said sarcastically, as she gathered her things and walked toward the kitchen. "I'll call you tomorrow," Lucy said shutting the door behind her and turning around, a wide grin on her face.

The Belltown family's history of grit taught Lucy the crucial need for unwavering resolve. Now was the time to shine.

Chapter Four

The Gordon Family Greed

John Mark Gordon watched the boats arrive from the high windows of Gordon Headquarters, as they slowly made their way around Gordon Point. John Mark waited, then turned toward the two other men in the room. "The Belltowns have always held that land. Lucy won't just give it up." He knew they'd see his sympathy as weakness.

Randall Gordon, his grandfather, cleared his throat. "She has no choice." He knew Lucy was ill, with no one to inherit the property; she would be forced to sell.

"Small towns, people talk." His dad, Stan Gordon, said, as he paced the floor.

"It's time you started showing some initiative in this company, John Mark." His dad never one for niceties spat out. "Gordon Developers has a legacy of three generations, and now, the fourth rests with you." Behind his father was an oil painting of Paul Gordon, John Mark's great-grandfather, the founder of Gordon Developers. John Mark had been raised on the company's history: Gordon Developers, one of the first businesses in Naples, and Paul

Gordon, a local legend. They had been building in Naples for over a century, starting with a small shack on the beach to luxury real estate. They had come a long way.

Gordon Developers Incorporated, a two-story, stucco building with all front-facing windows, was where his dad and grandfather practically lived. He looked around the room. Of course, it was opulent—velvet curtains, brass light fixtures, hand-stitched leather chairs. His grandfather had always liked nice things.

After his parent's divorce, his dad took over the bottom half of the building, turning it into a studio apartment—his bachelor pad. John Mark was sixteen when his dad invited him into the inner workings of real estate in Naples.

"Son, we need to trust you before we give you the helm of this great ship." John Mark moved away from the sunny window and took off his hat. He felt the bead of sweat drip from his forehead and wiped it away with the back of his hand. His sandy brown hair needed a trim. And, by the way his grandfather was looking at him now, he knew he thought the same thing. He quickly shoved his hat on and walked over to the thermostat to check the AC. Seventy degrees. Then why did it feel like a furnace in here? Did he tell his dad that he had his own proposal for the Belltown place? It would show that he was taking some initiative. He turned to face them both, locking his fingers together in front of him.

"Look," he began, his mouth parched, "I've done some calculations and talked to a surveyor. Property preservation is possible, but it would require changes. We'd have to bring the house up to code, do some landscaping—native plants, and to bring in certain bird species." His father gave him a skeptical look. "We could make it a Historic Preservation site, conserving wildlife and protecting biodiversity." He was met with two pairs of staring eyes.

Then, his dad rolled his eyes. "Here we go again, you're just like your 'eco-conscious' mom, always wanting to be in touch with the land and save the sea turtles; it's a pipe dream, John Mark." He felt the familiar stab. His father always knew where to cut.

John Mark wanted to defend his mom, but it would be a waste of time. It's why his mom finally left; a person can only take so much before they wither. John Mark knew that firsthand. He looked at his grandfather. His hands in his pockets, he rocked back and forth on his heels. His silence speaking volumes. John Mark knew it was about money; it was always about money.

"Do you know how much this deal will put in our pockets, John Mark?" His dad waved his hand in the air, a sarcastic yet serious gesture. He could take a guess. It was somewhere in the millions.

"If we keep that old place, we would be fools. It is always cheaper to tear down. I don't even want to think about the waste of money it would be to try and fix up that old hunk of junk. Read the writing on the wall, son. People don't want scraps, they want extravagance!"

As with countless original Naples homes, Gordon Developers would demolish and rebuild, replacing history with opulence. And he knew the Belltown place would receive the same fate.

"So, what will it be this time?" he asked dryly. "Condos or an all-inclusive resort?"

"You got it, my boy! With no expense spared, every luxury imaginable." The two men laughed, bantering back and forth, without giving a straight answer. John Mark stood and marveled at how different he was from his own flesh and blood. Greed, lust, conquest. He wanted no part of them, yet they reveled in them.

"The condos will have state-of-the-art sound systems, jacuzzi tubs, and if we build a resort, it will have an olympic-sized swimming pool plus tennis courts; I mean, we're pulling out all the stops on this one." John Mark knew there was no sense in appealing to his dad or grandfather. They had made up their minds. "It's what the people want, John Mark; you have to see that," his dad said, exasperated.

His grandfather rose and put his arm around John Mark's shoulders. "John Mark, we want you to spearhead this project, from start to finish." He was torn, unsure if it was a subtle jab or a genuine vote of confidence but leaned towards the latter.

"Grandpa, thanks, but I really think you and my Dad should manage this one." Something about it just didn't sit right. His grandfather turned him to the window, pointing at Lucy's place. "We're getting that land, no matter what it takes. And remember, all this will be yours." The Gordon Will. His inheritance, John Mark's future, secured by his grandfather's death, but only if he played along. Otherwise, he was out.

Randall slapped John Mark on the shoulder, almost knocking him over. He could smell the whiskey on his grandpa's breath. He was not a man who was shy about a mid-day drink. "And, just as your father had to prove to me that he had what it took to run this company, I'll ask the same of you."

John Mark felt the pressure of his grandfather's grip, squeezing his shoulder. Pressure to comply. It was typical Gordon fare, 'my way, or the highway.' And John Mark had already eaten his fair share of it. He didn't know if he could stomach another bite. He spun around, and his grandfather let go of him. John Mark looked at his grandfather then his own dad. His convictions were at war with his obligations. Sweat dripped down his back; the AC was definitely broken. His heart pounded. *Was it the heat or a rising*

44

anger? He wondered. Either way, he knew he needed to get out of there. And fast.

"So, son, what's your answer?" His father advanced, extending his hand, a gesture of a deal, not affection. John Mark refused, incredulous. Business before family, always. He turned away. "I won't disappoint you," he stated, his voice flat, his hands buried in his pockets, his back to them both. He walked out the door and back to his truck and climbed inside. He took off his white T-shirt and threw it on the seat. He would go surfing to blow off steam. Driving out, he looked back. His father was a silhouette in the window, arms crossed, a dark scowl etched on his face. There would be no convincing him. He was a stone wall. John Mark fumed, he knew he didn't have a choice. He turned right, taking the corner too fast, his anger getting the best of him. Someday, he would stand up to his dad. But it wasn't today. He would play the game a little longer. He would prove to them that he was a Gordon, even if it cost him dearly.

CHAPTER FIVE

West Coast to East Coast

The air, sweet and fragrant, filled the truck as Anna and Gus drove south on Highway One. The ride had been surprisingly comfortable. "We're almost there," she told Gus, whose head was now out the window, sniffing the air. "Can you smell that? Salt. It's the ocean." They passed the "Naples, Florida—Paradise" sign, and Anna smiled. Paradise was exactly what she needed. Perhaps, a day spent basking in the sun. Her thoughts were cut short by the smoke billowing from under the hood.

"No, no, no, this is not happening."

She checked the gauges, and they were darting back and forth. Anna quickly pulled to the side of the road as the truck inched along, looking for a place she could park. She steered the truck into the Naples Food Market parking lot, parking in a far corner. She hoped the engine just needed to cool down after the long drive. She put the truck in park. The truck let out a loud, ragged, strained sound, followed by a high-pitched, desperate squeal, and then silence. Gus looked at Anna. He groaned. Anna watched as more smoke poured from under the hood.

"This doesn't look good," she muttered, resting her head on the steering wheel. Turning to Gus, brow furrowed, "At least we made it." She was in a bind. She missed her parents; they'd know what to do. She could let her mind wander into worst-case scenarios or focus on the present. "We made it, and it stopped here, not on the road," she said to Gus. She appreciated the cool shade of her parking spot. Perhaps time was all it needed. She opened the door, unsticking her sweaty thighs from the hot seat. Even in the shade, the day's heat was obvious.

"Let's check it out." She reached over and clipped on Gus' leash, pulling him through the driver's side. They walked to the front of the truck and lifted the hood. More steam. The engine was hot.

"Well, I do know that we're not supposed to touch a hot engine," she looked down at Gus who was sitting patiently. "We can wait." The parking lot was a burst of color, with bougainvillea and tall, leafy trees. She gave Gus the last of the melted ice water from the cooler and sat on the curb, trying to strategize. Gus lay down beside her. She watched the flow of shoppers. They were all smiles and summer clothes, a picture of happiness. Not a single frown. Everyone was happy. Was it the sun? The warmth?

The warmth made her sleepy. Gus had already begun to fall asleep. A woman walked by holding her daughter's hand. They were wearing matching sundresses and appeared to be carefree, grinning and chatting as they went.

The sight of them triggered a memory, sharp and clear, the month after her father's passing. To alleviate some of their grief, her mother had taken them to the beach. Anna remembered, despite the sad circumstances, her mother's quiet sense of peace. For days, they walked for hours along the shore, her mother patiently naming each shell. Anna found solace in the sand between her toes, the salty air, and the cries of gulls—a slow, soothing balm. They crafted a sandcastle, adding to its magnificence with the shells they'd gathered. Anna recalled her mother, knees drawn up, eyes fixed on the horizon, a quiet stillness that was both comforting and strangely new. It was as if she were witnessing a secret past life unfold. On their final day, as they felt the cool sea around their toes, her mother shared a story of her childhood home, a window into a past Anna had never known.

"It was magical. It's hard to put words to it." She told Anna and Sam about the people—the cottages. "And, most of all, the sounds," her mother said. "The sea has its own music, you know." Her mother faced the sea, "one just has to stop and listen."

Anna observed a fresh radiance in her mother's face, a light that seemed to emanate from within.

Turning to them, she exclaimed with newfound enthusiasm, "and the sunrises, they were absolutely breathtaking!"

"Can we go there someday?" Sam asked.

"Maybe," she replied, her gaze wandering, as if lost in a distant thought.

"Perhaps, one day, I will take you there," she said, her face alight with a hopeful smile.

Gus barked, bringing Anna back to reality, the broken truck and hot parking lot were a stark contrast from her blissful daydream. She checked her watch; it had been twenty minutes.

"Excuse me, ma'am, but it looks like you're having car trouble."

She looked up and shielded her eyes from the ray of sun beaming through the tree and squinted. A tall man was towering over her. He moved to block the sun from her eyes. He was tan like everyone else she had seen, except he wasn't wearing flip flops, rather he had on what looked like work boots. His eyes darted back and forth between her and the front of the truck. "How did you guess?" she stood.

He sheepishly shoved his hands into his pockets. "The raised hood and sad look on your face, is kind of a dead giveaway." Gus was sniffing his ankles. He put out his hand, "Hi, I'm John Mark."

Gus barked and rammed his head into the man's outstretched hand.

"And, this is Gus," she stood and pulled his leash. "Sorry about that," she laughed. Gus sat next to her as she introduced herself, shaking his hand, "I'm Anna."

"Nice to meet you." He motioned toward the back of the truck. "California license plates, so did you actually drive all the way from the West Coast?"

Smiling, she nodded. "Yep, this old thing pulled through."

"Can I have a look?" he asked, gesturing towards the truck. The steam had dissipated, but it was likely still hot.

"Sure but be careful. It was so hot that I thought it was going to catch fire."

He walked over and leaned over the engine, like he was listening to it. He gently touched the oil cap with his palm and then re-touched it.

"Seems cool enough." He walked over to his truck and rummaged around. When he came back, he was carrying tools in a bag.

"What color did you say the smoke was?" Anna tried to recall, "It was a mixture of black smoke then turned into a white steam." She shrugged. She knew nothing about cars, and she wasn't embarrassed to admit it.

He scratched his head, thinking. "Well, by the color of that smoke, I'm guessing it has something to do with your water pump."

He used a wrench to undo the top of the engine plate.

"Wow, what year is this truck?"

Anna did the calculations quickly in her head. Dad got it a few years after she was born.

"I think it is twenty-three, maybe twenty-five."

"Yeah, your water pump has a significant leak. I can't see the entire tank, but the fluid dripping down is definitely from there."

"So, is that something I can fix quickly?"

"Only if you're a magician," he looked at her with a wide grin. "You will want a mechanic for this."

This issue was a serious setback. Carless was not part of the equation. Finding a place to live just became infinitely more difficult. She was counting on the truck for temporary shelter. Buying a car, even with the money she had available, was not feasible. She had to stick to the plan: rent a place, deliver the letter, maybe find a job.

She watched him fit the lid back on and screw it into place. He closed the hood and brushed his hands together. His white T-shirt was smudged with dirt. "Sorry about that," she said pointing at the grease rubbed on his clothes. "Oh this, it's nothing. These are my work clothes." He put his tools back into his bag.

"So, what brings you to these parts," he wiped his hands on a patch of grass close to where Gus was laying, rubbing at the black oil marks on his wrist.

"I'm here to meet some of my family." It wasn't a total lie.

"Cool." He sat down next to Gus and scratched him behind the ear.

"It's amazing if you think about it, that you had no trouble on the road. It's like the truck powered through to get you here." He pointed at the truck. "You were brave to take on such an adventure in that thing." From where she sat, she noticed the rust on the running boards. Maybe, this had been an unwise decision after all—one that she would come to regret. She couldn't let herself go down that trail. She needed to come up with a plan.

"Thank you for your help." She stood up, hoping he would take the hint that she was ready for him to leave. But really, if honest, she could use one more thing.

"Hey, do you know of any mechanics in the area that work on water pumps?" She opened the driver's side door and reached for her cell phone.

"I do, and I can give you a ride." He pointed to an old Chevy. "Oh . . ." She paused, watching him load tools into the back. *Get in a car with a complete stranger?* He seemed okay, and she'd have Gus. "Only if Gus comes," she said, as Gus stood beside her. John Mark leaned against the tailgate, waiting.

"He's coming, absolutely. We're not leaving him to bake in this heat." He smiled, pulling out his phone and dialing. "I'll get a tow truck sorted for you."

"Oh, thank you so much," she said, relief washing over her. She heard him give the driver their current address, as she gathered a few things out of the backseat: her purse and a bag packed with clothes, toiletries, and Gus' food. She gently placed the wooden box with her mom's ashes on the top in the duffel, zipping it closed, careful not to damage it. *This is not how I pictured my arrival.* But she had little choice. She walked over to John Mark's light teal Chevy, a mix of gratitude and apprehension in her steps.

"Sweet truck."

"Thanks, a classic, 1985; she belonged to my grandfather; he gave me this truck when I turned fourteen." He patted the hood. "The engine was shot. He told me if I could figure it out, it was mine. So, I did."

The truck was in pristine condition.

"There's the tow truck now." John Mark walked over to the man in overalls and shook his hand. They looked like they had met before. Anna walked up and John Mark introduced her to Mac. "I'll take care of it and meet you at the shop in a few minutes!" Anna reluctantly handed over the keys. Her dad's Smokey the Bear keychain was still dangling from the set. What would Sam say to her trusting all these new people? In truth, she had no choice.

She opened the door to the shiny Chevy and realized her dilemma: room enough for three. "Ummm, Gus doesn't know how to ride in the back. Are you okay with him sitting in the middle?"

"As long as he doesn't need a seatbelt." He winked. They both climbed in, and she shut the door with a thud; he started up the engine.

"So, did you just get into town, like today?" He turned toward her as he drove out of the parking lot.

"Just."

"Wow, sorry."

"It's okay, it just adds to the adventure."

"Well, I hope your time in Naples isn't all like this." He turned down the next road.

"Me too."

"Where are you staying?" he asked as Gus began to pant.

Anna watched as drool landed on the vinyl seats. Embarrassed, she started digging in her purse for a tissue. She knew the safe answer would be to say she was staying with her family, but that wasn't honest. "I'm not sure yet; that was my first order of business when we got to town, but well, you know . . ."

She wiped up the slobbery drips, knowing this would be a battle she would not win.

"Well, I know of a place; it's super close to the mechanic. I can take you by after that if you want?" Anna had no friends or family;

she did not know another living soul in Naples, except Casanova who was now driving her in his rad truck.

"Sure, can't hurt to take a peek."

They pulled into a parking lot where one side was lined with old cars. "This is Garrett's Place," John Mark said, "he's an old friend of our families; want me to go in with you?"

She didn't need handholding, she shook her head, as she pushed the door open, "I got this, but do you mind keeping Gus?"

"He doesn't bite, does he?" John Mark said playfully.

"Biting no, slobber, yes."

She closed the door and walked toward the entrance, the windows covered with advertisements for local activities and free resources.

Anna asked for Garrett, "That's me," a man said pointing to the name "Garrett," embroidered on his shirt. He took a bandana and wiped the sweat off his face.

She explained the situation with her truck, what John Mark concluded, and where she had left it.

"Well, if John Mark said it was the water pump, that's what it is." The older man looked out the window at where John Mark was parked. He pointed toward John Mark, "That boy knows a thing or two about trucks. That Chevy didn't look like that when he first got it." Garrett winked. He wrote several things on a sheet of paper, got her phone number, and then turned it toward Anna, "Just sign right there."

She took the pen and scribbled her name on the line.

"Looks like the tow truck just arrived," he pointed toward the window. "Don't worry, I will take good care of it."

"Thank you." She turned to leave but paused. So much had changed in a few days—she had left home, driven cross-country, now she was essentially stranded, handing over her dad's truck to a stranger. It was unsettling.

The man walked her to the door. "We will call you as soon as we get a diagnosis."

"Thanks, Garrett, I'll wait for your call."

She walked back outside, and John Mark was standing next to the truck, holding Gus by the leash. They both turned toward her and watched her walk up. Gus wagged his tail.

"Bad news?" John Mark knelt to scratch Gus behind the ear, but Gus laid down and rolled over on his back, asking for a belly rub instead.

"It is what we already know. He said you know lots about cars, so it is likely the water pump."

"Bummer, but the flip side is, it will probably be something he can repair, and it's not a total engine fail."

She was grateful for that too. She wasn't ready to let go of her dad's truck.

Now what? she wondered. *Cab? Hotel?* She'd never faced any big decisions alone; she had always been reliant on others for direction. Her family.

He gave her a thumbs up, "Ready to go?"

She forced a reassuring smile, "Yep!" Her stomach was in knots.

Gus jumped back in the truck and promptly sat in the middle.

"Wow, fast friends," she laughed, scratching Gus behind the ears as she climbed in next to him. She buckled her seat belt, still unsure what to think about this stranger.

Was the promise of a house luring her in? She could feel the tiredness in every bone of her body. She had to admit, after days of driving, it would feel great to have a shower and a bed to sleep in. She needed to decide. *What would Sam do?* she wondered. He would take a plunge. And I will let this guy know that at least one person knows my whereabouts in case he tries something. She buckled her seatbelt, "Let me update my brother, it will take just a second." She called his phone, knowing he was sleeping. After leaving a quick voicemail, she was ready to go.

John Mark turned on the radio. The beach boys blared from the speakers. He quickly turned it down. "Sorry." He ejected the cassette and tossed it on the dash.

"Okay, I'm ready to see the house for rent."

"Sure thing, it's super close!" he replied.

Her palms were sweaty. She could offer to walk there. He was already driving down a side street, too late for her to get out. Millions of scenarios were running through her head. She had to laugh at her tendency to expect the absolute worst. Maybe he was just a nice guy, she reasoned. She forced herself to look out the window at the palm trees, as they drove past.

Gus started to lick John Mark's face. He tried to push Gus away. "Down, boy."

She couldn't blame Gus. John Mark was likeable.

"I may have slipped him some of my emergency jerky stash while you were in talking to Garrett about your truck." He offered her the bag, "Hungry?"

"I'm good, I'll wait." A smile touched her lips, a testament to the day's unexpected turn for the better.

"So, about this rental, do they take dogs?"

"They do."

"Is it, by chance, partially furnished? As you have already guessed, I didn't pack a bed, but I'm prepared to camp out in my sleeping bag until I do."

John Mark seemed amused as he nodded his head.

"It's furnished."

"Furnished?"

"Yep, everything you could need. Down to a drawer filled with little tea napkins and pickle forks."

She didn't know what a pickle fork was, but she liked this place more and more by the minute. "Wow, I'm afraid to ask how much."

"Well, it's a month-to-month, and if I remember correctly, I think they were asking $100.00." John Mark drove down a tree-lined street; the palm trees looked like they had been there for decades. All the lawns were immaculate.

"These cottages are adorable!" She watched as they drove by shuttered homes—pale yellow, coral pink, and baby blue. Each cottage was distinctly different from the other—like an expert craftsman had built each one by hand.

"This is my favorite part of town." John Mark said, looking out the window. "Old Naples, is what they call it; some of these cottages are over a hundred years old." As he kept driving down the main road, Anna could see glimpses of the ocean. They were that close. John Mark slowed down and made a left turn onto a shaded road with big grassy lawns and a few more charming cottages, the ocean view was at the end of the lane.

"Here we are," he said smiling. As he turned into a driveway the truck tires crunched beneath them. "Crushed shell," he said, answering her question before she could even ask.

"This?" The cottage in front of her was a soft, butter yellow with white shutters. She looked to her left. It was two houses away from being oceanfront.

"I thought you said it was $100.00?" she asked. Maybe, he meant to say $100 daily; that would be more appropriate. She wasn't a complete dummy when it came to numbers. This was a nice place.

"Yeah, sorry, I know the yard is in pretty bad shape, but wait until you see inside . . ." He had misunderstood her to be ungrateful.

She interrupted him, "are you kidding me? This is adorable!" She was already picturing her walks on the beach. "To clarify, it is $100.00 a week, correct?"

"No, it's $100.00 a month."

They both got out, and Gus followed, bounding toward the yard. She certainly wondered who owned this place and would rent it for next to nothing. There had to be a catch. "Let's go take a look inside." He nodded toward the house. They walked up the path, old cobblestones, surrounded by beach sand. The yard was basic: crabgrass crawling over every inch of the lawn, trimmed short, and camellia shrubs with bright red camellias. The door was unlocked as John Mark pushed it open.

"Wow, people are pretty trusting around here." Anna replied.

"Well, I was over here yesterday working on some things," he shrugged. "I must have forgotten to lock it." He stopped in the threshold turning to her, which made her uncomfortable. "Naples is a close-knit community. People look out for one another." *I guess so*, she thought to herself. She had felt that firsthand when John Mark showed up and rescued her, stranded in a parking lot.

She followed him inside. It felt nice to have someone looking out for her.

"We have a lot of third and fourth-generation residents." He said, his voice laced with pride. "Some of these families have resided in Naples a long time." He flipped on some lights. "Everyone knows one another, that kind of thing."

"That's nice to know." She felt better about trusting him, knowing two or three neighbors were probably watching them, this very moment.

"I bet if you told me who your family was, I would know them." He stopped, waiting for her answer.

Anna was not ready to divulge her connection to Naples.

He waited for her to say something. "Sorry, I don't mean to pry."
She quickly changed the subject . . . "so, you work in construction?"
He caught the hint, "I do."

"Sorry, it smells a little musty." He said, sniffing the air.

John Mark switched on the wall unit, releasing a cool breeze, then moved on. She surveyed the living room: dated but clean furniture, just as he'd said—fully furnished, as if frozen in time. Matching floral sofa and loveseat, marble end tables, lamps with faded shades. Gus barked at the screen door, wanting in. She looked down, realizing she was standing on a colorful Persian rug, her sandy shoes a problem. She started to take them off as John Mark returned.

"Okay, that should do it," he said happily. "I turned on the other two wall units, it should cool down shortly."

"Thanks, coming from the Pacific Northwest, the humidity might take some getting used to." She turned toward the cool AC and let it dry the beads of sweat on her forehead.

John Mark opened the door for Gus, and he promptly came inside, sniffing every corner imaginable.

"So, whose place is this, John Mark?" Anna asked.

He smiled a silly smile, "It's mine." Anna's shock showed on her face.

She wondered if it was appropriate to ask him about the feminine couches or to just leave it be. Unsure, she defaulted to what seemed safe, raising her eyebrows, she said enthusiastically, "Great!" She was thankful for a place to stay, and the décor would grow on her.

CHAPTER SIX

The Sun is Shining Brighter in Naples

John Mark stood with his arms crossed, watching Anna's face turn from confusion into a half smile. "You?" she surveyed the cottage living room again. Her eyes swept over the furniture again, but this time slowly.

"So, what's with the floral print furniture?"

"Well, technically, this house belonged to my mom before she moved." He mumbled. Anna did have a point, most of his mom's décor was some type of flower.

"I think the floral 'style' was popular when my mom set up house in the '70s."

She looked like she wanted to laugh, instead she turned her face away from him and peered out the side window.

"Are you going to be living here as well?" she asked, her tone now serious.

He felt a wave of embarrassment. "Absolutely not." He was shocked she'd even considered it.

"Fine. But what's the catch?"

"It's been empty for a while. And I need to rent it. Sorry about the smell. It could use a good scrub. But, as we stand, the sheets are clean. I've kept the grass mowed. And everything seems to work!" He could tell she was still sizing the place up. She was trying to decide whether he was a total creep. He couldn't blame her. He stood still as she walked from room-to-room. She walked into the laundry room and came back out, her eyes the size of saucers.

"Is that the water heater?"

"Yeah, it's a little old, but it still works," he sucked in a breath, trying to reassure her.

"I would say that thing is ancient, not old." She walked back toward him and sat on the couch, a massive amount of dust came out of the cushion, enfolding around her.

Her lips formed the smallest smile. But she didn't say a word.

"Uh sorry . . . , like I said, it could use a good cleaning."

"I'll take it!" she exclaimed.

John Mark felt happier than he had in months. It felt good to do something for someone else. As far as he could tell, Anna knew no one in Naples, and destiny had pulled them together. He wanted to help.

"Tomorrow, I will bring by the rental paperwork, but no rush on the rent payment." The paperwork would give him an excuse to stop by again.

Anna chuckled and shook her head. "No problem, I can pay right now."

Her eyes sparkled. He liked knowing that he had something to do with that. He would have given the place to her for free if she had let him. But he got the sense she would never accept the gesture.

"So does that make you, my landlord?" she asked as she counted out five, twenty-dollar bills.

"Well, I suppose so. But it also makes me your first friend in Naples," John Mark extended his hand, and she laughed again as she took hold of it and gave it one big shake.

"You know, my brother, Sam would really like you." She placed the wad of cash into his other hand.

"Yeah, why do you say that?"

"You are funny. He has always appreciated humor."

"Well, I hope to meet him someday."

They stood there awkwardly, as John Mark remembered she would need the key.

He took the key off his key ring, and hesitated. That thing had been on there for a decade.

He smiled as he held it. Then handed it to her.

"Thanks! Oh, and I may need your phone number because if that ancient water heater breaks, I am calling you!"

"Done," he pulled a crumpled grocery store receipt from his pocket and looked around for a pen.

"Here," she took one from her purse.

He wrote down his number next to his first name. "You can reach me here, day or night. I mean, I'm available." He felt like an idiot. Now, she definitely thought he was a creep. She chuckled and stood watching him fumble with his words.

"I'm trying to say if something breaks, I will come and fix it."

"I catch your drift."

She brushed strands of hair away from her face, then tucked them behind her ear. He noticed her pearl earrings. They had a tinge of pink in them. Like the ones his mom used to wear. In fact, they were the exact same pair with rose gold fittings.

She noticed him staring at her ears. "A penny for your thoughts?"

"Oh, those earrings," he pointed, "there's a little shop on main street, Welden's, where Mr. Welden used to make earrings just like that."

"Oh really?" she reached up and fumbled with the small pearl.

"They were my moms."

Before he could ask what her mom's name was, her phone rang.

She reached into her back pocket for it and checked it. It must not have been important because she didn't answer. "So, anything else?" she looked at him smiling.

"Nope! The place is all yours!" He didn't want to go.

"Let me get your bags and bring them in."

"Thanks!"

He went outside and shouldered the large bag with Gus's food and bowls and carried her duffel in the other hand. He passed the shed and remembered the bikes. Maybe, Anna could use a bike to get around. He dropped the bag on the floor with a thud. "Oh, please be careful with that," she ran toward the bag.

"Sorry, I can be a little clumsy sometimes. I hope I didn't break anything."

She unzipped it and lifted out a small wooden box. She immediately carried it to the built-in bookcase and put it on the highest shelf. "It's okay." She assured him. Whatever was in that box was special. He felt terrible for dropping her bag and wanted to mend it quickly. "Hey, there are bicycles in the garage you can use! I'll check the air on my way out."

"Why are you being so nice to me, John Mark?"

She had a right to ask.

"Well, I'm a nice guy," he smiled. He was being cocky.

"Good answer."

He changed his approach. "It's like this." He leaned down and made a bowing motion. "Welcome to Naples."

Gus jumped up and circled around John Mark excitedly.

"We are a small community. We help each other. From what I could tell, you looked like you needed some help. And I needed someone to occupy this cottage, so it was a win-win for me."

What he failed to mention were the finer details of rental laws. If premises remained unoccupied for more than five years, the city stepped in and forced a sale upon the home. It was a stupid law. One that should be illegal. When the law passed, he watched the turmoil that ensued after his neighbor, Mr. Sams, died. The family could not decide how to settle the estate. No one wanted to take on the projects and annual tax. The home eventually fell into more disrepair during the mediation process. The city claimed it and forced their hand. The argument was that the house was a hazard and had become a place for squatters, although John Mark had never seen anyone ever live there. The decision: Mr. Sam's house would be demolished, and the land sold to the highest bidder. So, suffice it to say, he needed a warm body in this house and the paperwork to prove it.

"Well, thank you, John Mark." She looked tired.

"Hey, I'll go check those bikes out before I go. Do you need anything else?"

"A shower and a good night's sleep," she joked. Gus walked up to John Mark and licked his hand.

"His way of saying thanks."

"You're welcome, big guy."

They walked to the door together, and she opened the screen for him.

"Bye," he waved as he descended the steps toward the shed.

"Bye," he heard the door close behind him. He tugged on the wooden opening. He listened to the rusty hinges creak. There were two bikes: one belonging to his mom, the other his. Right where they left them. His bike would be perfect for Anna. He took a rag off the shelf in the shed and dusted off the silver frame. He checked the tires, ". . . these need some air," said into the empty shed.

He pulled the string overhead, and the lightbulb came on. He was grateful it worked. He found the pump in a box with two helmets and a bike bell. Bending down, he put air in the front tire. He remembered the morning events and how the day had taken an odd turn. It started with his dad berating him for being a coward yet ended with a reminder that he still carried his mom's goodness within him. His father was trying to turn John Mark into himself—a greedy, ruthless, and lonely man. John Mark would not let the darkness push out the light.

And it felt good to remember that.

Something about the land acquisition surrounding Old Blue was off. It wasn't business; it felt personal, driven by spite. He needed to uncover the motive.

His phone rang. He wondered if it was Anna. Was the water heater already broke?

He dusted off his hands and pulled his phone out.

"Hello?"

It was his dad. His shoulders slumped.

"Son, did you get the email I sent about the Belltown place? It hit the market today. I need you on this now. Don't let your grandfather and me down, boy."

His tone reeked of disappointment and John Mark hadn't even done anything. His dad was always good for the same old song and dance.

"Not yet, I've had a few things on my plate."

"Well get to it." His dad barked.

"I have a few things to finish up here. I'd better go." Snapping his phone shut and shoving it back in his pocket, he finished pumping up the tire.

If he had his way, he would preserve the Belltown place and gift it back to the community. But at the cost of what? Losing the absolute respect of his father and grandfather, no doubt. He checked the time. He needed to go. He closed the shed doors tight and walked to his truck. He knew he still had time to run by the title company to get copies of his land deeds.

Tomorrow will be a big day. He thought about Anna as he climbed in his truck. A breath of fresh air, like an Indian summer wind blowing, breaks up a cold winter.

He backed out of the driveway, and his eyes landed on his mom's rose bushes lining the side of the house. She loved those roses. He hesitated and wondered if it would be nice to pick a few to give to Anna. What was he thinking? He had to admit he was drawn to her. She reminded him of his mom, adventurous, free-spirited, and kind. He was curious about her story. Why had she driven all this way to Naples? He wanted to spend more time with her.

His phone buzzed on the seat next to him. It was his alarm, reminding him of the meeting with the bank. His thoughts were instantly drawn back to "the deal." Shaking his head, he forgot about the roses.

"I can't let anything distract me right now." And, like Anna, he needed a shower and a good night's sleep.

CHAPTER SEVEN

Lucy's Choice

Lucy walked the realtor to her back door and watched him walk down the steps to his Cadillac.

"Thank you, Mr. Thiessen; I'm sure all will go quite smoothly,"

He turned and waved at her, "Don't worry, Mrs. Belltown, a place like this will get top dollar." Lucy knew that, but it wasn't the money she wanted, now it was vengeance. Old Blue, now an accomplice in her plan to thrust a sword into the back of her enemy.

She walked back inside and found Sandy staring out the back window.

"Did you see that heron out there?" A blue heron had been landing daily at her pond. He spent his time scouring the surface of the water for fish. It had been a while since the Herons felt safe to return.

"Yes, I've taken to calling him Charlie. He is my new pet. And an easy one to boot."

"Your new neighbors must be finished with the last of their construction then?"

"I believe so. It has been so loud the past year; I think I learned to drown it out."

"Such a shame to see the old Wheeler place torn down like that. I don't think I will ever fully accept it. It was one of the finer homes on this stretch of the shore." Sandy clicked her tongue.

"Such is life nowadays, to build an enormous place and then only use it for a few weeks a year, some people have more money than sense." *What a waste*, Lucy thought. Houses were meant to be enjoyed, lived in, and shared.

Her house could be next.

"Whew, I'm tuckered out." Lucy announced, dropping into the blue velvet chair. The arm rest was worn to a thread, from years of use. The last two hours had been emotionally draining. Watching someone take stock of one's entire life and put a round number on it, depressed Lucy.

"Thanks for your help this morning."

"You know I wouldn't be anywhere else, Lucy. I hate to see this house go as much as you do."

"Can you believe it?" Lucy shook her head side-to-side, bewildered, "20 million dollars." She laughed. "Daddy would roll over in his grave if he knew what his hands had built is worth a fortune."

"It's incredible," Sandy agreed. "Things sure have changed around here. Jim predicted you would land somewhere in the millions, but I didn't think it would be that high."

Lucy lifted her legs from where they rested on the floor. One at a time she rubbed her calf. The tension slowly left as she rubbed hard.

"I know Old Blue needs a lot of work." Lucy sighed, as she noticed another corner of peeling wallpaper. "But I hope that as people walk through, they can see past all of that." She closed her eyes, as though making a wish. "With the fancy homes being built up and down this corridor, I know this place might pale in comparison."

"Your daddy was a craftsman; people can't find homes like this anymore," Sandy encouraged Lucy.

"Well, I'm trusting Thiessen on this one," although inwardly she doubted him. "He said the land is the selling point."

"Now I want to get my house assessed," Sandy exclaimed. "I could be sitting on millions, and I don't even know it!" She clapped her hands together, "Wait till I tell Jim we're millionaires!"

The two began to chuckle. Lucy was still a little shocked by the assessment as well.

"Did you know that my Daddy paid Paul Gordon $80.00 an acre back in 1900? That's $4,000 just for the land!"

Sandy shook her head, "Wow, and to build it wasn't much more in that day. Although at the time, I'm sure it seemed like a great deal."

"'My Mama used her small inheritance toward this house,' Lucy recalled. "My Daddy, always a dreamer, had painted a vision of paradise, a little slice of heaven on the Florida shore and mama obliged." Lucy remembered, it had been just enough to bring down beautiful oak beams, stained glass, and brass light fixtures, all the way from New York. Lucy recalled the excitement when the barge docked at the pier. The whole town would gather, helping to unload the cargo: giant barrels of flour and sugar, sturdy building materials, crates of squawking chickens, and bolts of vibrant fabric. Before the Naples Mercantile opened, folks relied on the land, their gardens, and the sea. They made do, lived simply. Lucy had grown up around hard work. Her family lived a comfortable life, but they were never over-the-top wealthy people.

"Daddy built mama her dream house." The memory sparked a smile.

"I think he always thought he owed it to her, since he dragged her from her family's fancy mansion in Pennsylvania." Lucy's mama loved this house. A wave of regret washed over her. What would her parents think? She'd just met with a realtor, forced to sell everything they'd worked so hard for. She felt helpless.

"Oh Sandy, I never thought in my wildest dreams that my home would have a for sale sign in front of it."

"I know honey," Sandy sighed. "If I could, I would buy it myself." Shaking her head, "I, too, have memories here, this old place has been a sheltering tree."

"Did you know mama was the one who gave it the name Old Blue?" Lucy chimed in. "She said it reminded her of a big blue sky, blanketing over us, a refuge of sorts." And Old Blue had been that for Lucy, and now it was time to step out of the home's safe embrace into an unknown territory, and it frightened Lucy.

"I never knew that was how it got its name," Sandy was smiling.

Lucy reassured herself this was the best choice. She was, in fact, all out of choices, so it was the only choice.

"When do you think Randall Gordon will find out you are selling the place?" Sandy interrupted her thoughts.

"Oh, you know how small towns are, Sandy, people talk." Lucy said waving it off, "I'm sure Mr. Fancy Pants realtor has loose lips. I wouldn't be surprised if Randall already knows." Lucy would turn down his offer, as fast as it came in. It gave her a sweet pleasure to think about jabbing Randall Gordon where it would count. His pocketbook and his pride.

"Maybe, for once, the Gordons will realize that not everything they touch turns to gold."

"You're a rascal, Lucy."

"Maybe, but we both know, he deserves it."

Sandy narrowed her eyes at Lucy.

"Don't look at me like that. Randall Gordon is a real piece of work. You know that."

"Do I need to remind you of the phone call I got last week?" Lucy decided she did.

"His secretary left me the nastiest message on my answering machine. They threatened me. And I can only imagine that Randall was mad as a hornet that I wouldn't give him water rights to my pond."

His condominiums on the point of the pier were still off the grid for city water lines, so Randall Gordon was pulling from his own cistern. However, water conservation was not on the top of the priority list for the wealthy and eventually they started to run dry.

"It's not my problem. He should have thought of that before building those monsters.

He will want this place, not only for the land, but for the large cistern. It's the largest for miles around, and 'oh boy' when I reject his offer, he is going to be seeing red."

"It's sad that you and Randall used to get on, and now you don't."

Lucy had to admit that it did hurt somewhat that he didn't call her himself and sent someone in his place to do the dirty work.

"Yes, but things change, and it feels kind of good to finally be the one to put a bee in Randall Gordon's bonnet." Lucy laughed so hard she started to cough. She put her hand to her chest and took deep breaths. Sandy watched her with raised eyebrows. Lucy reached for her water glass and took a big gulp. The water took the tickle from her throat. Composed, she continued:

"Honestly, they're going to have a high time figuring this one out. We all know the Gordon's are land rich and cash poor." They will have to sell off more than half of their properties to produce the money to even make a proper offer. The Gordons can't own all of Naples, and before I die, I'll make sure that gets across."

"You really are a crabby old lady."

"And you're . . ." Lucy didn't finish her sentence. It wasn't worth it. Sandy would never understand the predicament Lucy was in. Sandy still had her husband, children, and grandchildren all by her side. How could she understand?

"So, leaving it to Grace's children is still out of the question?"

"Yes! I've already told you they're not going to care one hither about this place if their mother never did. They'll sell it as quick as she would have to the highest bidder."

Lucy knew, at least this way, she could control who the buyer would be and convince them to preserve the house. She would even write in a clause, that whoever bought the house would get her inheritance upon her death to help with the upkeep. Her social security and savings were a handsome sum, as it just kept pooling in her bank account. It helped that she was as frugal as an ant.

"My intent," she declared, "is to direct the sale proceeds to the Naples Preservation Society, bolstering their work to safeguard historic homes. A double blow for Randall." She knew his pleasure lay in destruction. Her legacy, in stark contrast, would be one of preservation, a guardian of the city's past.

"You're not even going to give your grandchildren a chance?"

"No!" Lucy said sharply. *Did she need to say it again?* Lucy's heart was beating fast. She was getting worked up. Changing the subject, she deflected to the Gordons.

"In his sixty-plus years of running the company, Randall Gordon, the man at the helm of Gordon Developers, has dragged it through the mud." Lucy recalled the housing frenzy of the 1970s, when Randall took advantage of many of the older generation, who could no longer afford their property taxes. He made promises that he didn't keep. They sold their cottages to him. And as a local Naples boy, they trusted him. As they moved out, he moved in. He acquired their cottages and sat on them for years, before tearing each one down—one-by-one. The community was devastated. He bulldozed down large parts of Naples's history in moments. Once the debris cleared, he built condominiums, a hotel, and gaudy mansions. Catering to the wealthy who were taking Naples by storm.

"Randall and son, Stan, have disgraced what was once a dignified name. Paul Gordon was a man of principle and integrity." Lucy bellowed. "His son, Randall Gordon, is a greedy man. Paul would be appalled if he saw what his son has done to this town. Absolutely appalled."

Lucy wasn't done with her tirade. Sandy took off her reading glasses, folded them and put them in her lap. She rubbed her eyes.

"Do you remember when the new money came in?"

"How could I not? That was the year I saw more Rolls Royces and Bentleys parking in driveways and cruising down Main Street, than I had seen in my whole lifetime."

Lucy remembered it well because it had affected many of her close friends.

When the millionaires moved in, others had to move out.

"Jim went nuts when he saw our property taxes go through the roof; we weren't even sure we could keep living in our home."

Lucy suddenly stopped. She put her hand to her chest. It didn't feel right.

"Are you alright?"

"It just feels tight."

She took a deep breath. It was hard to breathe. She remembered how her daddy had the same complications as his sickness progressed. Lucy saw the concern in Sandy's eyes as Lucy tried to breathe. Sandy went to her and leaned over her. She grabbed Sandy's arm. "Maybe some fresh air would help." She said each word slowly. Sandy helped Lucy stand up. She tried to keep taking big breaths as they walked together toward the front porch. As Sandy motioned toward the wicker rocker, Lucy's eyes caught the ocean. Like a child's favorite doll, it began to soothe. She felt her chest loosening. Perhaps, the strain of listing the house and the news of Grace was putting stress on her body. She knew it was likely. The weight of it all felt like it was crushing Lucy; she felt utterly overwhelmed.

She pointed to her chest, "Daddy had this too."

She remembered, the few months before he passed, his breathing started to labor, leaving him stuck in bed which he hated. Lucy prayed that it would not be her fate. There was still work to do. She needed more time. Taking a deep breath, she silently prayed, "God, please give me more time."

CHAPTER EIGHT

Tragedy at Old Blue

A few days later, Lucy's whole world changed. "They did what?" Lucy yelled into the phone. She stood up so fast that she surprised even herself. Adrenaline would do that to a person. Lucy knew she frightened her realtor. He was a nice, gentle man, likely unused to someone screaming at him over the phone.

"I'm sorry Lucy," he feigned disappointment, but Lucy knew all he cared about was his payout. "It's the exact amount we asked for, Lucy."

Lucy dismissed him. She wanted answers and she wanted them fast. "So, how did he do it?"

"He used a separate LLC, people do it all the time." *What an underhanded, sneaky son of a gun,* Lucy thought.

"So, you're telling me the offer we accepted, the full price offer, was not the bachelor from Raleigh, looking to retire in a beachfront home that resembled his childhood summer cottage?" she said verbatim.

He sighed, resigned to his fate. "That is correct."

"How, how, how!" she banged her fist into her lap. She knew how. There were no other offers. The offer was full price. And Randall made up a sweet story to disguise his ruse. And she ate right out of the palm of his hand.

"It was sleazy, I agree."

"I just don't know how we didn't get a single other offer? There is nothing like this on the market, you said it yourself."

"Lucy, everyone knows Randall knows people in high places." He explained. "He twisted arms, blackmailed, I don't know what, but whatever he did, he made sure the house would go to him."

"Well, isn't there anything we can do about it!" she yelled into the phone.

"Lucy, I can't rescind the offer." He was exasperated. "It's illegal. I would lose my job."

"Well, then lose your job! We can't let Randall Gordon have everything he wishes."

Silence.

Lucy knew, the man who carries the gold carries it all.

"Lucy, I'm already breaking a code of conduct by disclosing who the buyer is so soon, but it's a small town, and you will eventually find out."

"Don't feel sorry for me; I don't want your pity."

She was growing weary of people feeling sorry for her. Word had spread out about her health; she couldn't walk down Main Street without someone giving her one of their pitiful smiles. "I don't need yours or anyone else's sympathy, thank you very much." She heard herself yelling, and she regretted it.

She hung up the phone with a bang. She didn't even let the realtor respond. Just as she was about to sit back down, the phone rang. You've got to be kidding me, she thought. She picked it up, "Leave me alone!"

"Lucy, it's me."

"Oh, Sandy, so the news travels that fast?"

The line was silent. Lucy unwound the phone cord and plopped herself in the comfortable chair. "Sandy, what am I going to do?"

"You're going to bury the hatchet, Lucy."

"I've lost it all."

"Lucy, don't do a thing until I get there."

Lucy sat quietly, slumped in her chair, with hot tears in her eyes, silent.

"Do you hear me, Lucy?"

She heard her, but she was speechless. Lost.

The last few weeks held more unwelcome news than most people experience in a lifetime. She needed to think.

Click. She put the phone down in the cradle. Even if she felt sorry for doing it, it didn't matter if she hung up on Sandy. Lucy knew Sandy was already grabbing her purse and shuffling to her car. She would be here in five minutes. That's how it was in their friendship. She leaned her head against the chair. Of course, she blamed herself for the mess she was in. If she could change things, she would.

Lucy remembered that day as vividly as if it had just happened. She could already smell the familiar smell of pancakes and coffee. A Saturday morning tradition in the Wright house, one they never missed.

"And where are you off to?"

Bill said looking at Grace as she hurried through her breakfast. Lucy watched from the corner of her eye as she stood at the stove and flipped another pancake. Lately, most conversations with Grace had been strained. They figured it was what happened when any child went through the adolescent stage.

"I'll be back before dinner." A lie. Grace hadn't eaten dinner at home in weeks. She had after school activities or opted to eat at a friend's house.

"Your mother and I need help today; we need to finish sanding the deck. We talked about it last night."

Lucy knew better than to interject. Bill could get through to Grace, where Lucy failed. Grace grabbed her breakfast plate and put it in the sink, the force nearly breaking the plate.

"I hate this house."

By now, Lucy had turned, catching Bill's eye, looking for reassurance. He stood, bracing for an argument. Lucy stepped into the arena, hoping to mediate. "Honey, this house is your legacy."

"The same pitch every time," Grace rolled her eyes. "One day, this will all be yours, Grace." She mimicked her mother's voice.

Lucy nodded her head in agreement with the statement, missing the sarcasm. She smiled inwardly; having something to pass down to one's children was a great feeling.

"Well, guess what? I don't want it." Grace spat out. She bore holes into Lucy's heart with her eyes. Resentment. Bill ran his hands through his hair, clearly exasperated. Lucy was speechless.

"You know what, Mom, I think you love this house more than your family."

"Why would you say that?"

"Remember my art show? You didn't come because you were painting the sunroom and lost track of time."

"Well, yes, but you had five other art shows that year that I did come to."

"Remember when I asked for new shoes for P.E.?"

"Not this again," Bill cleared his plate, setting it next to the sink.

"You told me we didn't have the money and that my old pair was fine."

Lucy laughed, "Oh Grace, you need to appreciate what you have. Growing up, I only had two pairs of shoes, one for going out and one for playing in, and last I counted you have at least ten pairs!"

"It's not fair." Grace crossed her arms like a spoiled toddler.

"We want to teach you to be a good steward of what you have, honey," Bill walked over and put his hand on Grace's shoulder. "Money doesn't grow on trees."

"Except, when you need to repair the house" she grumbled. "Somehow you had the money to replace the broken attic window."

"Grace, that was a necessary purchase; your choice in fashion is not." Bill said, laughing.

Lucy heard the sarcasm in his voice. For Bill, the conversation was over. Grace rolled her eyes at her dad; thankfully, he didn't see.

Lucy chuckled. Grace was being dramatic. Again.

"Honey, your father and I are not made of money. We have told you countless times. Joe said he would love it if you could help down at the market stocking groceries. You can always get a job." She winked at Grace. Lucy recognized this as typical teenage rebellion, a phase that would pass, she hoped. She was counting on it.

"I hate this house." Grace breathed out.

"Your grandfather built this house with his bare hands." Bill faced his daughter. His face stern. "You should be grateful to be living in such a fine house. We live within our means, Grace."

"Well, I am not going to inherit this hunk of junk someday. I will not give my whole life to a house; I will travel, go places, and live."

Lucy heard the condemnation in Grace's voice. The comment was directed at Lucy. It stung. Lucy turned on the burner to warm the kettle. She would brew a cup of tea. Better to ignore than engage.

Grace stormed out. Her goodbye was the slamming of the screen door. "I remember when she was such a sweet little girl. I never imagined she'd become so disrespectful."

Bill said, standing behind Lucy and placing his hands on her shoulders. "Teenagers."

Later that afternoon, Lucy was pulling weeds alongside the house when Bill drove up the driveway. He honked at her smiling, five huge beams stuck out the back of his truck. Lucy waved and brushed her hands off on her pants.

"Well, look who's home early!" She exclaimed, hurrying to greet him with a hug.

"Well, I am glad that I am." He kissed her, holding her close.

"What's all this?" she pointed to the wood.

"Oh, I thought I should brace up the back porch, I noticed it was starting to sag."

Bill had an eye for detail that Lucy was grateful for, and he could fix anything.

"I'm going to fix it first thing, Saturday. Oh, and I got some tar so I can patch the roof. They say another storm is going to roll through next week, and I want to get some of those loose spots on the roof secured."

Bill had always been a handsome man, but in Lucy's eyes, it was the quiet strength of his care that still drew her to him. She grabbed his hand and smiled.

"Can I make you a late lunch?"

"I would like that."

And in they walked, hand-in-hand, to the cool shade of the big blue house.

Lucy shaded her eyes as she looked up toward where Bill stood on the flat part of the roof.

"Bill, honey, Sandy and Jim will be here soon. I've got dinner almost finished."

An hour in the blistering sun on that roof was too long. He waved at her and gave her a thumbs up, but she couldn't shake the feeling of dread. He was too high up there without a rope. He cupped his hands around his mouth and yelled down, "No, Grace?"

"Not yet." And probably not ever.

She watched his shoulders slump. Even if Lucy made a five-star meal, it wouldn't bring Grace to their table. She was stubborn.

She stood watching Bill. He hammered several nails, securing the last shingle as he leaned his body toward the slant of the roof line. Lucy heard the buzzer go off on the oven. She took one more glance at him and hurried inside. Lucy pulled the casserole from the oven as the kitchen screen door clapped shut. She shot up, startled; it was Grace. It had to be. Lucy knew those steps.

"Oh, Grace, honey, you scared me."

Bill would be so pleased that she came home.

Grace looked softer than she had this morning.

"I'm glad you're home for dinner. Sandy and Jim are joining us, and I made one of your favorites, Tater Tot casserole," Lucy said, almost singing it as she set it on a hot pad.

Grace nodded with a half-smile, "Cool, thanks." She set her bag down and got a glass of water.

"Where's dad?"

"Oh, you know your dad, he saw those missing shingles and couldn't help himself, so he's up there replacing them. He should be down in a few minutes."

Grace sat at the round kitchen table while Lucy searched in the fridge for the lettuce she bought for the salad.

"I could have sworn it was right there," she reached in and moved things around.

An odd sound made her stop. She turned around and looked at Grace, who obviously heard it too.

"What was that?"

The sound was like a pickaxe on ice, scraping for a hold. Grace's eyes widened, "Dad!" she cried sprinting toward the back porch.

Lucy knew instantly. As the sound moved. A slow slide. A muffled yell, then a sickening thud.

"Oh, dear Lord," she clamped her hand to her mouth as she took off, following Grace's footsteps. By the time Lucy got to the porch, Grace had already reached Bill. Lucy froze on the steps looking down at the scene. She could see Bill's face from where she stood. Grace was kneeling next to Bill. He was on his back. "Dad!" Grace shook Bill's body. Lucy felt like she was moving slowly as she descended the steps. Blood was pooling under Bill's head.

"Dad!"

Lucy knelt next to Grace, never taking her gaze away from Bill. He lay motionless. Lucy knew, with a chilling certainty, that he was gone. Grace whimpered while clutching his collar, shaking him gently.

"Dad!"

He could not hear her.

Lucy's hands slowly moved to Grace's shoulders. Grace stopped. She let go of Bill and looked at her mom. She just shook her head and let Lucy pull her in and cradle her. Lucy felt the heat. Grace's body was on fire. "Shhhh . . . shhhh . . ."

She began to rock her in the same way she had soothed her as a baby. Lucy barely heard Jim above her own pounding heart,

"What the hell?" Then, "Oh, my goodness."

Sandy rushed to Lucy's side. No one talked. Lucy held Grace. Sandy held Lucy. Time moved slowly, like an old picture movie. Lucy watched Jim go inside and then return. He placed a thin sheet over Bill. "I called 911." Lucy nodded.

No tears came. Her body felt ice-cold. A warm breeze blew, Grace's hair whipped up, and strands landed in Lucy's mouth. Grace's face was buried in Lucy's abdomen.

Sandy tried to lift Lucy and Grace, "Come inside."

Lucy put her lips on top of Grace's head. The same sweet smell—honey and salt. She whispered, "Baby, let's go inside."

"I won't leave him!" Grace declared, pulling away from Lucy and settling cross-legged beside her father. Lucy stood, gazing out at the impossibly calm sea under the breezy sky. She closed her eyes, wishing this were all a nightmare.

The silence hung heavily in the air, as the minutes slipped by. No one spoke. It was broken by the cry of Grace's anguish. "It's all your fault!" Grace knelt over her dad. Sand stuck to her clammy

legs. The wind blew the edge of the sheet from Bill's feet. His shoelaces were double-knotted.

"No, sweetie, it's no one's fault," Sandy said, her voice gentle. Lucy startled and had forgotten Sandy was there.

Sandy crouched beside Grace, who looked like a cornered animal, ready to strike. Lucy watched, a detached observer, as Sandy reached out.

"Get away, all of you." Grace put her hand up, pushing away invisible enemies.

She laid her head on Bill's chest. Whispered something, then stood up. Lucy rose with her, unsure.

Grace looked directly at Lucy, then threw the first dart. "This stupid house, it's always been about this house."

She then stepped toe-to-toe with Lucy and pointed her finger in her face, "You have given everything to this house, and look what it has cost you."

Every instinct screamed at Lucy to gather her child into her arms, but she stood motionless, her arms pinned to her sides.

"The girl is in shock," said Sandy.

Lucy felt a wave of nausea move through her.

"We need to get Bill to a hospital," declared Jim. Lucy heard sirens in the background. Jim's call for help arrived. Lucy knew he was dead. No hospital, no ambulance could change that. But she couldn't bring herself to say the words.

Her daughter's eyes, steely and cold, were alive. They were Bill's eyes—blue, beautiful yet devoid of his compassion and warmth. Lucy lost herself in their depths.

Shock. It does funny things to people. Lucy tried to remember how she got inside. She sat across from Sandy at her kitchen table.

"The paramedics took Bill, Lucy." She wondered if that meant he wasn't dead. Maybe, he had just received a concussion, and he was going to be all right. Then she began to remember. Slowly. It all came back.

"Where is Grace?"

"She's okay, she is with Jim."

"I need to see her."

"I think she needs some space; you both do."

"But, dinner, aren't we all going to have dinner? "Lucy watched Sandy's brow furrow and her eyes dart down toward the table.

"Bill's coming back, Sandy; he just had a small fall."

Sandy shook her head.

"Lucy, you need to eat something."

Lucy wasn't hungry. Sandy rose to find a spatula.

"Help yourself, Sandy, it should be cooled down by now, it just needed a few minutes." Lucy had no sense of time. She looked out the window and saw that it was already dark.

Sandy opened the fridge and took out the pan, now covered in foil.

"I'm going to warm this up."

Sandy slid the glass Pyrex dish into the warmed oven.

"Jim and I will stay overnight in the guest room."

Lucy watched Sandy pull out her white floral plates and set them on the counter. She quickly counted them, "you only have four, you will need one for Bill."

Sandy came to Lucy and knelt in front of her.

"You're trying to process all of this, and it's too much, Lucy, just too much."

Lucy knew deep down what she had seen. But her mind refused to accept it. He was coming home. He had to be. Denial. This is what it looked like.

"I can't eat Sandy." Lucy was on the verge of tears.

"I know, me either. Let's get you into bed, it's late."

Sandy looped her arm through Lucy's. As they walked past the living room, Lucy peered in and saw Jim talking with Grace in a calm voice. She sat with her arms crossed, smashed between all the pillows on the couch. Her own pillow fort.

"Come on," Sandy nudged Lucy forward. They climbed the stairs together. One heavy foot at a time.

Sandy hesitantly pushed Lucy's bedroom door open. Lucy looked at the room, a storehouse of memories she wasn't ready to unlock for fear they would drown her whole.

"Do you want me to sleep in here? I can have Jim pull a mattress in?"

"No, I will be fine." *But would she be?*

I'll be down the hall if you need anything." Sandy said tenderly.

"I should be saying that to you." *I'm such a mess,* Lucy thought.

Sandy hugged her tight. Lucy climbed into bed and fell into a fitful sleep.

Lucy awoke in a stupor. She turned onto her side, facing Bill's side of the bed. She saw the sheets still tucked in and the pillows all in place from the morning before. Instantly, knots formed in her tummy. She felt sick. She looked at the clock and realized she had slept hours past her normal time. What time did she go to bed last night? She smelled coffee. She rose, her feet landing on the clean floor. Yesterday, it had been just another day, another chore: vacuuming, mopping. If only she'd known it was her last day with Bill, she would have spent it holding him close. She didn't bother getting dressed and went downstairs in her clothes from yesterday. She could hear light talking. She walked into the kitchen and the whispers went silent. Sandy and Jim were dressed; their hair done, ready for the day. And sitting with them, in her clothes from yesterday, was Grace. Lucy's heart melted at the sight of Grace's sad and tired face. It was obvious she hadn't slept a wink. Lucy rushed toward her and gathered her close. Grace remained unresponsive. Lucy kissed the top of her head before letting her go and looking at her.

"We will get through this. We need to stick together." No one replied.

Was she finally admitting that Bill was dead? Just hours ago, she was telling herself everything was going to be okay. Lucy felt awkward as three sets of eyes stared at her. She went to the fridge to fetch the carton of eggs. "Can I make anyone fried eggs?" Sandy shook her head, and Jim replied, "No thanks, Lucy." She gave a half smile, went to the stove, and cracked two eggs into the still-warm cast iron pan. She avoided the inevitable by making breakfast. It helped.

"Okay, speak up," Lucy said, forcing a smile, "You all look like big trolls sitting there."

The joke fell flat in the heavy atmosphere. Sandy's face reflected her disapproval.

"How can you joke at a time like this?"

Lucy's gaze shifted to Grace; her expression was unreadable.

But Grace would not look Lucy in the eyes. Lucy's breakfast was done cooking. She slid the spatula under the warm, gooey eggs and placed them on her plate. She sat in the last empty chair. She swallowed her bite and wiped her lips with her napkin. She reached her hand across the table to grab Graces, but Grace did not reach back.

"Grace, we need to start planning your father's funeral," Lucy said, surprised by her own directness.

"I'm leaving." Grace's voice cracked.

Lucy looked at Sandy and Jim. Sandy pursed her lips together and shrugged, and Jim stared down at the floor.

"What do you mean leaving?" she said, almost choking on food.

"I can't stay here anymore. Mom, I'm moving away."

Lucy swallowed and then laughed. "Good one, Grace, you're eighteen. Where would you go?"

"Anywhere. Anywhere but here."

Lucy took a drink from her juice glass. Sandy and Jim watched her.

"And how might you pay for this endeavor?"

"I will figure it out as I go."

Well, you can't go."

"I can and I will."

"Your dad is dead; what are you thinking? You're being selfish." Lucy said it.

And she would repeat it if she needed to.

"You don't see it, you never will, Mom."

"What don't I see," Lucy shouted. She felt her hands beginning to shake. Lucy felt overwhelmed, like a ship about to capsize. She was unstable, on the verge of collapse.

Jim cleared his throat and reached toward the center of the table. He used his hands like a volleyball net to keep the game fair. "Lucy, she's hurting."

"I'm hurting too, Jim, but you don't see me packing my bags and bolting." Lucy stood up and shoved her chair into the table. The saltshaker tipped over.

"This is a time to dig our heels into the ground. Bill would never want this, and you know it." Lucy looked straight at Grace. If anger didn't work, maybe guilt would.

"Dad's not here . . ."

The words hit Lucy like a blow.

The raw truth, that she couldn't unhear.

"He would never have wanted it to be this way, Grace, and you know it." He would have wanted them united, To solve this together, and to support one another. Work through things. Lucy knew her words were falling on deaf ears. Only Bill could reach Grace now, and that was impossible.

"Dad probably didn't want to be on that stupid roof either, fixing the shingles, but you forced him to. He had to take care of this house. Did it ever occur to you that perhaps he didn't want to?"

"Grace," Sandy laid her hand on Grace's wrist and tried to quiet her. Lucy's face turned a bright shade of pink. Disrespect. "Your dad never gave up on a thing, Grace. Not on this house, not on me, and not on you, even when we were at our wit's end." Lucy looked down at the floor after she had said it. Ashamed. She knew the words would hurt Grace. Grace shook her head. Lucy saw the tiniest tear dribble down her cheek. Maybe, she was finally getting through to her.

They were both riding an emotional roller coaster, plunging them down into its dark caverns and back up again for a glimpse of light.

"Grace, honey, I'm so sorry."

Lucy was sorry for what she had said, sorry that Bill died, sorry for being a bad mom, just flat out sorry. Lucy went to Grace, wanting to hold her, but needing to be held.

Grace put her hand up, and Lucy stopped. "Please, don't."

Sandy nodded, holding Lucy's gaze. Lucy gave Grace the distance she required. Grace had to come around; she always did.

Unable to compose herself, she blurted out, "like I said, we must focus on your dad. I prefer to have his memorial service here at the house. Jim, can you help arrange that?"

"Sure, Lucy," he looked unsteadily at his wife, Sandy.

Finally, Sandy walked over to where Lucy leaned against the kitchen counter. She put both hands on Lucy's shoulders and looked directly into her eyes.

"You need to listen. Really listen, Lucy. You need to hear Grace."

Lucy breathed out a large sigh, annoyed that they were back at this again. Exasperated, she breathed out, "Okay, Grace, I'm listening!"

"This is hopeless," Grace shoved her chair as she stood.

Sandy glared. Lucy cowered like a scolded child.

"Go ahead honey," Jim urged Grace on.

"This house killed dad." Grace said with emphasis.

Lucy heard the accusation, loud and clear, 'You killed dad.'

Ungrateful child. If Lucy could, she would ground Grace for the next month. Bill never would have stood for this type of language, yet Lucy held her tongue.

"I want nothing to do with this house or this town."

"We've already been through this; do you really need to keep driving the nail into the board?"

Lucy had to admit, sometimes she wanted nothing to do with the house either. She looked up at the ceiling at the same water spots that had been there for years. They came from the upstairs bathroom and had taken on the shape of a banana. Bill had promised to mend and paint them this year. Now the task would fall to her.

"Sell it." Grace looked directly at Lucy. "Prove me wrong, Mama."

"Sell Old Blue?" Was Grace kidding? She was acting out of shock and stress.

"That's what I said, sell it. Move away from here, start somewhere fresh."

"I would never sell this house; it belonged to my family. This is my home."

"I'm your family." Her voice was firm, yet Lucy heard the plea.

Sandy walked over to Grace, and stood next to her.

Lucy laughed, "what, now you're taking sides, Sandy?"

She went and picked up the kettle to make tea; it always calmed her nerves. Keeping her back to her audience, hiding the storm raging within her.

"Listen to her, Lucy!" Sandy said with force.

Startled, Lucy almost dropped the kettle.

Her hands tightened on the handle as she set it back down on the burner.

"What, Sandy?"

"Stop being so stubborn like your daddy," Sandy pleaded.

Stone-faced, Lucy met Grace's and Sandy's eyes. In response, Sandy moved Grace forward, holding her gently out to Lucy. "See your daughter. Hear her," Sandy said, her tone gentle but firm.

As Lucy's eyes rested on Grace, she saw her, she was ten years old. Suddenly, Lucy remembered the day Grace fell off her bike. She had come in with a bloody knee and a bruised ego. She was hurt. She wanted her mama. Lucy cleaned the wound and kissed her knee.

"You're one tough cookie," Lucy said as she put the band aid over the scrape.

She had to admit, Grace fell hard, and most kids would have yowled, but not Grace, she bit her lip when Lucy put the peroxide on to clean out the dirt. Lucy saw that same face, in this moment. Grace was hurt. Hurt kids always want their mama. And Grace's face wasn't asking for mom; it was begging.

"Grace, I love you. But I'm not selling this house." Lucy knew that the only way she would ever leave this house was over her dead body.

Silently, Grace bent down and grabbed her backpack and put it on.

"I won't set foot in this house again." Lucy wanted to tell Grace she had no choice in this matter, that she couldn't leave, but she wasn't staring at a little girl anymore. She was looking at an adult.

"Whoa, slow down; no one makes any drastic decisions now." Jim stepped in front of Grace, blocking her exit. He was Bill's best friend.

Lucy took a deep breath and softened. She turned toward the window and watched a heron land on the grassy bank of the pond. Bill loved herons. He didn't mind that they fished in his pond, he even stocked it for them.

"Grace, this is my home. It's your home. I can't give this up. It's all I've ever known. Our life is here, mine, yours, your daddy's," she barely choked out the last part, her back to Grace.

"It's hard for you to understand this, but we've built a life here, in this town, with these people, if I give all of this up, I'm giving up on them too."

Lucy watched the graceful bird lift up and fly away. His coming and his going providential. Eyes closed, breath steady, she turned back around, her gaze landing on Grace. She was poised, like a frightened deer, ready to dart. Sandy broke the silence.

"The pair of you are so alike. Hardheaded. Loyal. You love each other. But you're too stubborn to admit it."

"I'm nothing like her," Grace's disdain burned for Lucy, burning furiously in her eyes.

Lucy had to stop this emotional freight train before it crashed, but the price was too high: her home, her legacy. She remained unmoved. Grace looked at Lucy. "Bye, Mama."

"Oh, Grace, don't be irrational; we have too much to do. Your father's funeral is going to take a lot of planning. Then there is the list of chores we must divvy between us." Lucy had already decided how she would get through her pain. She would stay busy. Avoidance: her path through the pain.

Lucy watched Grace hug Sandy. Then, walk over to Jim and do the same. They whispered a few words to one another that Lucy couldn't hear. Lucy was the outsider. Sandy reached for Grace's hand, a silent offering of consolation.

Lucy wanted to scoff and tell them, *She'll be back. She's just overreacting.* But she knew she had said enough.

Jim grabbed Grace in one more bear hug and said, "We're here if you need anything, kiddo. Are you sure this is what you want?"

She stepped back from him and nodded her head, yes. Grace looked at Lucy. She gave a half-smile and shrugged. She took one long look around the kitchen, turned, and walked out the door. And Lucy let her.

"Lucy," it was Sandy.

"In here." A brief pause, and she pulled herself back to the moment.

Sandy set her purse on the piano bench and shook out her jacket.

"Is it raining?"

"Just a lite sprinkle. You know the routine, it will last fifteen minutes, and the sun will be shining once again."

Sandy sat down across from her.

"We've been here before, you and me."

Lucy groaned and rubbed her face with her hands. "History does have a way of repeating itself sometimes."

"Lucy, it is important to preserve the past, but when it is at the expense of those in the future, I just don't think it's the way."

Lucy had heard these exact words before. Sandy spoke them to her decades ago. The day Grace left home. Lucy knew. Deep down, she had always known. She picked her house over her child—her family's legacy. Sandy was right then, and she was right now.

"How is it that you're always right?"

Sandy laughed. "You were right, too, it just took you longer."

Lucy's resolved herself to the truth. "All along, it wasn't a pile of bricks and wooden slats; it was Grace. She was my legacy." *And, I blew it*, Lucy thought.

"It's never too late to change things, you know."

"Oh, those kids won't want this, I'm sure of it."

"You will never know if you don't try."

Lucy felt trepidation. She knew Sandy had a point, but she wondered if her heart could take one more stab. She wasn't sure this time it would hold up to more rejection and loss. She would put on a good face for Sandy, even if she was trembling at the thought of finding her grandchildren.

Lucy grabbed Sandy's arm, "I have an idea! With the twenty million, let's fly to Belize, a girl's trip and live it up!" She was half-kidding, but kind of serious.

Sandy smiled, "One day at a time, Maverick."

CHAPTER NINE

An Unexpected Development

The next morning, Lucy pushed herself out of bed, even with a full night's sleep, she already felt exhausted. It was one of the awful side effects of cancer, and the sale of the house to the Gordons only amplified the exhaustion. Today, she needed all the energy she could muster. Just yesterday, a man had arrived at her door with a certified letter. It was the letter she had dreaded--the title company had formally notified Lucy that Old Blue had been sold. The purchaser's name: Raleigh Bay LLC, also known as Gordon Developers LLC. Bill would be shocked if he knew Randall Gordon would be the owner of their grand, old house. Without fully reading the letter, she crumpled it and tossed it away.

It's time to get up, she told herself. She stepped lightly across the upstairs landing, the cool hardwood familiar beneath her bare feet. Descending the wide stairs, her hand glided along the banister, each groove a memory etched in wood, a braille book of her childhood. In the mudroom, she slipped into her daddy's worn red wool sweater, its familiar scent offering a comforting embrace over her pajamas. The kitchen light flickered on, casting a warm glow, and the coffee maker gurgled its last, familiar drops. She had to hustle. Sandy and Jim would be right on time. They always were. Today was going to be draining—emotionally and physically. Decisions had to be made. What to sell, what to donate and what to give away. The Naples Preservation Society would welcome some family heirlooms. Many of her mama's items were "firsts" for Naples, such as the Steinway Piano that she had shipped from up north. Folks said it would never survive the humidity, but it did. And Lucy still played the keys from time to time. She could have sold it, of course, but she didn't need more money. She still had to decide what to do with the hefty sum she would accumulate from the sale of the house. After she died, it would need somewhere to go.

Coffee in hand, she sat on the porch. The sunrise turned the water into pink diamonds. The water's glow, warming her from the inside out.

Lucy heard a faint knock at the door. Her hearing wasn't up to par but she wasn't deaf. What in the world was someone doing at her house at this hour. Sandy and Jim were not due for at least two hours. She waited, maybe they would go away. Then she heard the doorbell. She set her cup down on the side table, looking at the clock as she walked by—6:10 a.m.

It's an awful time to pay someone a visit. She opened the front door. Frowned.

It was another delivery. But this time, the man standing before her offered a gentle smile. He was wearing a blazer and black slacks. Behind him was a black, official-looking Cadillac. Lucy forgot she was in her pajamas and wrapped her arms quickly over her chest. She narrowed the door's opening, leaving only her face in view.

"Good morning, Ms. Belltown, is it?" he asked, looking directly at her. He held up a large square envelope.

"Yes, I am she."

"Then, this is for you."

He put a clipboard before her and pulled a pen from his pocket.

She reached through the door opening and took the clip board.

"I'll need you to sign here and here." He pointed to the two blank spaces. He handed her the pen.

"And what is this all about? It better not be another letter from that scoundrel." She said, thinking Randall sent yet another notice.

"Official letter, ma'am. Notarized and hand delivered."

He held the envelope up once again for her to see. Her name and address were printed on the front. She knew she shouldn't shoot the messenger. The guy was just trying to do his job.

"Okay, young man, give me the pen." She reached out her hand. "So, this form, I am signing is to verify I am in fact Lucy Belltown?"

"Yes, ma'am."

She took the pen and signed on the dotted line. He pointed to two places. She obliged. He smiled and nodded and handed the letter to her. "Sorry for the early morning call, it's just that I drove in from Miami late last night, and I have a few more of these to deliver today."

He tipped his hat and strode away.

Turning around he waved, "Good day, ma'am."

"Good day, indeed."

She turned to go back into the house. She put her reading glasses on and read the return address. "Harvey and Snyder Law Offices, San Diego, CA."

Curious, she made to open it, but thought she would wait a moment and finish her coffee while it was still warm.

"Yoo-hoo, it's me!" She looked at the clock. An hour had already gone by. Sandy came through the back screen. She must have walked to the house.

"I'm in here," Lucy said as she reached for her letter opener, and slid it just under the flap of the envelope.

Sandy stood with her hands of her hips, staring at Lucy. Her hair was windblown, her cheeks were rosy. "Did you just get up?"

"No, I just got interrupted. By you!"

"What's that?"

"I don't know, I was just about to open it."

"Well, don't let me get in your way, I've got a bag of beach treasure to wash off." Sandy pointed toward the laundry room, "Do you mind?"

"You know where the utility sink is, just make sure you wash all of the sand down."

Lucy looked around, "Where's Jim?"

"Oh, he's driving over. He borrowed Jeff's truck. He thought you would need us to haul things away to the thrift store." She bustled away with her treasures, leaving Lucy to the letter.

Lucy unfolded the papers. Sandy was humming from the other room. Lucy was sure she had gathered more sand dollars, scotch bonnets, and sundial shells for her collection. *How many shells can a person have?* Lucy wondered. Sandy had at least seven decades worth. Lucy read the first line on the letter. Sandy walked back out, drying her hands on the bottom of her dress.

"You always have the biggest sand dollars down your way. I found one the size of a grapefruit!" Lucy didn't look up. Reading further, she realized this was entirely unrelated to Old Blue changing hands.

Sandy eventually sat down; Lucy's eyes never left the page.

"Lucy, what is it?"

"I don't fully know yet; I'm still reading."

Finally, Lucy looked up, "I can't believe it."

"What?"

"You've got to be kidding me." Lucy was bewildered by what she was reading.

"What is it, Lucy?" Sandy questioned.

Lucy's eyes glowed, "Sandy, it's Grace, the children."

"A letter from Grace?" Sandy look confused.

Lucy started to ramble, thinking out loud.

"Grace never wanted a relationship with me. She did not want her children to have a relationship with me." She paused and felt the lump rise in her throat, and took a deep breath.

"I mean she would send me the occasional school picture with a few sentences, but that was it. In Grace's eyes, I was unsafe." Lucy paused and looked at Sandy. Unsure of how to go on. Here they were again, revisiting the valley. Sandy waited.

"But, now I get this," Lucy held the letter out for Sandy to read.

Sandy took it, and slowly began to read.

"Oh, wow." Sandy put her hand to her mouth.

"Exactly." Lucy's shoulders slumped and her body relaxed. Sandy began to read the letter out loud.

> "Ms. Belltown, as you are surely aware, upon the death of your daughter, Grace Gentry, her estate was bequeathed to her two surviving children, Samuel and Anna Gentry, with the exception of one item, which was bequeathed to you. Somehow, our office overlooked Ms. Gentry's addendum to her will. The inclusion stated that Mrs. Lucy Belltown should inherit the Pennsylvania Shelton stock bonds, and all monies should be put toward a structure named Old Blue, in the town of

Naples, Florida. We have contacted Shelton Industries and processed all the formalities, putting the stocks into your name. They will contact you directly to discuss particulars.

We apologize for overlooking this, and we hope that this letter finds you well.

> *Our deepest condolences and apologies,*
> *Darrell Harvey,*
> *Attorney at Law, Harvey and Snyder*

She looked at Sandy. "She left me her inheritance money." Lucy was speechless. "It's mama's family stock, set aside for each grandchild. And Mama, had just the one, Grace." It was the same money Lucy's mama had used to build Old Blue. Grace's allotment had likely grown into a large sum by now. What baffled Lucy the most was that Grace had wanted it to go toward Old Blue!

The letter had given her more energy than a cup of coffee or a weeklong vacation. Something had altered in Grace, a shift Lucy was not given the privilege to see. Then, in an instant Lucy was overtaken with a swift sadness. Grace's gesture, a peace offering offered too late, revealed the vast, unbridgeable gap. Grace was gone. The moment for understanding and reconciliation had passed.

Regret. It was the word that hung onto Lucy like a hangnail. Disturbing and always coming back. Sandy kept shaking her head in disbelief.

"Lucy, I wish I could say I'm happy for you, but I'm not sure those are the right words right now," Sandy admitted, her gaze reflecting Lucy's profound sadness. "A bittersweet moment," Lucy agreed, her voice strained. The letter revealed a buried tenderness in Grace, perhaps even forgiveness, but it was overshadowed by the weight of what could have been.

Lucy folded the letter and tucked it back into the envelope. "I'm speechless, really." She shook her head looking at Sandy. Surveying the room, she saw what lay before them—

Mountains of work. "Let's talk while we work." Lucy said. "We have a lot to do."

"Okay," Sandy agreed. Lucy needed to work her way through this one. She reached for the masking tape and a pair of sewing scissors. She was ready to attack her first pile of knick-knacks and pack them up.

Sandy walked over and grabbed a box and began to fold it into a cube.

The two were silent for a while, wrapping and packing, both thinking about the letter.

Finally Lucy broke the silence.

"This is a complete turn of events," Lucy said, her voice faltering.

"Grace is speaking to you, Lucy. Her last words."

"I have to find them, Sandy. Everything here—it's theirs."

"If they want it," Sandy said, offering the tape.

"Do you think she mentioned me to the children?"

"There's no way to know."

"Hey gals," Jim walked in interrupting their conversation.

"Well, finally, I thought maybe you got caught up in an undertow or something," Sandy winked at Jim. He walked over and hugged Lucy. "You're getting too skinny." Lucy slugged him in the stomach, "Yeah, and you're getting too fat, and I'm not hassling you for it."

"You two cut it out and get back to work," Sandy shot Jim her look.

"Right-O, Boss," Jim nodded at Sandy.

"We have to get most, or all of this labeled and boxed by tonight for the movers."

Lucy ran her hand over the top of the wooden buffet, nestled against the wall. It had belonged to one of daddy's great-aunts. Now, it would grace the hallway of the Naples Preservation Society. She could not bear to see her family's items sold off, and she was grateful the society welcomed such heirlooms, particularly those with a storied past.

"Jim, come with me. Lucy, you focus on the items for the society. I'll show Jim what needs packing in the guest room."

Lucy felt a wave of gratitude for her friends, especially today. She'd never been able to part with Bill's clothes, moving them instead to the guest room closet. When grief overwhelmed her, she'd open the door, burying her face in his worn work shirts, inhaling his lingering scent. Aside from the few shirts she held back for herself, it was time to let them go.

After getting Jim started, Sandy returned and began to unfold sheets and shake them out.

Lucy instructed Sandy, "once we label the society items, we will cover them up. They are making room for a few of them at Palm Cottage, the rest will be saved for the new addition."

Sandy gave a thumbs up.

Lucy studied her mother's curio cabinet, *save or sell?* She wondered. Sandy paid no attention and tossed a sheet over the top almost covering Lucy in the process.

"Hey wait!' Lucy said pushing the sheet away. "I haven't gone through the contents inside."

"I'm sorry," Sandy said as she whipped the sheet off. Lucy, had a sudden urge to revisit the past and unearth it's treasure. She unlatched the hook, revealing her mother's linens, china, and napkin rings. Sandy stood next to her. "Your mama's special dinner set," Sandy said excitedly. Reaching in and pulling out a napkin, she held it out to Lucy. "Remember your sweet sixteen?"

"I could never forget," Lucy smiled. "The table, the candles, everything was perfect."

They purged and cleaned, discarding and boxing. Lucy reached deep into a dusty shelf, pulling out her find. "Great-Grandma Sundry's candlesticks, from Poland!" she announced, her excitement palpable. It was like Christmas morning.

Sandy grinned. "You know what this means?" Her joy was contagious. Lucy looked puzzled. "Silver polish?" Sandy nudged her. "A party! A going-away party!" Lucy groaned. "More work." But she knew Sandy was right. Old Blue needed a proper goodbye, even if its new owner was . . . less than ideal.

"What do you say, Lucy?"

For Old Blue's sake, Lucy would do it.

"I think that would be fine," she nodded, not sure how she would pull it off.

Lucy continued walking from item to item, deciding what would go where. She felt every bit her age as she taped one more box. "Let's take a break before starting on the next room."

Before Sandy could answer, Lucy grabbed her side and yelped.

"Sit down, Lucy," she helped her to the couch. She pushed aside the stack of books and made a place to sit. "You rest; I'll finish this out."

She walked to the foot of the stairs, "Jim," Sandy yelled.

Lucy didn't want to admit that the pain in her side had been increasing by the hour. Sandy walked back in and handed Lucy a glass of water. Jim joined them.

"I just need to sit for a moment."

"We all do," Jim sat down and wiped his brow. From the look on his face, going through Bill's clothes had been hard.

"I'm grateful for you, Jim." She smiled over at him. He winked, understanding.

She let her body sink into the chair. As she looked around at the few boxes they had packed and the covered furniture, she thought, *what if Grace had reconsidered? And what if now, somehow, she was trying to tell Lucy to wait.* Lucy had never met her grandchildren, they could be her next-door neighbors for all she knew, and she would never know. She didn't even know where to begin her search, and if so, would they want any contact with her? Would they want all this old stuff? Could she wait? No, time was a luxury she couldn't afford. Death was at the door.

CHAPTER TEN

A Promise to Help

Anna ended the call and snapped her phone shut. She tossed it onto the floral couch, then hopped up. The clock confirmed it was early but thankfully she was a morning person. John Mark would be at the cottage any minute. She needed to brush her teeth. She tossed on a sweater over her tank top. The air conditioner worked great, except it kept the cottage about ten degrees cooler than what the gauge said. After gulping down some water, she hustled to the bathroom to finish her morning routine. Just a few minutes passed before Gus's barks let Anna know that someone was at the door.

"Quiet boy," she shushed him as she walked past. She opened the door; A smile brightened John Mark's face as he held out a basket brimming with various items.

"Thanks!" Anna exclaimed, glancing into it. He'd created a charming welcome basket.

"This is the best coffee you'll ever have. They roast their beans right here in Naples."

Tucked into the basket beside the coffee beans were chocolate bars, a jar of honey, and a coffee mug declaring, "Pelicans are my Friends."

Anna laughed, "nice, I do like pelicans. Is this from a nature conservation?"

"Yeah, but not a local one. I wish we had a local branch. This one's for Fort Myers."

She took a deep breath, enjoying the smell of the coffee, and then noticed something else in the basket. Underneath the beans was a set of socket wrenches. Anna gave John Mark a questioning look.

"Oh, these!" he said, gesturing to the wrenches. "Well, I figured I could teach you a few things about your truck. Just the basics, you know? So if something goes wrong again, you won't be stuck on the side of the road."

"That is thoughtful," she wasn't sure if she should laugh or take him seriously.

"It feels nice out here, mind if we sit on the porch?"

"Yeah, sounds great." He replied.

"Can I get you something to drink?"

"Maybe a glass of water?"

Back inside, she filled a glass with tap water. A twist of the ice tray released a few cubes, which immediately began to shrink as she dropped them into the glass. *Everything here melts so fast*, she thought. As she walked past the living room shelf, her eyes landed on the letter she had placed there last night. Without thinking, she grabbed it and stuffed it in her back pocket.

"Here we are," she handed John Mark the water.

"Thanks."

"Sorry, I should have put more ice in it. The water here doesn't cool down much, does it?"

"Nope, it's always a tepid 75." He said, laughing, drinking it all one in a swoop. "So, how were your first few days in the cottage?" he asked a hopeful look on his face. "Everything work okay?"

"Yes, it's been good."

They sat in silence for a few moments.

"Alright," John Mark said, breaking the quiet, "what's going on?" He'd probably been wondering what she wanted to talk about since she'd invited him.

How do I begin? She wondered

"So, you said you grew up here," she stated confidently.

"Yes, I did," his reply curious.

"And your parents? And grandparents, are from here too?"

"Guilty, as charged." He put his hands up in the air, surrendering.

"Well, I was wondering, since you're a local and all, that maybe you could help me figure something out."

"Try me!"

She pulled the sealed letter from her pocket. Anna thought back to finding it—a mystery, unsolved, that had started all of this. It had brought a mix of confusion and a strong sense of curiosity.

"Remember when you asked who my family was?"

He nodded yes.

"Well, that is what I'm trying to figure out."

"Okay," he shifted uncomfortably in his chair.

"It all began with this letter," she clutched it, then set it face down on her lap.

He was watching her. His eyes landed on the letter in her lap.

"This is why I came to Naples." This letter, the unexpected start of the bunny trail, she prayed would also be where the trail finally ended.

She flipped the letter over and let him look at the name and address.

"Whoa," his brow furrowed. Something by the way his eyes shot open made Anna wonder if he knew the address.

"Do you know this place?" She asked excitedly, ready for any lead.

He reached for his water glass. The last few ice cubes had left a small sip at the bottom. Probably very warm by now, but he drank it anyway.

Licking his lips, he leaned forward, resting an elbow on one of his knees. "Can I ask you a question?"

"Sure."

How are you connected to that address?" His voice was no longer casual, but serious.

"Well, that is what I don't know. I'm trying to find that out."

"Where did you get this letter?" He pressed.

"Wait, why are you asking me questions?" The tables had suddenly turned making Anna uncomfortable.

"Sorry, you're right." He took a deep breath, running his hands through his hair.

Anna chuckled trying to lighten a serious moment. "Well, my mom wrote it before her accident. I found it when I was packing up a few things," she said fidgeting.

"I think this is the address for the home she grew up in." Anna looked at the envelope again.

"Wow . . . geez." He inhaled deeply. "You know what? Could I get another glass of water?" He cleared his throat and stood abruptly. Anna could feel the shift in the air; something about her question had clearly made him uneasy. As he went inside, a pang of regret hit her. *Maybe I shouldn't have pushed it.* John Mark reappeared moments later, carrying two glasses of water. "Here you go," he said, gently handing her one. She took a long drink. He settled back onto the wicker bench, his hands going behind his head in a deliberate stretch. His eyes scanned the sidewalk, where locals and visitors alike were making their way towards the beach. The silence stretched again before them. Anna wanted to change the conversation, but before she could, John Mark spoke.

"Anna, what happened to your mom?" This question caught her completely off guard.

"Uhhh," was the only sound she could manage.

She was grateful when Gus whimpered, peering through the screen door, panting.

"Hey boy, you want to come outside too?" She stood and pulled the door open. Gus wagged his tail, turning in circles around the porch and excitedly sniffing each corner and crevice. Eventually Anna sat back down, and Gus meandered over and lay at her feet.

Besides Anna, only Sam knew the details of the accident. The memory remained too raw to share with anyone else. They had always had one another to confide in, and that had been enough. That was before continents came between them.

"Sorry," he scratched his chin. "I didn't mean to pry."

"It's just not easy for me to talk about."

"Understood."

He took another drink and leaned down to scratch Gus behind the ears, a small snore as the dog began to doze.

"You know," John Mark said, looking around, "being here always makes me think of my mom."

Anna was relieved that he didn't continue to press her.

"You must miss her terribly."

"Yeah," he said quietly. "She died when I was eighteen, right after I finished high school."

"I'm sorry, John Mark." Anna replied, her voice filled with sympathy.

"My parents had been divorced for a while. This is where mom lived after the divorce," his eyes swept past Anna to the side yard where tea roses bloomed. "I lived with her up until she passed."

Anna looked down at her linked fingers, a familiar ache stirring within her. She understood the depth of John Mark's grief. The loss of a parent was a wound that never fully healed, a truth she understood by her own loss.

"Cancer," he said simply. "They tried to remove it all, but it kept returning." He shook his head slowly. "She fought it with everything she had, every single day. And even then, she always found a way to be happy, to look for the light even in the darkest times."

"Those roses are beautiful." Anna said pointing to the pink and yellow petite roses, blooming against the house.

"Mom loved flowers, but I'm sure you gathered that from those rad floral-covered couches."

They both laughed.

"She loved life."

"She sounds like she brought a lot of joy to those around her."

"She never had an enemy." A gentle smile crossed his lips, as he said it.

"I don't know what she ever saw in my dad though. He's a real jerk."

His jaw twitched. He rubbed his hands on his thighs and looked out again toward the sidewalk. They sat once more, in silence, letting the slight breeze cool them on the shaded porch.

"And, you know what, she would be glad you're living here." He smiled reassuringly.

"Thanks," Anna whispered, a pang of longing hitting her. How could he speak so openly, so calmly, about his mother? For Anna, the mere thought of her own mom brought a lump to her throat.

Maybe the key is simply to begin, she told herself, but the words felt impossible to form. She brought her water glass to her lips, finding it empty. The birds happily chirped in the tree branches above them, as the sun grew higher in the sky. Anna felt the little golden rays on her bare feet and moved them into the shade.

She would try. *Just start talking,* she told herself. Anna's heart raced as she began to speak, "Mom was driving back from a convention in Southern California, something to do with forest conservation. A drunk driver hit her head-on. She died on the scene." Her body tensed. She wasn't sure if she was going to throw up or pass out. Trying to regain control she folded her arms in front of her and closed her eyes.

John Mark turned toward her, a look of tenderness in his eyes.

"Anna, I'm really sorry." He reached out, then quickly pulled his hand back, unsure of the right thing to do.

I've done it; I have shared. I can do this, she thought. "My brother, Sam, and I were notified that evening. I thought it would break Sam apart. But we held up okay."

Anna's eyes were drawn to a man pulling a wagon down the sidewalk. Two children giggled inside, alongside a panting dog, all shaded by a wonderfully jerry-rigged umbrella keeping off the late-morning sun. The scene tugged at her heart, reminding her of her own dad and the lengths he'd go to for a smile from her and Sam.

"I can't even imagine, Anna." John Mark looked at her. "How did your dad take it?"

Should she tell him? Dig even further into her past, offering it to a new friend? She would keep it brief. The familiar tightness formed in her throat, "John Mark my dad passed away when I was really young."

"I am so, so sorry. I don't feel like I have any words of comfort to offer." Her story was heavy. But, she wasn't looking for comfort. If anything, she was ready for a pause after diving deep.

"Anna," John Mark paused. "Losing a parent is just downright crummy," he murmured.

No kidding, she thought wryly. Discussing her dad had softened with time, sometimes even offering a strange comfort. But her mother's death remained raw. She hoped, as she'd been told, that eventually talking about it would become less unbearable.

"It's left a huge hole, as far as Sam and I know, we're the last of the last."

John Mark breathed a huge sigh.

"But that is one of the reasons I am here." She glanced at the envelope in her lap. "This might be the only way Sam and I can find any of our living relatives."

"That letter is everything, it's what drove you here." John Mark stated.

"Absolutely. It feels like a vital piece of the puzzle that's been missing for too long," Anna said, her resolve growing stronger.

"Whoever this letter is for," she stated, a renewed strength in her voice, "they have to know something about my mom, about our family's past." As she said it, she felt some of the weight of their heavy conversation lift.

"And my mom was a Naples native, John Mark, so this has to be a link." The thought fueled Anna's hope of finally finding the family she craved.

A buzz from John Mark's pocket interrupted the moment. He retrieved his phone, his brow furrowing as he read the notification.

"I'm so sorry to cut this short, but I really need to get going."

She nodded, understanding, yet feeling slightly embarrassed that she had confided so much in him. She needed to clear her head.

John Mark picked up the water glasses and took them inside.

When he came back out, Anna was putting on her running shoes and hooking the leash up to Gus.

"You two going somewhere?"

"Well, I've got to put that bike to good use, you spent all of that time working on it!"

"Okay, just watch the left brake, I'm not entirely sure it is working right."

"Got it, brake right, not left,"

He nodded. "And watch out for potholes, Naples is notorious for them!"

As he walked down the steps to his truck, he paused and turned. "I'll help you play detective with that letter, Anna," he called back with a smile. *How thoughtful. He just keeps getting better and better,* she thought.

"Just . . . maybe don't mention the letter to anyone else in town just yet." He waved as he climbed into his truck. She gave him a thumbs up from the porch.

Weird, she thought, a little annoyed. *Why the hush-hush about the letter? And who does he think he is, telling me what I can and can't do with it?* Rolling her eyes at his suggestion, she went inside and changed into a tank top and her running shoes. She decided to bike into town and ask the first nice person she saw where Old Blue was. She gave the clean envelope one last glance before shoving it into her backpack. Up in the corner was her California address, and right in the middle, the reason she was in Naples, written carefully in her mom's handwriting:

Mama
Old Blue
Naples, FL 34102

She looped Gus's leash around her elbow and wheeled her bicycle onto the sidewalk. Before pushing off, she flipped open her phone and tapped Sam's number.

"Hello?"

"Hey, it's me."

"Anna, do you even know what time it is here?" he said in a groggy voice.

"You'll be glad I woke you up, trust me."

"You say that every time."

CHAPTER ELEVEN

The Friends of Old Blue

John Mark slammed on the brakes, the tires screeching as his truck veered sharply to the right. He'd narrowly avoided hitting a dog that darted across the road. He watched, heart still pounding, as the animal trotted into a meticulous yard and began sniffing the grass. A small girl stood on the opposite side yelling something he couldn't quite make out.

He pulled his truck over and got out.

"Babcock, come here right now," she hollered.

John Mark noticed Babcock was ignoring her completely.

"Need some help with him?" he offered.

"Yeah," she said, gesturing to the side of her yard. "He dug out under the fence." She pointed to the tiny hole, a testament to Babcock's surprising agility.

Finding the short rope in his toolbox, he figured it was worth a try. He held it up, then said, "I'll try to leash him."

She responded with an encouraging thumbs-up. He crossed the street, deliberately slowing his approach to the oblivious dog.

"Here, boy," he whistled bending down.

Babcock looked up, assessed him, and continued sniffing through the neighbor's grass, hunting for something.

"He loves jerky, mister! Do you have any?" she called out excitedly.

John Mark recalled giving his last piece to Gus. Thinking quickly, his gaze fell on a nearby leaf.

Babcock wouldn't know the difference. He crumpled it in his hand, offering it gently. "Here you go, Babcock." He held his palm open, presenting the crinkled leaf to the curious terrier.

Babcock's ears perked up, intrigued. The girl crept across the road, as Babcock inched closer to John Mark.

"Does Babcock bite?" John Mark suddenly wondered as the small mutt moved closer to John Mark's outstretched hand.

"Only if you don't give him the jerky."

Great, John Mark thought, *I'm definitely getting bit*. Babcock was within reach.

John Mark held out his hand a bit longer, as Babcock cautiously sniffed the leaf. With the dog preoccupped, John Mark slipped a cinch knot around his scrawny neck.

"Got ya!"

Babcock sniffed the leaf again and realized he had been duped. Impressed, the girl whistled between her teeth, "Nice work, mister."

John Mark handed the rope to the girl. "You'll want to fill that hole," he advised. "Maybe put some larger rocks in it to make it harder for him to dig out again."

She thanked him and crossed the almost deserted street, gently coaxing the dog along. John Mark brushed the dirt off his hands and climbed back into his truck. As he drove in the direction of the bank, he realized that acquiring Old Blue was no longer a straightforward matter. The situation had become more complicated, and it had a name: Anna. She was Lucy's granddaughter.

And John Mark was the man who would own and eventually tear down her family's house. His father's words resonated in his head, sharp and unwavering: "Business is business. No room for feelings. Move forward."

He doubted himself. Condos? Was that what he truly wanted? Was he destined to be another cold-hearted businessman in the family line? He'd only just met Anna, but her beauty hadn't escaped him. A thought arose, *perhaps I could get to know her,* which he quickly dismissed. It was a pipe dream, especially if he was the one bringing the house down.

This opportunity had been a long-awaited feast for his dad and grandfather. Like sharks patiently circling, they'd always known their prize would come. Yet, the question of "Why?" wouldn't leave John Mark. What was so significant about this land that it had caused such a rift between two local families? It felt strange. He'd never seen his father and grandfather so openly gleeful about any other Gordon Developers deal. This one was clearly the cream of the crop. The bank was just a drive away. He could sign the papers, keep his head down, and let the acquisition proceed as intended. But a stark question arose: was that honest? What would happen when Anna discovered his identity? She would see him as a fraud—a deceiver, a swindler, a liar. He would become the very image of the two men he loathed most: his grandfather and father. He'd just offered her his help in finding her family. Lies. When had this casual dishonesty begun? A wave of shame washed over John Mark. Perhaps he was fooling himself. Deep down, he was a Gordon, through and through.

He jerked his truck into the parking lot, bouncing over the small curb. He parked in between the two lines, facing the entrance. Frustration building, he leaned his head on the steering wheel, *this deal is getting muddled*, he thought.

He had ten minutes before the bank opened. "Ugh, why was I born into this family?" He shouted into the empty cab.

Looking out the window, John Mark watched an old couple walking slowly, their hands clasped, each leaning gently on the other. A simple act of connection something never witnessed between his own parents. He wondered about the quiet comfort of such a bond, and the journey of growing old together. John Mark's mom was one of those naturally good people everyone loved. Even after his dad hurt her, she never became bitter. He once asked if she regretted marrying him, and she just smiled and said no.

"I just kept building my home, life, and my family." She had looked at him, with love in her eyes. "Just because something is in disrepair, or has some broken parts, doesn't mean we need to tear it down." A laugh escaped her lips, accompanied by a wink. "Well, some might have a different opinion on that," she said, her gaze hinting at John Mark's father's methods. "But we can always build *on* what's here. Maybe just . . . reshape it a little. Work with what you've got." Her sharp blue eyes held his.

Unlike his father, who thrived on tearing things down, his mother's nature was to always build and nurture. He watched as a man unlocked the front doors of the bank, reminding him of where he was.

"Ugh!" he groaned, pounding his hands on the steering wheel.

He couldn't sign any paperwork today. The pull toward truth and honesty was unrelenting. *Maybe I'm not all Gordon?* He smiled to himself. He turned the ignition, letting the truck rumble to life for a moment. His hand tightened on the clutch as he shifted into drive. He would call the bank. The appointment needed to be rescheduled. He needed more time to think.

He looked at the clock. *Hopefully, she will be awake*, he thought. He knew what he needed to do. He pulled out of the parking lot and onto Gordon Drive. She might turn him away. It was even likely she would slap him on the face. But he would not let that deter him from trying to speak with Lucy Belltown. His whole life, the story had been the same: greedy Belltown's, thieves who stole from the rightful Gordons. Maybe it was all true. But before he made any more moves, he needed to know. Truthfully, if she was as bad as they said, signing the papers would be a whole lot easier.

As John Mark drove down Lucy's driveway, he took in the vastness of the legendary Old Blue.

He had never been this close to it. The house itself was a marvelous feat of craftsmanship; the grounds, although in need of care, were a magical forest of trees, shrubs, and flowers. He parked and got out.

"I could never tear this down," he said, looking toward the pond where two blue herons were standing, still as statues.

"What could dad and grandfather have been thinking?" He stood, with his hands on his hips, and surveyed the lush fifty acres. It was a rare sight to see a place preserved, nestled into wooded acreage, and so near to the ocean. Before he could reach the steps, the door opened.

"What do you want?' Lucy's voice was soft but bold.

"Hi, Mrs. Belltown, I'm . . ."

"I know who you are; I read the papers." Grandfather and dad had been right; she was feisty.

He swallowed the lump in his throat. "I was hoping to speak with you for a few minutes, if you have the time. I have some questions I'd like to ask."

It had been a long time since he last saw her. She was smaller than he remembered. As a kid, he passed her a few times on the street. He was always told to avoid her. Gordon's did not associate with Belltown's.

The door was only slightly open. She looked him up and down. "Son, you've taken the last thing I have, and I am not giving you one more thing." She was right. She didn't owe him a thing. She turned to go.

"Wait!" He stepped forward. She stopped, turning around, she opened the door wide, her tiny frame enshrined in the peeling door frame. She eyed him with a stern look.

She rendered him speechless. As her eyes bore into him, he shoved his sweaty palms into his pockets. He looked down at his feet, then back at her. There she stood firm, holding her ground. *It is now or never*, he thought.

"Lucy, our families have been at odds for almost a century, and I was hoping you could tell me why."

Her brow furrowed and she stepped back, caught off guard by his question. He shuffled his feet, unsure what to say next. He smiled at her. The initial reserve in her expression began to melt away, replaced by a small, welcoming smile that formed delicate lines around her soft grey eyes.

"I don't know you, John Mark, but I know your father and grandfather." She shook her head, "And to be honest, I don't like your father, and your grandfather is the worst of them all."

John Mark didn't disagree. He saw her size him up. Her internal wheels spinning. Resigned to her fate, she gave him a half smile.

"Please, come in. I imagine you're curious to see the place you'll own soon enough." She waved him forward.

"Thanks," he replied, the tension leaving his body, as he moved towards the door. But before he could step inside, her hand rested lightly on his forearm, halting him. She looked up, her grey eyes steady. ". . . however, your great-grandfather, Paul Gordon, was truly a wonderful person."

He was surprised to hear the tenderness in Lucy's voice as he followed her into the hallway.

"Paul was one of those rare, good souls." She spun around quickly, a movement so sudden John Mark briefly thought she'd changed her mind and was powering up her arm to slug him. He was at least tall enough that the hit would probably only reach his shoulder or chest.

"Do you like coffee, son?" she smiled sweetly.

"Yes, ma'am," he swallowed the lump in his throat. Relieved, yet still watching her every move.

"Then come on." She kept moving forward through the hallway. "As you'll see, I've started packing, so the place is a disaster."

John Mark felt guilty about that. He stepped inside and saw boxes everywhere, stacked neatly along the wall. He wondered if she had anyone helping her. He could help her. As Lucy guided him into the kitchen, the sweet, warm scent of cinnamon filled the air. She gestured towards a chair, and he watched as she carefully pulled a golden-brown loaf of pound cake from the oven.

"Isn't it funny you arrived just now?" Lucy remarked, a hint of a smile in her voice. "You must have inherited Paul Gordon's nose. My mother used to bake this, and he'd appear at our back door like a little lost puppy. It was his absolute favorite. He always told her he could smell it wafting over from next door." John Mark had to admit; the aroma was heavenly. Lucy set the steaming cake on the table, setting a knife beside it.

She pointed toward the kitchen window, "You do know that Paul and Nancy lived just over there."

"You mean across the pond?"

"Yep, my daddy and Paul were best friends, more like brothers, really." Lucy coughed, a loud rattling sound, wincing with each intake of breath. The pain obvious on her face.

John Mark stood to help. "Can I get you something?"

"No, just old lady maladies, nothing to be concerned about," she waved him off. He noticed her steps were more delicate.

She took two porcelain cups from the drying rack and placed them on their saucers. After pouring coffee, she set one in front of him. "Here you go." She then placed two plates on the table, ready for the cake.

"These are my special occasion plates." They were painted with a delicate floral motif. "I've been washing and re-washing them. Hope that's alright with you." She sat down across from him. "My Daddy, bless his heart, if he were here, he'd say having Paul Gordon's great-grandson gracing our table absolutely called for the best china."

A feeling of relaxation began to spread through John Mark. Lucy poured milk into her coffee. She then cut a thick slice of the still warm pound cake and placed it before him. The fragrant steam reaching his nose, making his mouth water in anticipation. He savored the first bite, closing his eyes. He was so captivated by the flavor that he didn't notice Lucy watching him. When he opened them. He saw her joy. A broad smile reaching from ear to ear.

With his mouth full, John Mark mumbled, "Yeah, I can see why he liked this cake."

It was buttery and warm with spicy, citrus flavors. Lucy took a small corner from her cake and nibbled it. If he were alone, he would devour the cake in a single bite, but he didn't want to be rude. John Mark decided that anyone capable of creating something so tasty, couldn't possibly have a bad bone in their body. He placed the final square on his tongue, savoring the last crumbs before wiping his mouth clean. He knew he was treading dangerous ground. If his grandfather knew he was sitting at Lucy's table, the old man would likely cut him off entirely—a deep sense of betrayal.

"Now, about your question," Lucy said, leaning slightly forward, her attention fully on him. "I'm all ears."

Chapter Twelve

Friendships Built and Friendships Broken

As Lucy watched John Mark eat the last bite of cinnamon cake, she shook her head, still bewildered that Randall Gordons's grandson was sitting across from her. When she had looked out her window at the man, stepping out of his truck, it caught her off guard. Because, the last person she expected to see was a Gordon, in the flesh. A surge of anger had filled her and the thought of punching him in the face flashed before her eyes. Yet, the boy was the spitting image of Paul, and the fear in his young eyes gave her pause. He had looked terrified, and she hadn't exactly been welcoming. He had questions. She knew she had answers. When he had walked towards her, his slow, focused stride was undeniably Gordon. They were a family that moved forward, rarely looking back. Maybe this one was different from his father. Lucy, a believer in second chances, decided to offer him one by inviting him inside. Old Blue was hers for a little longer, but soon he would inherit it.

He swallowed his last bite, and Lucy pressed him about his question. Watching him, she noticed his dark hair and bright eyes. He was handsome, just as Paul had been, a fact that surprisingly warmed her. He cleared his throat and began to share what he knew of Paul Gordon. A few superficial details were all he offered, confirming for Lucy that John Mark was unaware of his great-grandfather's deeper character.

"So, like I said, that is all I know about my great-grandfather." He reached for his plate and began to dab at the crumbs putting each one on his tongue.

"Do you want another slice?" she had already started to cut it.

"Oh, I couldn't."

She cut it anyway, smiling she slid the pan toward him.

"Thanks," he said, using his fork to lift out the crumbly cake, putting it onto his plate.

"This stuff is out of this world." He talked with his mouth full again and Lucy tried to decipher the words.

"For some reason, my grandfather doesn't like talking about his dad."

"I can only imagine why," Lucy said sarcastically.

John Mark had the deer in the headlights look, "I take it you know why that is," he said, as a piece of cake fell from his mouth onto the table.

"Did your dad or Randall ever tell you about this plot of land? How it used to be one large parcel before Paul and my daddy divided it?"

He shook his head no.

"This land belonged to Paul, your granddaddy, before it belonged to us."

"Wow." John Mark look surprised. "So it's true, this was always our land."

Lucy was certain Randall had filled the boy's head with lies about the Belltowns stealing the land, and she felt ready to set the record straight. Lucy twisted her napkin in her hands forward and back, then set it on the table.

"If I'm going to do this right I have to start from the beginning," she said.

"By all means," John Mark replied, wiping his mouth with the back of his hand.

"Let's begin with Naples and how its originated," Lucy said. "This settlement isn't that old. 1885 or '86—roughly. Two men came down from the North. They saw the empty land and formed an idea." Lucy knew the story by heart. "They told some friends and soon enough a scarce group of rough necks, who loved the breezes and sunshine, decided to lay down roots."

Lucy explained, "The journey south was met with swampland, swarms of giant mosquitos, and barren sand."

"Ah," the boy said, a hint of understanding in his voice, "so Paul was one of the first, bought all the land, and then sold it for twice the price?" Lucy laughed, realizing he had no idea who his great-grandfather truly was.

"Wrong, indeed." *Very wrong indeed*, she thought.

"Everyone needed each other. Whether it was for help with work or sharing what they had, they were all in the same boat. Bartering and trading were how things got done. Lucy explained, her tone taking on a storytelling quality. "My father and his younger brother co-owned Belltown Lumber out of Pittsburgh. It wasn't a grand operation, but it provided them a living. When my father got the 'go south bug,' he figured out a way to have lumber shipped to Naples via large barges, quite a feat in those days. Only a select few had the means to purchase it, so most traded other goods, and that's where your family comes in."

John Mark shifted in his chair, his eyes fixed on Lucy.

"You can probably see where this is going, right?" she asked, a smile playing on her lips.

"Yeah, I think so," he agreed.

"Well, your great-grandpa, Paul, owned a hundred of the prettiest acres around. Gordon Point.

This very spot."

Lucy stood and grabbed the coffee pot, setting it on the table.

"Help yourself, honey." She poured more for herself.

"Paul needed lumber, my Daddy needed land, so they cut a deal."

"What was the deal?" John Mark questioned.

"My Daddy bought Paul's acreage at a reduced cost and Paul got his lumber for next to nothing."

John Mark took another sip from his small cup. It looked like a tea party cup, held in his big hands. "Paul was one of the first to put up a little house—practically a shack by today's standards—and boy, did he have a gorgeous view. His place was right over that way." She nodded towards the side of the house.

"I think I remember learning about that in grade school," John Mark added, with a glimmer in his eye. "Naples history. They call them the founders, and they really had to rely on one another to get by."

"That's right," Lucy agreed with a nod. "This place was so remote, getting anything down here was nearly impossible. And those who did manage to bring supplies shared them." Lucy hadn't learned Naples' history in a classroom; she'd lived it. "When I was a little girl, much of Naples was swampland, believe it or not!" She chuckled at the memory of chasing alligators with brooms.

"I've lived long enough to remember the year they started building a proper road, the year the barges finally became a thing of the past and our supplies came in on trucks." A hint of nostalgia warmed her voice. "We relied on a spring for water, both to drink and to wash, we fished for food, and we scratched a living from the sandy soil—if you could even call it farming." She cherished these memories. "Naples was so raw back then, so untouched. The day Old Blue finally got indoor plumbing was a cause for celebration in the Belltown house. The outhouse was finally gone."

John Mark's face brightened as Lucy revealed a Naples he'd never known.

Lucy looked at him and asked, "Has anyone ever told you, you look like Paul?"

"My mom used to say that." A half-smile touched his lips.

"I was sorry to hear about your mother's passing when it happened," Lucy said.

"Thanks. It left a big hole," he replied.

"She was a darling in the community. What your father did to her was terrible." Lucy had known John Mark's mother through their shared involvement in numerous charity events.

"So, Paul got the lumber, and you all got some of the land." John Mark shifted the conversation.

"Yes, to clarify the land was purchased from your great-grandfather." She smiled. "I still have the deed. But these facts are facts your grandfather, Randall, would beg to differ with," she winked. "So, that's the story of how we ended up as neighbors." A fond smile touched Lucy's lips; these brighter memories were a joy to revisit. "So, eventually, Paul and my father, Howard, became the closest of friends. Their wives followed suit, and as you can imagine, so did their children."

"You and my grandfather were friends?"

"Hard to believe, isn't it?"

"Very."

"Your grandfather wasn't always the way he is now. At one time, he was a carefree boy." Lucy remembered the dark-haired boy, who used to play hide and seek with her in the woods, a friend who was more like a brother. A sadness came over her as she remembered that season when they were just two, playful kids. Randall Gordon once held a dear place in Lucy's heart.

"We used to run up and down that patch of beach with our kites, seeing who could get theirs to go the highest."

"The word 'carefree' doesn't fit the grandfather I know," John Mark said, his brow furrowing.

He sat forward, his attention unwavering. *Should I risk revealing the full story?* Lucy debated internally. *Perhaps it's the key.*

"If your grandfather knew I was sharing this with you, his blood would boil."

John Mark laughed, "Lucy, that man's blood is always set to boil. It's nothing new."

Eager for any insight Lucy could offer, he leaned forward. She plowed ahead, unearthing memories.

"Well, he might tell you otherwise, but there was a time your grandfather was sweet on me; oh, that man pulled out all the stops trying to win me over."

John Mark shifted uncomfortably in his chair. "Obviously, it didn't work," he added.

"You guessed it. I never saw him in that way. To me, he was like the brother I never got to have." Lucy twisted the gold band on her finger.

"Then, after my senior year, my Bill came along and swept me off my feet. Randall couldn't stand it. He never spoke to me again. After that, Randall never set foot on Belltown property."

Lucy did occasionally see Randall downtown, but he'd either turn away or pretend she didn't exist. It had been a wound that never fully healed.

"You have to understand, something broke in him," Lucy sighed. "The Randall I knew was a good man. Over time, he grew bitter and resentful. His anger was not directed just at me, but also at his father, Paul." Lucy's face fell in sadness, "it was a terrible thing to witness."

"Wow, my grandfather really took that hard . . ." John Mark shook his head, disbelief etched on his face.

"Do you think you broke his heart, and he never recovered?" John Mark asked.

Lucy chuckled. "I was cute and fun, but trust me, I was no heartbreaker, John Mark." She chuckled again. "I think Randall had different ambitions than his father envisioned, maybe he felt like a disappointment. I can't say for sure." She hesitated, rubbing her hands on her thighs. "But I do know disappointments can accumulate, year after year. And when the money started flowing, that's when things truly went wrong."

"How did grandfather come into all his money? Paul sounds like he was a simple man." John Mark questioned.

"He was, through and through. But as time went on, his land became increasingly valuable. You know how desirable ocean views eventually become. Paul's main asset, his land, became worth a great deal."

"So, my grandfather inherited all that land after Paul's death?"

"Well, yes and no." Lucy hesitated, a weight settling in her chest. This wasn't her story to share.

"John Mark, you really need to have this conversation with your father."

He leaned forward, his voice urgent. "Lucy, they won't tell me anything."

Lucy exhaled, tapping her fingers on the table. *What would Paul want? The truth.* "Okay. This might be difficult to hear." *And difficult for me to say,* she thought. Sometimes, stirring up the past felt like a dirty business.

"I want to know. No, at this point, I need to know."

Lucy trusted the young man. His sincerity seemed genuine.

"Give me a moment to find the right way to tell this." The story was a tangled web of pride, selfishness, arrogance, and the sting of petty cruelties. Lucy needed to ensure she was ready to tread that difficult ground again.

She stood and went to the sink and filled a water glass. She drank deep, finishing the last drop. "Do you want some?" she turned toward him holding an empty glass in the air.

"No, thanks."

She sat back down. The motion of bending brought pain through her stomach up into her chest. She caught her breath and waited a moment for it to subside. It always did. The spasms were unwelcome reminders that her clock was ticking.

"When your great-grandfather, Paul, took sick, my Mama and Daddy opened their home to him and cared for him until the end."

"What about his wife and family?"

"Nancy, your great-grandmother, had died a few years earlier, and your grandpa, Randall, was somewhere up north, making deals in real estate. He couldn't find the time to come."

Couldn't or wouldn't? she silently wondered, hoping it was the latter.

"It was a sad but beautiful time. A few days before Paul passed, he made my Mama draw a sketch." Lucy recalled that day, it was as vivid in her mind, as though it had happened yesterday.

Lucy's Mama and Daddy, Howard and Deborah, dismantled the twin bed from upstairs, carrying each piece carefully into the sunroom. They reassembled it, positioning it to face the sea. Deborah arranged two nightstands on either side, lovingly placing framed photos, a lamp, a pitcher of water, and Paul's few medications. In the afternoons, Lucy would sit beside Paul, reading aloud his cherished stories: *The Adventures of Huckleberry Finn* and *Pilgrim's Progress*, his most frequent requests. One evening, as Lucy and her mother cleared the dinner dishes, Lucy heard Paul's voice, quiet and firm, "Deborah, Deborah."

Lucy tapped her mama on the arm, "Mr. Gordon is calling you."

"Oh," she tossed the dishtowel on the counter leaving Lucy to finish the task.

A few minutes later, she returned to the kitchen and pulled a pad of paper and colored pencils from the drawer. She rested her hand on Lucy's arm, the soap suds reaching up to Lucy's wrist, "Let's finish these up later. Paul has something he wants to share."

She rinsed her hands off and followed her mama out of the kitchen.

Through the huge picture windows, as the sun was setting, a purple glow filled the horizon. As it bounced off the walls of the sunroom, it left a rich, golden hue.

"Now, Deborah, you must draw it exactly as I describe it."

"I will Paul," Deborah rested her hand on his, giving it a squeeze.

Paul mustered his strength to push himself up to a sitting position. Lucy quickly adjusted the pillows behind to support his back.

"Thank you, Lucy girl," he winked at her.

Paul began to describe the property, more specifically the Belltown place:

"The grass that grows a little long near the south side of the pond where the herons like to hide—make sure you put that in there. And how the light catches through the trees as it lands on the soft lawn, can you draw that?"

Deborah started to laugh. "I'll do my best, Paul."

Her hand scribbled on the sheet.

He waved his hand in the air, imagining something they could not see.

"The smell, oh, we must capture the smell of the sea as it blows in after a rainy day."

Lucy imagined what the smell would look like. She drew a blank.

"Now, the pathway. The one that leads from your back door to mine. The crushed shells—Howard and I spent hours on a Saturday afternoon hauling each load, then we evenly spread them out."

"What about the flowers, Mama? The wild irises and the bird of paradise?" Lucy added.

"Shhh, you two. Give me a minute. I can only draw as fast as my hand will let me."

Paul looked at Lucy with an ornery smile and raised his eyebrows.

"Now Deborah, see if you can't draw a big old yacht parked just yonder from the house, my dream yacht you know, and we shall call her *Paul's Paradise.*"

Mama stopped what she was doing and stared at Paul. She couldn't tell if he was joking or serious.

He nudged Lucy who was standing close to the bed.

"I'm fooling around. You should know better. I've always been a land lubber."

He licked his dry lips—a huge smile on his face. Mama gave Paul her serious look, like you're seriously in trouble. Lucy knew it well.

"Okay, what's next for you two jokesters?" Deborah said, a hint of amusement in her voice.

Paul motioned for Lucy to help him sit straight up. Deborah helped shift him.

"Ah better, now I can see all the way out."

"What do you kids say we leave this land to the people when we're gone?"

"What do you mean, Paul?"

"A preserve, all 100 acres."

He must be talking about the Gordon's fifty acres and the Belltown fifty, Lucy thought.

Deborah paused, "And what about Old Blue, our home? Where will we live?"

She chuckled as she said it, catching eyes with Lucy. Lucy was wondering the same thing.

"You'll live right here. For as long as we are around. Deb, these homes are going to outlive us. We built them that way. When I'm gone, I don't want things to disappear. To go poof, like a wisp of smoke."

"Oh, that would never happen; people always need homes, and our homes would be great for another family."

"Something tells me things aren't always going to be as they are now." Paul leaned back into the pillow mound.

It was dark outside when Howard walked in.

"What did I miss?" he asked Lucy, as he tossed his coat on the chair.

"Mama has been putting her art skills to use," Lucy said as she held up the drawing.

"Wow, honey, that looks great." He kissed the top of Lucy's head as he examined the picture. He took it and leaned in squinting, ". . . is that a turtle in the pond?"

"Yes," Deborah said blushing. "I was having a little fun, but after the turtle, everything else is Paul's idea."

Howard kissed his wife as he sat next to Paul's bed.

"What have we here, old man?" he said jokingly to Paul.

"Just a dying man's last wish."

"Which is?"

"Howard, I want to ensure that when I'm gone, it remains intact."

Howard looked at Deborah, his brow furrowed.

Deborah pointed to the picture, "these," she said, pointing to the two houses.

"You always did love this piece of soil. I cannot imagine a hundred years from now that this house or yours will be gone." Like Lucy and her mama, Howard also couldn't fathom their homes being sold or torn down. "It will take a strong hurricane to knock these old gals down." Howard laughed a hearty laugh. "We built them to last, remember? Like the castles in Europe, to be handed down to the next generation and so on and so on."

"But that's what I'm afraid of." Paul coughed into his handkerchief.

He did not need to say more. All three Belltown's knew he was referring to his estranged son.

Howard stood up and looked at the picture once more, "a dying man's last wish," he mumbled. Sympathy in his eyes. "So how do we do that? What's your plan Paul?" Howard knelt next to the bed, looking at his friend.

Deborah answered, "Honey, Paul wants to turn the whole 100 acres into a nature preserve."

Paul gave a thumbs up. Lucy poured water from the pitcher and handed him the cup.

Howard nodded his head up and down. He was thinking. "Hmmm . . . not an idea I had ever thought of, but not a bad one." Howard sat down and undid the tie around his neck.

"Howard, I want you to take my land. Please put it into a trust. Give it to the people."

"Paul, you've always been a generous man, but I can't do that."

They all knew that if the rumors were true, Randall Gordon would sue them silly until the land was his, and he had a right to it.

"You can and you will." Paul would not speak badly of his son or of the rupture of the relationship, but they could see the sadness written on his face.

Howard clicked his tongue, deep in thought. His mind turning. "If you're sure about this, than I will get ahold of Jeb tomorrow and see if he can write something up." Howard ran his hand over the stubble on his chin. Concern written all over his face.

Paul grabbed Howard's hand and squeezed it, bearing a huge grin on his face. "As sure as I've ever been."

"I'm no lawyer, but I think we would need to combine all one hundred acres, that way it would be locked together." Howard held the picture, taking in the idea.

Paul saw something they did not see. Paul was betting on the Belltown legacy over his own. While Howard and Paul discussed the remaining details, Deborah filled in the colors, there was not a blank space.

The cerulean blue on the house popped out amidst the greens and browns of the ground. Her mother had done an exquisite job detailing the windows and lattice work. She had added other details that Paul had not described: benches for people to sit, more trees, and more parking spaces. Deborah seemed to catch where Paul was going with this.

"There, that should do it. Our two homesteads, should we no longer reside here, preserved—for the people and future generations to come. I like it." Deborah signed her initials at the bottom.

Lucy finished the story and John Mark, hearing it for the first time, leaned back in his chair and took a deep breath. "So, what happened when Paul passed?"

She detected the slight tremor in his voice. He knew, or at least suspected. Still, she continued. "Before Paul's passing, they drew up a deed. In essence, it granted my father the entire hundred acres upon . . . Paul's death."

"So, they believed your prospects were brighter than Randall's," John Mark murmured, thinking aloud.

"Paul saw me as a daughter," Lucy said. "And, yes, he likely assumed Randall would sell off everything for the highest bid and never glance back."

"Whereas you," John Mark looked at her, "would keep it and pass it along."

"Yes, that was the plan."

"But, when you had no one to give it to, you were forced to sell?"

Lucy nodded.

"But this is only fifty acres?" John Mark was beginning to track with Lucy.

"Yes, so that is the part I'm getting to." The part she would rather move right past.

"Your grandfather caught wind of what was going on, and after Paul passed, he hired some convincing lawyers, and we were only able to retain this fifty. And, as you already know, the other fifty went to your grandfather and he turned it . . . well into exactly what Paul didn't want."

"Condos." John Mark shook his head. "Did my grandpa know what his dad's wishes were?"

"Sadly, yes. They were stated clearly in the deed."

John Mark bit his lip, "his flesh and blood turned on him."

"Well, I would state it differently, but essentially, yes."

"Unbelievable."

Lucy waved her hand around, "This place, this land, it was never meant to become a point of dispute, but rather a partnership, a pact. Paul wanted Randall to want that. I think that deep down he never wanted Randall to be alone. He knew if he could tie him to the land, then he could tie him to us."

"But the land wasn't his, it was all deeded to your dad."

"Yes and no. There was one stipulation. If Randall would come home and live on the land, then the deed had an addendum which would allow him to take over half of the one hundred."

"Thus, the even split of fifty-fifty," John Mark understood.

"Exactly! The lawyer was able to find one loophole and ensure that Randall acquired what was due him. Those two were smart. And to be honest, my daddy didn't have enough money to fight for long in court. By then, Randall had a small fortune and would drain our coffers in lawyer fees."

"So that's why grandpa has a condo in Starfish Estates."

"Yes, essentially fulfilling the deed's requirement of 'living on the land.'" Lucy knew he never slept there; it was all a pretense.

"As you can now guess, Paul and my daddy didn't create an airtight deed."

"Which is why grandpa wants this last fifty so badly." John Mark's eyes darkened.

"It's prime real estate, but I think he also thinks most of it already belongs to him."

Lucy reached across the table for John Mark's plate. He had eaten every crumb. She stood and walked to the sink. From her kitchen window, she could see the top of the condos that had replaced Paul and Nancy Gordon's modest cottage.

She set the plate down gently and turned around. Her arms crossed across her chest, leaving a ruffle in her linen shirt.

"But if Grandpa knew his father's dying wishes, why would he completely disregard them?" The boy had circled this point before, but Lucy saw his genuine distress and decided to approach it differently.

"Randall distanced himself from his parents after college, relocating to New York." Lucy recalled his departure, abrupt and lacking any emotion.

"Nancy's death had left a huge void, and I don't think Paul approved of some of Randall's business ventures in New York." Lucy kept silent about the triple fees Randall charged low-income families. "Paul, very clearly, accused him of dishonesty. They parted ways with much unresolved, if I remember correctly."

"Whew," John Mark ran his hand through his hair. Clearly disturbed.

"A few months after Paul passed, Randall turned the deed upside down, swooped in and cleared the fifty acres."

John Mark pushed his chair back and stood up.

Lucy felt compassion for the boy. "Your grandfather was in pain."

"He was heartless." John Mark shot back.

She longed to offer him comfort but was unsure of how to do it.

"Here, let's go sit in there." She motioned toward the living room. She needed to sit down in a soft chair. They sat across from each other—a coffee table between them. "Ah, that is better."

John Mark fidgeted with a string on his shirt that hung from the hem.

"How are you doing?"

Shaking his head, "a lot of things are beginning to make sense," he answerd. *Should I go on?* Lucy wondered. Sensing her hesitation, John Mark relaxed his posture. "If you feel up to it, I would like to hear the rest of it."

"Okay, but it doesn't get any better." She frowned.

"Well, after Paul passed, I tried to talk with Randall, to comfort him, but he wouldn't have it. I was the last person he wanted around. I broke his heart. He pushed our family away. Got married. Had your father."

Lucy recalled Randall's wife, Sally James, a New York beauty. "Randall brought her to Naples, and oh, how she loathed it. It wasn't the Naples you know now, still quite rustic. She returned to New York five years later, taking your father with her. Eventually, she and Randall divorced. I'd see him downtown, an engine about ready to blow, always angry. With each passing year, it seemed to grow, like a heavy weight pressing him down. I learned to give him space. We haven't spoken since."

"What a sorry excuse for a man,' John Mark muttered. "And, that is the line I come from."

"Son," Lucy said gently, "one bad apple doesn't spoil the whole bunch."

"Thanks, but it's not just grandpa; Dad's no better."

"John Mark, we don't have to accept the hand we're dealt. We can change." She tapped her chest. "Speaking from a seasoned mistake-maker." John Mark smiled, a flicker of hope in his eyes. "You know,' "Lucy continued, "you're more like Paul than his own son or grandson. You're a Gordon, but with all the best parts."

She watched his slumped body straighten. "I want to show you something, it belongs to you anyway."

She stood and walked over to a chair covered in a white sheet. She tugged at it, but one corner had wedged under the wooden leg.

"Here, let me help you," he jumped up.

She stepped aside and let him finish.

Beneath the sheet was a beautiful high-back chair—hand-carved feet and armrests. And every last inch was covered in needlepoint. A work of art.

"Your great-grandmother Nancy did this. Isn't it exquisite?"

She ran her hand over the stitches, feeling the wool.

"It took her the better part of a year. Paul loved this chair. When we moved him here, that was the only thing he brought. He never sat in it. I think he liked to imagine Nancy sitting there."

John Mark bent down and looked at the legs. They had been carved into lion's paws.

"Paul hand carved those. It's yours if you want it."

He smiled and walked to the back of it, admiring the detail. "I would be glad to have it."

"Great, take it today!" she smiled, "one less thing to be moved." She hesitated, "John Mark," Lucy began, "there's something you should know. I have two grandchildren. I understand the house is yours now, but should circumstances change, there are still Belltowns living, family to inherit the property."

He spun around, his eyes widening like saucers. "Have you met her?"

"Met who, dear?"

"Your granddaughter," he stammered.

"I have not," Lucy admitted, a flicker of pain in her eyes. She looked away. Her face turned hot. The shame crawled up her neck.

What grandmother has never met their own grandchildren? A bad one, that's what. She thought.

He was about to say something when Lucy began to cough. She couldn't catch her breath. It sounded like she was choking. She walked to the couch and sat back down.

"Water, please," she choked out to John Mark.

He looked frightened and ran to the kitchen and back just as fast, with a large glass of water, spilling some on the way.

He bent down next to her as she drank. She could see Paul in his eyes. Her cough stopped, and she took slow, deep breaths. She reached out her hand and placed it on his cheek. He smiled reassuringly at her, "I think we need to take you to the hospital."

"No, I'm fine. It's just something that has been happening. Old age."

He gently touched her shoulders like she was a fragile vase.

"Are you sure? I've never heard anyone cough like that."

She brushed him off. "Now, as I was saying."

John sat down next to her.

She swallowed a few times, letting the water soothe her throat. It wasn't her throat that was the problem, it was her lungs.

She swallowed the remaining water. "I don't even know where to begin in finding my grandchildren."

"Well, maybe I can help." He suggested.

Lucy wondered why he, of all people, wanted to help her.

"By offering help, are you saying you would back out of the deal if we found them?" Her boldness caught him off guard.

"Not exactly, but I think you should find them."

He looked at his watch and stood.

"Have you tried searching online?" he asked.

"What is that?"

"Like, on a computer, the internet."

"Oh, no, I don't know how to even go about it."

"The library is a great resource, and maybe I can help dig up some of the information you're looking for."

She looked at him thoughtfully, baffled by the turn of events.

"John Mark, I'm still wondering why you want to help me?"

He thought for a moment before speaking.

"I think it is what Paul would do."

Lucy kept her eyes on him, a cautious yet hopeful look in her gaze.

"I think it's time for me to head out," he said, pushing himself to his feet and thanking her once more for the cake.

She walked him to the door, as he walked to his truck, he reiterated his promise to Lucy.

"I'll reach out within the next few days," he said, as he climbed into his truck.

Lucy went back inside and pondered what all of this meant. Things were definitely taking a turn. She laughed softly to herself at the irony: Paul's great-grandson, her unlikely knight in shining armor. She felt hopeful for the first time in months. Maybe something will go her way.

She walked back into the living room and her eyes landed on Nancy's needlepoint chair. She heard the house creak in the stillness. She sat down on the deep burgundy cushions on the couch and closed her eyes. She leaned back into the sofa, letting her head rest against it. She had to admit, it had been an emotional roller coaster these past few months with her health, the house and the loss of Grace. Maybe that was why she was so exhausted. *A nap would refresh her,* she thought. She curled her legs up on the couch and stuffed a pillow under her head. Her mind drifted back to her childhood.

She was a little girl again. Paul had stopped by to borrow some of her daddy's nails from the shop but couldn't find them. He walked down to where Lucy and her mama had set up their picnic spot on the beach. Lucy was building a castle. Mama sat under their striped umbrella, reading a book.

"Hey Deborah," he hollered as he got closer. "I'm trying to track down Howard," Paul said, waving at Lucy, as he walked down the steps into the sand.

"Oh hey, Paul," Deborah waved back.

"Howard had a meeting in town, he should be back soon."

"Okay, I am going to borrow the last of these nails if that's okay," he said, holding up the brown paper bag. "I will get some more at the hardware store tomorrow. "Yes, of course," Deborah smiled, going back to her book.

Paul waved goodbye and Lucy, absorbed in her task, kept building her sandcastle. As she put the clamshell on the top, a wave snuck up and washed her hard work into a puddle.

"Drat." She hadn't even gotten to build the moat. She stood up and walked toward the water to go and rinse her hands off. When she turned to walk back, Paul was there, and he had rolled up his pants and shirt sleeves and was sitting cross-legged next to the ruined castle. With his hands he was scooping sand and packing it into a big mound. Overjoyed, she ran up to him.

"These waves don't play by the rules, kid."

She sat beside him and used her shovel to scoop and add more sand to the pile.

"You looked like you could use a little help."

Lucy laughed, and together, they rebuilt what had fallen.

CHAPTER THIRTEEN

Welcome Home

After her morning with John Mark, Anna was more determined than ever to track down the owner of the letter. She slowly biked down the bustling Main Street of Old Naples, taking in the stores and cafes. People were window shopping and strolling along the sidewalk. She smelled fresh bread as she passed a bakery with a yellow and white striped awning out front. Under the cool shade, people sipped their coffee. *I wonder if anyone here can help with this address,* she mused. Anna hopped off her bike and walked towards the outdoor seating, where Gus immediately collapsed, panting from their ride.

"Hi," she approached a nice-looking woman in her sixties.

Her lipstick-rimmed cup was empty, and she was gathering her purse and hat. "Hello," her smile was warm and inviting. Anna was relieved she had picked the right person.

Anna whipped out the now wrinkled envelope. "I'm looking for this address."

The woman squinted at it. "Honey, I can't make heads or tails of that without my glasses."

"It says, Old Blue, Naples, FL."

"Ah, Old Blue, yes, yes," the woman replied, nodding. "Anyone and everyone from around here knows where that is. You're not too far now."

Anna's face lit up. "Great!"

"It's on Gordon Drive. It's the last one on the right, just before the curve. A beautiful place."

"Does it have a street number?" Anna asked.

"Oh, you don't need it, sweetie," the woman replied. "Big houses like that have names, you can't miss it."

"Thank you so much."

"Of course," the woman said, standing up ready to leave, and placing her empty cup in the bin by the door.

Anna couldn't wait to get started. The smell of fresh croissants lingered in the air, making her stomach grumble. Gus looked up at her expectantly.

"Not right now, we are on a mission," Anna murmured to him.

Gus perked up, wagging his tail. "It's just up the way, you heard the lady." They left the slow bustle of Main Street and turned onto Gordon Drive.

Here we are at the curve, she thought as they reached the bend. Now her choice was either to veer left and follow it around or stop in front of a bunch of trees and shrubs.

"Hmm . . . no house," she murmured aloud. The last building was aways back.

"Maybe that sandstone one was Old Blue." Unclipping Gus, she let him explore while she filled his water from her pack. "Gus? Where'd you go?" she called, realizing he was gone. A bark made her turn. A driveway, previously unseen, now cut through the foliage. *"That wasn't there,"* she breathed. It was subtly hidden by overgrown bushes and a dense tree cover. But there it was, marked by a small metal sign swinging gently: 'Old Blue.'

Elated, she zipped up her backpack and wheeled her bike down the narrow driveway.

"Gus," she said, her voice tight and firm, barely audible. "Get over here!" She saw him sniffing intently in a corner. He looked up at her, tail wagging happily, and trotted over. "Yes, I know, you found the house, but that doesn't mean you can just run off like that." She clipped his leash back on. "Now stay with me." She wrapped the leash around her wrist and continued wheeling the bike.

Abruptly, she paused. Questions flooded her mind: *What if she's trespassing? What if whoever lives here doesn't want to be found? And once I go further, there's no turning back.* She bit her bottom lip, glancing from side to side. Gathering her courage, she moved forward. As she reached the end of the driveway, the shade vanished, and the scene opened up before her. It was like entering a secret garden—an open space unfolded before her eyes.

"Wow," she whispered, a slow turn encompassing the scene. Gus barked once. "Quiet," she said, guiding him to an old shed. She propped her bike against it and secured his leash to the frame's base. "Be good."

It was like seeing a painting for the first time, each detail new and exciting. A big, blue house sat off to the right several feet from a pond. Mature trees shaded the house and dotted the boundary lines of the property. The yard had recently been mowed, leaving bushy patches of grass around the trunks of each tree. The circular driveway led up to the back steps and the shed where Gus was now resting. Rose bushes and patches of birds of paradise grew up next to the house forcing their way through the weeds. Impressive in its three-story height, the house had white trim that outlined the house and each window was flanked by neatly positioned storm shutters. As she stood still, she noticed how quiet it was. The settled silence then focusing her ears into the sound of the waves. *The ocean must be close,* she thought excitedly. She walked around a bit more, waiting for someone to come out and question her. She approached the shed and slice of shade where Gus was lying flat on his side, half asleep. She peered in through the single pane window, no car. "Hmmm . . . looks like no one's home," she murmured, turning around. A moment of hesitation caught her before she moved toward the back door, the butterflies in her stomach causing the brief pause. Taking a deep breath, she stepped forward with boldness, ascending the steps with determination. She tapped a few times on the white wooden door.

She waited. Silence.

She knocked again. Still no answer. *Maybe the house is abandoned?* she wondered. Or worse, perhaps whoever lived here was watching her from un upstairs window, with no intention of answering.

Anna had come all this way, and she wasn't about to back down so easily. She walked over to the sleeping dog and bent down, gently rustling him awake. "Gus, you need to come with me." She had to admit, the house did feel a bit eerie, and she intended to use Gus as a deterrent if anything went sideways.

"Let's go around to the front." Gus stood, shaking loose dry pieces of grass from his coat. She unhooked his leash, and he lumbered along beside her as they walked toward the front of the house. Anna paused at the side, where a row of rosebushes clustered together, their overgrown bases suggesting an age that matched the house itself. Clearly, someone with a talent for roses had planted and meticulously pruned them over the years. As they came around the corner to the front of the house, the breeze caught Anna's hair, swishing it in front of her eyes. She brushed it aside, tucking the loose strands behind her ears. Lifting her gaze, she was met with a view of blue sky and ocean in front of her.

"Wow, look at this view!" She exclaimed. Gus wagged his tail excitedly as he ran ahead of Anna, then bounding up the steps he arrived onto the front porch. She took a few more steps, slowly absorbing the expanse before her.

Anna figured that if anyone were home, they would have emerged from their hiding place by now. She decided she would take her time and enjoy this scene a little longer.

"It's like our own private cove," she whispered.

Standing still, she closed her eyes and inhaled deeply. She felt her body relax, like she was lifting off years of heaviness with one breath.

"Ouch!"

A sudden, sharp sting on her leg made her flinch. Glancing down, she saw the source: she was standing squarely on a low mound of dirt, and a legion of tiny ants was already making its way up her leg. "Ouch!" she yelped, slapping her leg with the same reflex used for a mosquito. "I didn't realize ants could bite!" she exclaimed, her fingers now flying to brush the crawling insects from her leg and shoe.

A low groan escaped her lips. Her leg was now sprinkled with tiny, inflamed red bumps. She rubbed them absently. Turning, she understood. The unassuming mound she'd been standing on was an intricate ant city, the small opening where her foot had pressed down now a flurry of frantic activity as the colony rallied to protect their disrupted habitat.

Unlike other regions, the West Coast was blessedly free of fire ants, however sugar ants were common and harmless. The red bumps on Anna's leg had begun to itch. Seeking relief, she looked for a hose to cool the burning. Near the rose bushes, she found a pipe with a spider-web-covered handle sticking out of the ground. It wouldn't budge when she tried to pull it, stiff with rust. Bracing herself, she pushed up on the lever with her shoulder, finally moving it. A small stream of brown water trickled out. Desperate for anything, she cupped her hand beneath it and patted it onto her leg. Soon, clear, chilly water emerged.

She put her entire leg under the cool water, letting it soak her foot and shoe. It was worth it, even if her running shoes got sopping wet. *Relief, at least for a little while.* She thought. She pushed down on the handle turning it off, grateful it still worked. *Now where did Gus go off to?* She wondered. As she went back to the front of the house, and up the steps, there was Gus sound asleep next to a wicker chair. Anna laughed aloud. "Well, at least we know we're the only ones here," she said to Gus. *Seriously, if someone had watched the last thirty minutes, there's no way they could have stayed silent. It's not like we've been very discreet*; she chucked to herself.

The porch was long and wide, extending across the entire front of the house. Anna noticed the delicate lattice along the railing. The white paint on the railing and the house itself was chipped and peeling in large sections, clearly weathered by the harsh ocean winds. It needed repainting. Gus looked up, his tail giving two contented thumps. Deciding on one last attempt, Anna walked toward the porch door to knock loudly. However, as she stepped toward it her shoe caught on a warped board, and she tripped, stumbling against the wall.

"This place is booby trapped," she laughed. She would move more cautiously from now on. She shook herself off and knocked on the door. The delicate window shook with each tap. She tried turning the glass doorknob. Locked. She bent down, so she was face-to-face with the doorknob. It too showed that someone had paid special attention to every detail when building this home. Cut into the glass knob, was a small sand dollar. And the brass plate had a big B that encircled the skeleton keyhole. One final knock, louder this time, met only with silence. Anna shielded her eyes and peered through the window. A sharp intake of breath followed as she jumped back. Inside, various large items were draped in white sheets, creating a distinctly creepy image. *Haunted house, minus the zombies,* she thought.

"Well, isn't that something," she commented, a wry amusement in her tone.

She moved to the large window to her left and peered in. The interior looked completely deserted, as if someone had abruptly left and never returned.

"Okay, Gus," she announced, a note of finality in her voice. "Looks like this is our cue to turn back. Dead end."

From his new perch, he watched her as she paced, lost in thought. She was wrestling with the puzzle of her mother's connection to this place. Finally, she sat down in the wicker chair beside Gus, scratching her head in contemplation. It was then that she noticed the wool blanket draped over the back, a detail she'd missed earlier. A sudden thought struck her. *That's odd.* For a deserted house, the chair looked as if someone had just been sitting there.

Anna knew this was the house. She was sure of it. *But why send a letter to an abandoned home?* She thought. Clearly when her mother had written it, she had expected it to be delivered. *Perhaps, the letter was written as an afterthought, something her mother intended to be left at her own mother's headstone?* Thoughts raced through Anna's mind. "I just don't get it!" She said, frustration in her voice. Instead of providing answers, the house only presented Anna with more questions.

She surrendered to the truth, that there was nothing more to do here. There was no one to talk to and no clues. She would need to do research and see if she could locate who had last occupied this house. She rocked back and forth, Gus still by her side. The sound of the waves lulled her into a state of contentment.

A feeling of peace washed over her. "A place like this," she sighed softly, "I could stay here forever." Despite the lack of progress, a small, happy breath escaped her lips.

"Let's head out, buddy," Anna said, reaching down to touch Gus. He rose, and they walked down the steps. Anna kept her eyes on the ground, not wanting a repeat of her earlier experience with the deadly ants. Her bike was where she'd left it by the shed. Clipping Gus's leash and swinging her leg over the bike, she turned for a final, lingering glance at the house. *Magnificent.*

"Mom," she breathed, "how could you ever leave this?" The question hung in the air, increasing the mystery. The thought of the old house being abandoned or worse saddened her—such a loss of history, so many stories untold. She was left wondering why her mother had kept it hidden from her children; surely things hadn't been that bad. There was more to unearth here, a truth she was meant to find. As she pedaled away, she felt a quiet pull. Though the house wasn't hers, and the connection she had to it, distant, she had a distinct feeling it was calling her back, a silent welcome home.

CHAPTER FOURTEEN

When Fate Triumphs

Morning arrived, bringing with it the reminder that Anna had forgotten to buy coffee yesterday. The thought of biking to the store and back without caffeine felt like climbing a mountain. The delightful smells of the downtown café popped into her mind. She grabbed a long-sleeved shirt and decided to call John Mark. Maybe, he'd be interested in hearing about her discoveries. He *had* said he wanted to help. She dialed his number, hoping it wasn't too early.

"Hello?" He answered his phone after the first ring.

"Want to grab a coffee?" Anna asked.

"Hey, good morning!" John Mark replied, sounding genuinely enthusiastic.

In the background, she could hear loud hammering. "No pressure if you're busy," she added quickly, "I know it's last minute and it's early."

"Eight o' clock isn't early at all! I've already been at work for an hour. In this kind of heat, most contractors start their day at four to avoid the late afternoon scorchers."

"What's the best place?" Anna asked, her heart not particularly set on the quaint café. She'd let John Mark choose; she could always visit the cute cafe another day.

"Hey, have you ventured downtown at all?" he asked.

Without waiting for her reply, he began describing the very café she had visited yesterday when she asked the woman for directions to Old Blue.

"Yes, I know the place," she said, a wave of relief washing over her that they were thinking of the same spot.

"See you there in ten."

She hung up and tossed the phone in her backpack, alongside her wallet, a water bottle, and a baseball cap.

Anna arrived at Rogers just as John Mark was pulling his truck into the parking space out front. He looked handsome, even in his work pants. She leaned her bike against the metal railing.

As he approached, she couldn't quite read his intention—hug or high five? Deciding on the safer option, she raised her hand for a high five. His arm, however, connected with the side of her head as he belatedly realized what she was doing.

"Oh wow, I'm so sorry." His face flushed crimson. He quickly backed away as Anna kept her hand suspended in the air.

"It's okay," she chuckled, "like I said, it's early." *Contact.* The high five finally landed.

At the door, John Mark reached for the handle and held it open for her. The rich aroma of baking dough and sweet sugar immediately enveloped her.

"Everything is fresh in the morning," he said, gesturing inside. "I bet Roger's been baking all night."

The display case was filled with donuts, bear claws, cinnamon buns, and an array of other pastries. The shelf behind the counter had been stacked with different breads and rolls.

"I could live here," Anna joked, turning to look at John Mark. "Roger does!"

Roger walked from the back, "Hey, John Mark, how's it hanging?"

Roger wore a Hawaiian T-shirt and shorts, with a white apron tightly covering his tummy. He must have enjoyed many of his offerings, as he had a round belly to show for it.

"Hey, Rog, it's moving along." He smiled, as he gestured toward Anna. "I would like you to meet my friend, Anna."

"I would shake your hand, but I'm afraid I would leave it completely covered in flour." He gestured with them before wiping them on his apron. Anna's gaze flickered to the tell-tale sign of his craft—a sprinkle of flour on his mustache—and she nearly laughed.

"I'm pleased to meet you." She gave a small wave. "And whatever that smell is, it is heavenly."

Leaning over the glass display case, Roger's chubby fingers tapped the top. He glanced back and forth between John Mark and Anna, a wide smile spreading across his face. "They're my signature cinnamon rolls." He said triumphantly.

"They're basically a conglomeration of butter, flour, sugar, and more butter," John Mark joked, a playful grin on his own face.

"shhhh," Roger put a finger to his lips, "that is my secret recipe," he declared with a sarcastic glare.

"Well, whatever they are, I know I'm getting one!" Anna smiled.

John Mark and Roger bantered like old friends.

"You two ready to put in your order?"

"How about that one," she said, pointing at the biggest cinnamon roll in the case. "And a coffee with cream, please."

"Fine choice."

He reached into the case and pulled out a gooey roll. "And, for you, my man?"

"I'll take the same."

Roger lifted his eyes at John Mark.

"Oh, changing it up a little, huh?" He put another cinnamon roll on a plate.

"I can't always eat maple bars. I've got to live on the edge a little, Rog."

John Mark grabbed the plates while Anna waited for the coffee.

"Here ya go," Roger set two, filled cups on the counter.

"Help yourself to the milk over there." He pointed to a small side table with straws, napkins, forks, and creamer for coffee.

"Thanks, Roger."

"Enjoy!" He waved as he went to the back, whistling a happy tune.

She walked outside; John Mark had picked a corner table with an umbrella for shade.

Anna realized she hadn't given him any money. "John Mark, did you pay him?" she set the coffee down and reached for her backpack. "Don't worry, I got it!" He sat down.

"Roger and I kind of have an agreement." He stirred his coffee, letting the cream mix with the rich drink.

"I have an open tab here."

"What do you mean?"

"Oh, last year, Roger's main oven went out; it was a little bit of a crisis, if you know what I mean. Considering he supplies our whole town with his amazing bread." John Mark winked. "I do a little electrical work on the side and was able to get them up and running in hours. He was grateful." He smiled sheepishly.

Anna had already taken a large segment of cinnamon roll and stuffed it in her mouth.

"I would say so," she drank a sip of coffee, to help swallow her large bite.

"Good, huh?"

"I don't think I've ever eaten anything so delicious."

She wiped her face with her napkin.

He put a bite into his mouth and closed his eyes.

"He's been making these since I was a kid." He nodded in appreciation. "The taste never changes."

He looks like he's in his happy place, Anna thought.

"So, what's up?" He took a drink of his coffee. Setting the cup down, he looked at her.

"I have updates for you. I think I found the house."

He choked on his drink. "What?"

She laughed, then spoke slowly, "I found the house."

He leaned forward after clearing his throat.

"Yeah, how did that go?" He looked about as uncomfortable as a cat in a wash basin.

"Well, there is, in fact, a big, old, blue house on Gordon Drive, just like my mom had written out on the envelope."

"Uh-huh," John Mark mumbled around a large bite of cinnamon roll, his cheeks bulging.

Anna decided to politely ignore the stream of white icing making its way down his chin. "So, you *do* know the place I'm talking about?" Anna asked, her gaze briefly flicking to the icing as it fell from his chin to the table.

John Mark leaned back, his hands behind his head, he nodded, "yeah I've been there."

"Okay, so were you going to tell me that eventually?" Anna inquired, a touch of impatience in her tone.

He looked down the street, then back the other way. He seemed distracted. Maybe, he wasn't supposed to take a break after all.

"I know you need to get back to work." Anna offered, giving him an easy way out.

"No, no I'm fine," he added quickly, "just been a busy morning."

"Okay, well, I just thought you would want to know." Anna continued, watching him, "I get if you don't want to help me with this."

She noticed a shift in his demeanor, an unease as she continued to press the matter.

"Is there something wrong?" She asked, her brow furrowing.

"I just think you should leave it alone," he said, his face suddenly showing a hint of defeat.

"Leave what alone?" Anna asked, confused.

"The house."

"Seriously?" She exclaimed. "But I'm quite sure it belongs to my family. I'm not just going to walk away from it."

"Well, maybe you should." His response slightly threatening.

Who was this guy? What is he trying to cover up? She wondered.

"Why, was someone murdered in that house or something creepy that you're trying to shield me from?" She chuckled. "Because guess what, I'm not a kid, I can handle it." However, as she said it, she wasn't so sure.

The silence was tense.

"Listen," John Mark said, his tone now edged with irritation, "it's better if you just walk away now. You saw your family home, what else do you need?"

"I don't know," Anna retorted, rolling her eyes. "To find the owner? To deliver the letter?" She added, the sarcasm thick but her underlying seriousness clear.

A wave of regret washed over Anna. Sharing the letter with John Mark now felt like a mistake; his resistance was obvious. Her initial excitement at finding the house and sharing with him had now evaporated, leaving a bitter taste like unsweetened tea.

Why is everyone so against this? Even mom had tried to bury her past and any connection to the blue house. Maybe, it was time for Anna to take the hint and let it go.

"John Mark," she said, a note of apology in her voice, "I'm sorry I involved you in this. Let's consider this the end of our discussion about that old house." A flush of embarrassment crept up her neck at having shared so much, so quickly.

"You didn't do anything wrong, Anna. You just showed up a little too late."

He seemed troubled. He took his napkin and wiped his mouth. Thankfully, the napkin also caught the remaining crusted icing smudge on his chin.

His comment sparked her curiosity. "Late for what?" She asked, genuinely surprised.

"Anna, the house has been sold; no one lives there anymore," John Mark stated flatly.

"Yeah, that much I figured out," she replied, a touch of impatience creeping into her voice. "But I want to know *who* lived there. It was occupied at some point; there's a ton of furniture still inside."

"I don't think I can be of any help to you," he said, avoiding her gaze. "I understand why you're here and that this is important to you, and honestly, I'd advise you to consider moving on."

Moving on was not an option for Anna. Once she set her mind on something, she was like a dog with a bone. She would uncover the truth behind this, no matter what it took. But John Mark didn't need to know that. And, he didn't need to be involved, going forward.

Anna pushed herself up from the table, a bead of sweat tracing a path down her spine. She began collecting her empty cup and plate, heading towards the tub marked with a "bus your own table" sign.

"Anna, wait." John Mark stood as well, offering a hesitant half-smile as he tucked his hands into his pockets.

She walked over to where he stood.

He started to explain, "It's just that . . ." when a woman's voice cut him off.

"Good morning, John Mark!" The voice came from behind him, a woman standing on the sidewalk just beyond the outdoor seating railing. John Mark's back was to her, but Anna watched his face drain of color. The woman was elegant, with white hair and an air of quiet sophistication, her hands resting on the black metal railing.

"Aren't you going to say hi?" Anna prompted him, a little confused by his reaction.

Slowly, John Mark turned around.

Anna stood beside him, offering the woman a friendly smile, while John Mark remained utterly silent.

The woman seemed perfectly pleasant, yet John Mark looked genuinely terrified.

"Good morning to you, too," Anna replied cheerfully, filling the awkward silence for him.

The woman nodded politely at Anna, then turned her attention back to John Mark, a knowing glint in her eye. "Well, John Mark? Aren't you going to introduce me to your lady friend?"

Anna cleared her throat lightly. This woman assumed she and John Mark were a couple. An item. Dating. How awkward,

Anna thought. She debated whether to correct the assumption or let it slide. Instead, she turned to John Mark with a teasing smirk, deciding to let him squirm a little. His jaw had practically unhinged. He stammered, finally managing, "Forgive me, Lucy; this is my friend who's visiting from out of town."

CHAPTER FIFTEEN

A Hopeful Heart

Lucy had started early this morning. She got a good night's sleep and was feeling in high spirits. She parked her truck a block from the library, knowing she was ten minutes too early, she would stroll down Main Street. She felt inspired to try her hand at the internet, and the library had free computers for anyone to use. She hoisted her purse up on her shoulder; she could smell a savory aroma as she stepped closer to Roger's. And, there sat John Mark.

What a happy coincidence, she thought.

She would let him know that she had taken his advice and would be searching for her granddaughter on the world wide web. He appeared to be with someone. A young lady from the likes of it. Lucy felt her pulse quicken, maybe John Mark had a lady friend. *How exciting*, she thought. She had enjoyed being courted by Bill. Lucy cleared her throat, interrupting their discussion, John Mark looked as though he'd seen a ghost when he turned around, she could see that he was uncomfortable. He stared at her for so long that Lucy thought the cat had gotten his tongue. Or perhaps she had caught them in the middle of a serious conversation.

Finally, John Mark introduced the young woman to Lucy, referring to her as his friend. Lucy squinted through the sun, looking at the lovely young lady, as she extended her hand, toward Lucy.

"Good morning," she said. Lucy held onto her warm hand, cupping it with her other.

"Are you new to town, honey?"

"Just recently."

"She drove cross-country to come and check out what we Floridians have going on," John Mark chimed in.

"Ah, now the boy talks!" Lucy joked.

Anna snickered at the comment. Lucy watched her tuck her hair behind her ears.

"Sorry, you surprised me," he said. "It's been a full morning, and I need to get back to work." John Mark's eyes were clouded over, as though he were irritated.

"Yes, I won't keep you. You young people always have somewhere to be." She winked.

Lucy looked at the young woman. Something about her seemed familiar. A little embarrassed, Lucy admitted to herself that the girl reminded her of Grace. It was the shape of her nose, with the same small bump on the slope, like a bunny's jump. But it was more than that. She also had Grace's eyes, the slant of her shoulders, and the high cheekbones. If Grace hadn't died, Lucy would have sworn she was staring at a twentysomething version of her.

Lucy glanced at her watch and saw the time. Five minutes until opening.

"I better scoot soon." She put her hand on John Mark's shoulder, "this fine young man told me about a thing called the internet, and today, I'm going to give it a go. I'm going to search for some missing people."

Lucy wanted to be at the library first, hoping that Linda, the librarian, would be available to show her the ropes. She had never used a computer before. The girl tossed her backpack over her shoulders and looked at John Mark with a sly grin, "What a coincidence; I'm looking for someone, too."

With robotic movements, John Mark turned back to the table and gathered his cup and plate and walked to the gray tub, now filled with discarded saucers, water glasses, and small plates.

"Well, you have come at a lovely time," Lucy smiled at the girl. "Naples will surely provide you with our signature cool breezes this time of year."

John Mark walked back to where Lucy stood, she gently adjusted her purse as it slid off her shoulder.

"Well, ladies, it's been lovely," he said, a clear indication he was eager to leave.

He must be late for something, Lucy mused, watching him. *I'll have to teach him how to properly say goodbye to a girl,* she thought to herself, a small chuckle escaping her lips.

"Alright," Lucy nodded. He sure was acting strange. They both watched him get into his truck and pull away. They remained silent. Without thought, Lucy blurted out, "Honey, you're new to town; how would you like a brief history lesson of Naples?"

"Wow, really?"

"Yes, I'm due to give a tour of the cottage, I've been shirking my duties lately. How does this afternoon sound?"

"That would be amazing!"

It warmed Lucy's heart to see a young person so excited about history. Her history.

The two exchanged phone numbers. "Let's plan on 3:00 p.m."

Lucy gave her directions on how to get to the cottage.

"I will look forward to it."

Lucy turned to walk away, then stopped, realizing she hadn't asked her name.

"Oh, honey," she called, "what is your name?"

Anna bending down to zip up her backpack, looked up, "Anna," she smiled at Lucy.

Lucy took a step back. Her mouth went dry. Anna. Her smile. Her name. Her voice. Could it be? Lucy thought she was going crazy for a moment. The resemblance to Grace was uncanny. Could finding her granddaughter be this simple?

"What a lovely name," she breathed out.

"Thanks," Anna turned her head sideways, but smiling.

Lucy couldn't tear her gaze away. She felt an overwhelming urge to hug Anna, but trepidation and doubt held her back. Not yet. Her heart was pounding. *Wait.* She needed to be sure. She needed to be prepared.

"Okay, Anna," Lucy said, forcing a casual tone. "We will see you then." She didn't want to leave, but she willed her feet forward toward the library. She wanted to keep talking to Anna. To learn more about her. She would still conduct her search. Perhaps, in her investigation, Anna would appear with a picture, and it would confirm her growing suspicion. As she walked away, she turned around to catch one more glimpse of the girl. She saw her hop on a bike and ride away. How in the world did this happen? She shook her head, flabbergasted. As she crossed the street, Linda was opening the library's wooden double doors. Lucy quickened her pace, moving her purse to her other shoulder to balance out the weight, still perplexed by the encounter with Anna. As Lucy reached the steps, Linda was waiting, holding a lime green watering can.

"I swear these things think they live in the Sahara, by the amount of water they need."

The two potted azaleas framing the entryway had been there for as long as Lucy could remember.

Lucy walked up the steps and embraced Linda.

"Good to see you."

"As soon as I finish with these, I'll be right in."

Lucy walked into the overly cooled space and shivered. She browsed a few shelves while she waited. "All right, I'm all yours," Linda piped up from behind her desk.

Lucy gave a wry smile, "I was hoping you could teach me how to search on the internet."

"Of course," Linda laughed. "What are you hoping to do?"

"Well, I don't know quite yet, but if you could show me how to search for a person," Lucy trailed off.

But maybe it doesn't matter because I have already found her. She smiled thinking to herself. At least she would confirm her findings using one of those big square boxes, called a computer.

"You got it." Linda led the way as they walked over to the wall of Mac computers.

Linda pulled the chair out and Lucy sat down. Linda pulled another chair from the table next to them. As Linda typed a bunch of words onto the screen, Lucy began to formulate a plan. An idea had sparked, today, at the cottage tour, she would subtly guide Anna, offering her clues. She would reveal Anna's heritage, starting with Naples, the very strip of land her family had called home. She would lead and direct Anna down that path, the path of her own legacy. Maybe it would spark something within her. She knew she had to set Old Blue aside. It could no longer be her motivation. This was Lucy's second chance, and she was not going to blow it.

"Here we are," Linda announced, a search engine displayed on her screen. Lucy carefully used her index finger to type in her grandchildren's first and last names, along with the address out

West and their parents' names. "Okay, now we wait a moment as it searches." Linda arranged some of the papers and pens next to the monitor as Lucy watched the spinning hourglass, tip back and forth. Then poof, a picture appeared, it was Grace, her husband their two children. She felt a lump in her throat. "Lucy?" Linda asked, a hint of concern in her voice, "is everything okay?"

Lucy had found her. Or perhaps it was the other way around, a twist of fate bringing Anna unknowingly to her doorstep. Lucy could no longer offer Old Blue; it wasn't hers to give. But she knew she would offer something far more significant, even if the thought made her heart pound. She would offer Anna herself—Lucy Mair Belltown, wrinkles and all. That was the most valuable gift she could give. The only gift she could give.

CHAPTER SIXTEEN

John Mark's Conflict

John Mark could feel the panic subside as he drove away from the streetside café. When Lucy walked up to him at Rogers, it had caught him completely off guard. As John Mark drove off, he watched Lucy and Anna exchange phone numbers, a wave of bafflement washing over him. How could they not see it? The resemblance was striking. Lucy's smile, he noted with surprise, was the perfect likeness to Anna's, softened only by the fine lines etched around her mouth from years of laughter. He must be more like his own father than he cared to admit. A pang of guilt twisted in his gut as he saw Lucy's genuine happiness, knowing he was keeping secrets from her. Things were coming together on their own. Like a greater force was at work. A honeybee to a flower, they were destined to meet. And he knew he couldn't stop it. Anna and Lucy were being drawn together by an invisible thread. He had to think fast.

He needed a plan. It was getting complicated. Surely, one or both would think he was a con artist when they found that he was using them. Why must he be such a hero and help the damsel in distress? He wouldn't be in this situation if he had just put his head down and finished the deal like his father had said.

He felt his father's disappointment one too many times. He was not willing to channel down that river again. Like in high school when his father wanted him to play football. Despite his protests, John Mark went to every practice and every game. And he hated every minute of it. It wasn't the game he despised but the lectures after it.

"John Mark, get your head in the game; you missed that pass."

Or his dad's favorite line, "A Gordon never loses."

To his dad, John Mark was a total bust. If John Mark could secure this deal, his dad would approve of him. But he would lose the respect and friendship of both Lucy and Anna. If only Paul Gordon's wishes could be fulfilled, along with Lucy's and perhaps even his father's. Was there any way this deal could benefit everyone involved? It seemed impossible. As he thought through it, he realized there may be one last effort.

"Grandfather," he said aloud.

John Mark wondered if even a tiny shred of sympathy remained in the older man's heart.

He would soon find out.

CHAPTER SEVENTEEN

Anna's New Friend

Later that afternoon, Anna walked along the shaded sidewalk, toward the cottage. She smiled at her luck in meeting Lucy this morning. Maybe, Lucy would be able to fill in some of the blanks on her family's past. So far, talking with John Mark had been like hitting her head against a brick wall. The sweet jasmine scent led her to the white picket fence. A plaque identified the cottage as a preserved museum. "Cool," she said, looking up. She walked beneath a flowering arbor, stepping onto paving stones marked with names and dates. "Remembrance Stones," another plaque explained. The lawn was perfectly green, and a few visitors relaxed in the rose garden or on benches. *Quaint*, she thought; it reminded her of John Mark's mother's cottage.

"Yoo-hoo!" Lucy stood on the screened-in porch, waving at her.

Anna smiled and walked towards Lucy, a sense of anticipation bubbling within her. She had indeed been looking forward to this.

"You found us!" Lucy exclaimed, pushing the screen door wider to allow Anna to step inside. With her other hand, she reached out and gently took Anna's, guiding her across the threshold.

"Come in, come in."

Anna looked around the screened-in porch; it was like she had stepped back in time. Green Astroturf carpeted the ground. Wicker chairs with deep seats and cucumber green cushions were scattered about. The walls, made of what looked like stucco, were painted white. Anna walked up to touch the thick plaster wall.

"Wow, that's surprisingly cool to the touch."

"That's called tabby." Lucy followed her and put her palm against the house.

"It's made of shells. It's the toughest stuff out there. This tabby house has withstood some large storms, and somehow it is like a natural air conditioner." Lucy smiled.

"How old is this place?"

"Older than me, if that tells you anything."

Suddenly, Lucy gasped and grabbed her side. Anna moved toward her, worried.

"Are you okay Lucy?"

"Oh, yes, this nuisance." She pointed to her tummy and then motioned them toward the chairs.

"Let's sit down."

Anna followed Lucy; she had a dozen questions but waited patiently for Lucy, not wanting to overwhelm her.

"Was it something you ate?" She questioned.

Anna sat in the rocker, letting it slowly glide back and forth. *People around here know what a good chair is,* she thought, thinking back to the same rocker on Old Blue's porch.

"You could say that," Lucy chuckled, then added, "honey, when you get as old as I am, your body will talk to you too."

Anna smiled sympathetically. Lucy adjusted herself in the chair. Anna saw the intensity in her eyes. The pain was not subsiding by the way she methodically moved.

"Okay, honey, I'm all yours. By the looks of it you look like you're about to explode with questions."

"How can you tell?" Anna laughed.

"I know that look. Curiosity."

"I suppose so. I know nothing about Naples except the few tidbits my mom passed onto me." *Which weren't many*, Anna thought.

Lucy nodded her head understandingly.

Lucy looked like she was thinking, "I know just where to start." She stood and motioned for Anna to follow her inside.

"You sure? You looked like you were in pain a few minutes ago." Anna said with concern.

"As sure as I'll ever be. This thing comes and goes, like an ocean tide. I don't let it keep me down."

They went inside and Anna noticed the dust particles, motionless, in the air, as the sunlight spilled in from a side window. Lucy walked gracefully toward the dining room like she owned the place; her prior aches and pains had vanished.

"Ah, here it is," she pointed to a picture tucked in amongst others.

She tapped it. "See this?"

Anna stepped closer and saw ten people standing in an extensive line. One of them was holding a newspaper, but Anna couldn't read what it said.

"Who are these people?"

"These are the magnificent ten," Lucy said triumphantly. "And that one right there is me!"

Anna leaned in and looked again. She turned and looked at Lucy and looked at the picture again. Lucy was beaming in the picture and as she stood beside it.

"Not to boast, but we saved this cottage from being demolished."

"Really, why was it going to be torn down?" Anna wondered why anyone would tear down something so wonderful.

Lucy pursed her lips, "A few decades ago, there was this big move to renovate the town. The city told us these old buildings were dangerous and must be torn down. So, our city council started what would become a decade of destruction. It was fast, and irreversible. We lost a lot of beautiful buildings, but we didn't lose this one."

"What did you do?"

"We formed a committee, raised money, and bought the place." Lucy continued. "The magnificent ten turned this into a preservation home, and now we give tours and try to help others see the importance of the past."

A subtle pride entered Lucy's posture as she spoke. "This house is almost a century old," she declared, "and she is as strong as ever." With that, Lucy rapped her knuckles firmly on the wall.

Behind Anna was the long, dining room table, with seating for twelve; it was polished and set with china and crystal.

Did you ever eat at this table?" Anna asked, impressed.

"I did."

"What was it like, you know, back then?"

Lucy turned towards the office. "Let's sit down again for a bit, shall we?"

A gentle worry creased Anna's brow. "Lucy, are you sure you're up for it? Maybe we should do this another time." Anna didn't want to tire her out.

"Nonsense." Lucy plopped into a worn leather chair.

Lucy looked tired. Anna wondered if Lucy was telling the whole truth about her health or holding back.

"Anna, you asked about life 'back then,' and I'm guessing what you're referring to is when I was about sixty years younger?" Lucy said with a playful smirk, raising her eyebrows at the youthful Anna.

Anna nodded, returning her smile.

"Life was simpler," Lucy began. "People helped each other. Neighbors knew one another." Lucy painted a picture of a bustling town, where demanding work was balanced by a quiet Sunday, and each day was met with a certain resilience.

"It sounds like something out of a movie, Lucy." Anna said softly, absorbed in the picture Lucy was painting with her words.

"In some ways, it was, honey." Lucy looked off into the distance. Anna wondered if she was remembering those 'good ole days.'

"However, with the joys and togetherness, also came suffering and brokenness." Lucy frowned. "I suppose what I want to say is life never gives you a free pass from suffering."

Anna knew that truth intimately. A wave of emotion tightened her throat. She had known great loss. Lucy, perceptive and kind, watched Anna, a gentle smile gracing her lips. Then, she reached out a weathered hand and rested it lightly on Anna's knee. The simple gesture nearly brought tears to Anna's eyes. Such a small touch, yet it resonated deeply, a quiet acknowledgment of an unspoken grief. Anna felt that feeling again, like someone or something was welcoming her home.

Lucy sat back in her chair, resting her hands in her lap. "Now, where were we?" she asked.

Anna appreciated the change in subject, allowing her to compose herself. She straightened in her chair and began, "actually, Lucy, I was hoping you could tell me about a house I found. It's called Old Blue."

A visible shift came over Lucy. The easygoing warmth from moments before vanished, replaced by discomfort. She hesitated, her words catching in her throat before finally emerging in a rush, "Ah, yes . . . that old place."

"So, you know it?" Anna leaned forward in her chair.

"Everyone knows that place, honey, it has been around as long as I have." Lucy shuffled her feet back and forth on the rug beneath her. A familiar pattern emerged in Anna's mind. Once again, the mere mention of Old Blue elicited a palpable unease in the person she was speaking with. Anna wondered if she should continue with the subject or drop it again. *It's now or never Anna, if you don't ask, you will never know,* she thought to herself.

"I think it belonged to my family." Anna blurted out.

"Who is your family honey?" Lucy's brow furrowed.

"Well, that is what I am trying to find out. I was hoping you could tell me."

Lucy's fingers gripped the sides of her chair. Anna saw her knuckles go white. Lucy cleared her throat, the house eliciting another strong response. It was obvious Lucy was not feeling well today. Anna felt selfish for pressing the sweet woman. This topic was causing obvious agitation. *Again, I better let it go,* Anna thought her frustration mounting that she still didn't have answers.

"Lucy, you have been so helpful and kind." Anna looked at the clock on the wall, "you know, I better get going." She stood and began to gather her things. "Thank you for the tour!"

Seeing Lucy sit motionless, Anna now regretted, even more that she had brought it up.

"Sit down, we're not done here." Lucy said with force.

Anna looked at her, surprised.

She set her bag on the floor and sat down once again in the chair.

"You look as if you've something more to say," Lucy observed gently, her eyes fixed on Anna.

Anna hesitated, biting her lower lip. "It's just that . . . whenever I've mentioned this house, people seem genuinely scared."

Lucy nodded slowly, a thoughtful expression on her face. "And perhaps they are. Sometimes, revisiting one's past can require a great deal of courage. Tell me, what do *you* know about the house?"

A wave of vulnerability washed over Anna as she confessed, "I think the house once belonged to my grandparents." The statement felt sad, exposing her family's long-standing estrangement more than she intended. "I never knew them; they passed away when I was little."

Lucy's gaze dropped to her feet, her posture slumping slightly, like a balloon losing air. A sadness flickered across her face at this, but just as quickly, her eyes lifted, meeting Anna's with a renewed intensity. "Tell me more, honey," she urged softly.

"Lucy, there are a lot of holes in my family history. And I'm on a journey to figure out why." Anna, like Lucy, felt a surge of energy to keep going, despite the complexities of the conversation.

Lucy nodded, "A worthy feat, child." Lucy closed her eyes a moment, breathing deep. "I can tell you that Old Blue belongs to the Belltown family, and it always has."

Finally, someone gave her a clear answer. Anna's heart pounded in excitement.

"You said has . . ." Anna looked perplexed. "So, are you saying a Belltown still lives there?"

"Yes," Lucy drew out her reply. "At least for a few more days." A sly look in her eyes.

"What does that mean?" Anna asked, confused.

"The Belltowns are in a position of having to let go of their family home," Lucy stated, clearing her throat, a visible wince of pain crossing her features.

A flood of questions surged through Anna's mind, leaving her unsure where to even begin. Looking at Lucy's face, it was clear the topic of the house was causing her distress. "You must know them well then," Anna commented softly, remembering the close-knit nature of the community in Naples. Lucy nodded her head, yes. "I'm so sorry, Lucy, that's truly sad." Just as Anna was about to delve deeper, a sharp knock echoed at the front door.

The sudden knock startled Lucy, causing her to make a little jump in her seat. "Just a minute, honey," she said, surprised. "Let me see who that could be." She rose to answer the door.

Anna stood and peered around the door frame. A young couple stood together, shoulder-to-shoulder, both dressed in tennis attire. Huge smiles plastered on their faces. Lucy stood holding the door open, "Yes, may I help you?"

"We heard that a docent might be available to give us a tour this afternoon."

Lucy turned and looked at the grandfather clock, "oh my, is it that time already?" She shook her head, "time certainly does get away from a person if we don't keep an eye on it."

Anna chuckled; it was true. She watched as Lucy welcomed them in. She walked them over to the living room.

"Give me just a moment." She motioned to the two high back chairs, "take a seat there, if you'd like."

Anna sensed it was her cue to leave. Lucy had been incredibly generous with her time, providing a tour and answering her questions.

"I'm sorry, honey, but duty calls," Lucy replied, her expression genuinely apologetic.

"I understand, Lucy. Thank you so much for everything," Anna wanted to hug her, but felt silly.

Lucy reached out and placed her hand gently on Anna's arm.

"What a lovely young woman you are, Anna," Lucy said, her wrinkled hand surprisingly warm, offering a small but welcome comfort. Anna longed to tap into Lucy's wellspring of local history.

"Perhaps, I could swing by later this week?" Anna ventured.

"Of course," Lucy replied, then paused, a thoughtful look in her eyes.

"I have a better idea; do you like to watch the sunrise?" Suddenly, the room felt like a dream—like a déjà vu moment. As though Anna had been waiting for this invite all along and didn't even know it.

Anna looked at Lucy's face. Her features, so warm, open, and friendly, also familiar. She reminded her of someone she knew. But she couldn't place it.

Lucy's offer ignited Anna's curiosity. At this point, she felt she'd agree to anything for more answers. Like a hidden trap door suddenly revealed, she stepped through Lucy's offer, being the next crucial step in her mission.

"I cherish sunrises."

"Well then, have I got a treat for you." Lucy winked.

CHAPTER EIGHTEEN

Lucy's Offering

There was no doubt that Anna was Grace's child. As the girl walked from picture to picture at the cottage, leaning in close to each one and asking the names of people, Lucy's heart felt like it would burst. She was this close, and everything in her wanted to envelop Anna in a hug—her granddaughter, Grace's baby girl. However, she knew it wasn't the time. Anna wanted answers. Lucy had them. Crumbs. She was going to give her crumbs. *Slow down Lucy*, she told herself. As they were settled into the office, Lucy began to unfold her story. Just as she might have revealed more, a sharp knock at the door startled both her and Anna, abruptly breaking the moment. Lucy rose to answer the door, and a chiseled couple stood in front of her, asking for a tour. She knew she had to do it.

"Come in," she opened the door with a smile. Her body was tired, but she would press on.

One last tour, she thought.

She settled the couple in the living room and returned to where Anna was waiting in the study. She stared at her, studying her; her cheekbones were Grace's cheekbones. Her hair tucked behind her ears just as Grace had done in high school. Lucy saw the same resolve and determination that her daughter had once carried. Lucy felt it. It was time. She invited Anna to watch the sunrise.

Anna was surprised and pleased and asked for her address, assuming Lucy meant from her home.

Smart girl, Lucy beamed inwardly. *I can't give her the address quite yet.* Lucy thought.

But she knew she needed to act soon, there was no telling if she would be around tomorrow. Every day her body felt weaker. *How to get Anna to her house without revealing what I know right now.* Suddenly, she remembered the daily walk she would take with her daughter, Grace. Grace would leave school and make her way to the beach. She would stroll home using the sand as her sidewalk. And, nine out of ten times, Lucy left the house a few minutes past three to meet her halfway. It became their ritual. They would walk the last stretch together, often with their eyes to the ground, looking for beach glass to add to their already growing collection. It was their common ground, even if they were at odds, the sea and the sand was their white flag. Things would be different today if she had surrendered to the walk, their halfway point. But the day Bill died, Lucy had been stubborn, unyielding. This was her second chance. She would be a fool to waste it.

"Do you know where the Pier is?"

Anna nodded, "yes."

"Good, start there. Walk to the sand and turn left."

"Okay, what next?" Anna was getting excited.

"Just start walking; I'll meet you and walk with you."

"Cool, so you'll meet me halfway?"

Lucy felt the knot in her stomach and the lump in her throat.

"I will meet you halfway." She closed her eyes as she said it.

Her heart felt like it was cracking.

Anna hugged Lucy tight. Lucy held both joy and sorrow in her arms. She felt her knees wobble beneath her, and Anna held onto her.

"Whoa, sit down, Lucy."

This was not the time or the place for her to crumble. She used all the strength she could to stand.

"I'm okay. I'm just tired."

She knew her body was slowly giving up. But she wouldn't let it go, just yet. She would fight this. Time, that precious commodity, was slipping away. After assuring Anna she was okay, she watched her leave, and then, with a gentle sigh, turned to her waiting guests. "Welcome," she said, her voice filled with the echoes of years past, leading them into the dining room. Over the next hour, she told the stories, the retelling of Naples' history. The Stories of Palm Cottage, the people and the founders lived on, whispered like prayers through her lips. When the tour was done, her "thank you" was soft, she knew this would be her last tour, her benediction. The lock turned, and she leaned against the door, grateful she had finished well. Behind her, she heard a soft tap on the glass. She turned and there stood Sandy, a vision of familiar comfort, holding out a plate. "Dear friend," Lucy breathed, opening the door.

Sandy, she always turned up at just the right time.

"I had an inkling you might still be here when I saw the lights on."

Sandy's house was across the street from the cottage.

"Late tour?"

"Yes, a sweet couple. A lot of questions." Lucy smiled; relief written all over her face.

Lucy and Sandy walked into the outdated kitchen and sat at the small, lacquered table. The food was still warm and smelled good. She was thankful she still had a small appetite. Sandy sat down across from her.

"It's nothing fancy; Jim wanted spaghetti tonight, surprise, surprise." Sandy said sarcastically.

Lucy took the foil off and used the fork Sandy had taped to the top of the plate to take a big bite. The pasta tasted delicious. She stabbed at the wilted salad. The heat from the pasta had made it soggy.

Sandy leaned back in her chair, watching Lucy take small bites. She folded her arms like an army general.

"What aren't you telling me?"

Sandy could always read Lucy like a book.

Lucy finished chewing her bite and swallowed.

"I found her, Sandy."

Sandy leaned toward Lucy, "What?"

Lucy took another bite and spoke with her mouth full.

"She's here in Naples, and she's charming."

"You've met her?"

Lucy nodded triumphantly. Between chewing, she told Sandy everything about meeting Anna at Roger's bakery and then inviting her to the cottage. And, most importantly, about her plan.

"I can't believe it. It's like she just fell into your lap."

"It's miraculous. She's searching for me, Sandy, but she doesn't know yet."

Lucy felt the pain in her chest and abdomen; like sharp knives, prodding, pressing into her. She winced.

Sandy's eagle eyes saw the short burst of pain.

"Let me drive you home."

Lucy rested both her hands on her abdomen, holding them still.

"I'll be okay; it comes and goes."

"But it has been coming and going more often, hasn't it?"

She hated to admit it, "Yes, it has."

The pain slowly subsided. Lucy rested her hands on the Formica table.

"And the oddest thing about all of this is, Randall Gordon's grandson, John Mark, knows Anna is my granddaughter. I know it. He was with her. They've already become acquainted."

"What makes you think he knows?"

"It's written all over his face. Guilt. The same guilty look his grandfather wore when he challenged Paul's will in court." Disgust twisted Lucy's features, directed more at herself for being twice duped by a Gordon. "You'd think I'd be smarter." She offered a dismissive shrug.

"Don't beat yourself up," Sandy replied. "It's hardly surprising the grandson is cut from the same cloth as the grandfather. Paul was the only good one in that bunch."

"How could I have been so daft, Sandy?" Lucy lamented. She had welcomed John Mark into her home, even offered him her cake. "He's my enemy. He'll be the new owner of Old Blue. And he's going to tear it down, piece by piece." Lucy inhaled deeply. "I know, I can't even focus on that right now." Her attention needed to be on more important people, Anna being one of them. John Mark would have to wait.

"I'm sorry, Lucy." Sandy gave her a sad smile. "But, on the positive side, you found your granddaughter!" *Yes, this was a cause for celebration*, Lucy thought.

Sandy clapped her hands together in anticipation, "I have so many questions. Like, how did she get here? Did she know about Naples growing up? Does she know about you?"

"I know, me too. But the questions will have to wait."

"So, tell me about tomorrow, what's your plan?" Sandy asked.

Lucy looked out the window and the sun had begun to set. The warm glow changed the color of the room.

"I'm dropping my last crumb for her. She will get to choose what she does with it."

Lucy felt her chest rise and fall, in one big breath.

"I am going to walk with her to the house. She's coming for the sunrise." Lucy felt the lump in her throat, she swallowed it. "I'm meeting her halfway on the beach."

Sandy nodded knowingly, a familiar path she herself had trod many times. "That's quite a walk, Lucy."

Lucy knew it would take every ounce of reserves she would have that day.

"Do you hear that, Sandy?" She thought she heard the church bells ringing. *What an odd time of day for the bells to go off*, Lucy thought.

"No, what is it?"

"It's bells!" The sound was distant, but Lucy was sure she heard it. "That's the sound of freedom," Lucy beamed, her face alight. "The arrival of a new day." The bells held significance, their ringing typically reserved for funerals, weddings, and Easter—moments marking transition or transformation. What was odd was that they were ringing now. The last clang rang out then no more.

Sandy reached across the table and grabbed Lucy's hand. "Honey, let's get you home."

"Okay." She agreed. Lucy felt the weight lift. Today marked the day she had finally let go, choosing instead to embrace what truly mattered.

Before standing up, Lucy wiped her eyes, small tears forming.

"Sandy, I always thought Grace owed me something, because she let me down." As Lucy said the words, she felt lighter and lighter. "What I see now is . . ." her voice trailed off. She began to cry. Through muffled words, Lucy choked out her truth. "There should be no owing anyone." She shook her head. Sandy stood and walked to the side bathroom bringing back a tissue for Lucy.

"Thank you." She blew her nose. "We inflict pain upon each other, then assign a value to that hurt, a price that has to be paid. If the person who caused the pain can't pay the price, forgiveness is withheld." Lucy's price had been high. Too high for Grace.

"If I could take it all back I would." Lucy's voice was laced with regret. "Sandy, I feel like I've been given an opportunity to right things."

"I believe you have." Sandy agreed.

"I can't go back and change things with Grace, though God knows I wish I could."

A wave of emotion threatened to surface, but she held it back. "But now, I can do this *for* Grace."

"I'm proud of you, Lucy."

"I'm not afraid anymore, Sandy." The fear that had held her captive—rejection—had lost its power. Now, Lucy was gripped by a desire to pour out her life for another, and in that very act of selfless giving, the long-held captivity would finally be overcome.

Sandy looked pleased as she folded her arms.

"I can see it in you," Sandy chuckled.

"What?" she questioned.

"In forgiving others," Sandy observed, "you have also learned to forgive yourself."

Lucy slowly nodded, absorbing Sandy's words. "I suppose I have." She pondered, a thoughtful expression on her face. *Perhaps. in forgiving oneself, we lift the heaviest burden?* A quiet certainty settled within her; she knew it to be true.

"Do you want me to go with you?" Sandy asked.

"Thank you, but I need to do this on my own."

"I understand." Sandy's smiled, knowingly.

They both stood, gathering their things. "I guess I will take that ride," Lucy said.

Sandy nodded, then looped her arm through Lucy's. As they walked to the front door, Lucy stopped.

"You know, Sandy," Lucy said with conviction, "when she sees the house, she'll understand. The puzzle, solved." Lucy's throat tightened thinking about it. She placed her hand over her heart, reminding herself. "But I'm not afraid." They walked out the door, as Lucy turned and locked it from the outside, she took a deep breath and looked out, Sandy waiting patiently. "What happens after that is up to her. All I can do is help guide her home."

CHAPTER NINETEEN

A Fight for Good

John Mark crumpled up the paper bag and tossed it in the trash. He crammed the last of the meatball sub into his mouth. The sandwich he'd grabbed on his way home clearly hadn't satisfied his appetite. A foot long and he was still hungry. As he walked to the fridge to forage for more food, his eye caught on the one lone picture he kept on the refrigerator. Held in place by a magnet advertising a local pizza place. The picture was creased down the center and dog-eared at the corners, yet it was the only one he didn't toss after his parent's divorce. Seated on a couch were his father, mother, and seven-year-old self. Their arms were around one another; everyone smiling. He remembered that day being a good day. All was well in his world. His mom's sickness hadn't reared its ugly head.

John Mark looked at the clock. It was 4:00 p.m. He knew he was only delaying the inevitable. Maybe he was attempting to deceive himself into believing he didn't need to do what was required. After years of living under his dad's thumb, breaking free would be a monumental task. Anything outside of Stan Gordon's plan would get instantly crushed.

He took the picture off the fridge and studied it. His dad was actually smiling. He laughed, it was hard to believe they were one in the same. These days, his father's smiles were reserved solely for the growing numbers in his bank account. A shudder ran through John Mark at the thought that with each passing day, with every choice he made, he was transforming into his father: heartless, greedy, and emotionally distant. His gaze softened as it landed on his mother in the picture—the strong, generous, and resilient one.

"I'm like her," he whispered. *I have to be,* he told himself.

He touched his chest, a silent wish in his heart. He knew, deep down, it was a choice. John Mark stood at a crossroads. Would he feed the wolf inside or the lamb? He put the photo back under the magnet.

He glanced at his mother's image one last time, drawing strength from the photograph. "I know . . . and I will," he murmured, a quiet promise hanging in the air.

John Mark grabbed his keys off the counter and ran out the door, letting it slam behind him. He slid into the truck's cab and shoved the key in the ignition. As he backed out of the driveway, he felt his hands shaking. He put the truck into drive. The incredible sunset caught his attention, a vibrant canvas of gold bleeding into pink and purple. He thought of his great-grandfather, Paul. If Lucy's words held any truth, then somewhere deep within him, John Mark knew he possessed that same inherent goodness. The thought strengthened him. He pressed down onto the accelerator, the car surging forward down the road.

Reaching his grandfather's imposing gate, he steered his truck down the winding driveway that led to the spacious four-car garage. His grandfather always had a thing for cars, dedicating most

Saturday mornings to their meticulous care with a terry cloth and a tin of polish. Even if the vehicle never left the confines of the driveway, it had to be perfect. Just like everything else he owned. John Mark parked in front of his grandfather's mansion. It had been built, sparing no expense. A prestigious architecture firm from Boston had meticulously designed every square inch of the three-story residence. The house featured two widow's walks offering ocean vistas, private ensuite porches for each bedroom, a state-of-the-art in-home movie theater, and a gourmet chef's kitchen. *And the comical thing*, John Mark thought, *is he has this huge, gorgeous home and he is rarely here. What a waste.* As John Mark climbed out of his truck, he waved at Al, his grandfather's gardener, a familiar figure on the estate since John Mark's childhood. Al returned the wave as he tipped the fresh garden soil from the wheelbarrow into the flower bed, carefully spreading it around the base of the plants. John Mark saw his dad's BMW parked in front of the garage. Predictable. John Mark knew they were having pre-dinner cocktails. *Great,* he thought, *at this rate, I'll be surprised if I leave this place alive.* He walked toward the elaborate wooden door, the sound of distant waves causing him to pause. His grandfather's house, like Lucy's, was in a lucrative location, seaside, with expansive views. His grandfather often boasted about having the finest ocean views in the entire county. Randall Gordon, after all, was a man who settled for nothing less than the best. John Mark wondered if that were true anymore. After seeing the view from Lucy's front window, perhaps, he would beg to differ.

He knocked on the door.

Angeline, his grandfather's housekeeper, opened it, happily greeting him, "John Mark, how wonderful to see you!"

Her accent, soft and welcoming. "Your father and grandfather just sat in the front room with their drinks."

She ushered him in.

"What can I get you," she walked briskly ahead of him while speaking over her shoulder.

"I'll just take some water. Thanks, Angeline."

"You sure? You look a little pale; want me to make you some tea?"

"No, no, I'm fine; water is good."

Was his face a dead giveaway? Inside, he felt like a dog backed into a corner, timid yet braced for a fight, even before the confrontation had begun.

"You got it; go sit down; I'll bring it to you."

"Thanks."

He walked in, and the two men he loved and hated most in the world sat across from each other in black leather chairs. They were still in their suits, the ties unknotted, and their shirt sleeves rolled up. They called this their casual look. John Mark had few memories of his dad wearing anything other than a suit.

Clearing his throat, he announced himself, "Hey, Grandfather. Hi, Dad."

Instantly, he realized he had forgotten to take off his shoes. He was sure the rug he stood on cost more than his truck and house combined. Maybe, his grandfather wouldn't notice.

They both looked at him, surprised.

"Son, what brings you here?" his dad set his drink on a marble coaster.

Before John Mark could answer, his grandfather stood and motioned for him to sit down.

"Join us."

His grandfather was likely two or three drinks in, judging by his flushed cheeks and jovial manner. A subtle tension eased from John

Mark's shoulders; he knew the alcohol would help soften the sharp edges of the conversation to come.

He swallowed the nervous lump in his throat and drew a deep breath. His thoughts turned to his mother, Lucy, and Anna. And, once again, to Paul. His grandfather stood waiting, his offer of joining them lingering in the air.

"I was hoping I could talk with you," John Mark said, moving toward the chair but not sitting down.

"Anything, anything," his grandfather said as he sat back in his chair. John Mark could smell the alcohol; it was strong. It confirmed John Mark's suspicion: yes, they had been sipping cocktails for a while. He noticed a small, framed photo next to him on the side table, and picked it up. He instantly recognized the man: Paul, his great-grandfather. In the picture, Paul was young, robust, handsome, and happy. He was perched atop a huge, felled live oak tree, a two-man, cross-cut saw held casually in his hands.

John Mark set it back down. Curious.

"Grandfather, who helped your dad cut down that live oak?" He said, motioning to the photo.

"Oh, who knows? I think he did it himself." His grandfather cackled. "That photo was taken the day my dad felled the first tree on his property." John Mark knew the story, but would his grandfather tell him the truth? "He cleared the whole one hundred acres, a true lumberjack."

John Mark knew the truth. Paul Gordon certainly did not clear the land himself. "No one helped him?" John Mark asked. "Nope, like me, he was an astute businessman, he didn't need anyone to do his work for him." Pride. Arrogance. Lies. John Mark was done with them. John Mark wanted to blurt out what actually happened: the Gordons and the Belltowns cleared their land together. They were friends. Instead, he remained silent.

Randall put his hands on his knees and rubbed his palms up and down over the top of his thighs. His face bore the marks of time: aged, worn.

"Well, what brings you over this way, John Mark?" His grandfather picked up his drink and took a long swig—pursing his lips. A whiskey sour—his drink of choice.

John Mark closed his eyes and took a deep breath.

"Well, spit it out, kid," his dad's voice demanding. John Mark glanced one more time at Paul's picture.

"I'm dismantling the deal. I've something different in mind for the Belltown place."

There, he had said it. He watched as their expressions shifted, the blankness replaced by smiles. This was not the reaction he had anticipated. Suddenly, his dad began to laugh, leaving John Mark utterly bewildered.

"Well, well, look at you, finally growing a little backbone." His father smirked. "Not a big one, mind you, just a teeny, tiny sliver." He held up his thumb and forefinger, leaving a smidge of space between them.

John Mark knew his remark was anything but a compliment.

Stan turned toward Randall, "Maybe, just maybe, he will turn out okay."

His grandfather's laugh was deep and husky. And it turned from a laugh into a raspy cough.

Randall turned toward the door, "Angeline, I need some water."

John Mark remembered he'd asked for water too. Before he could ask, Angeline was already entering with a tray.

"Well, that was fast," his grandfather remarked with a smile.

"Sorry, I was taking dinner out of the oven and completely forgot your water, John Mark."

She set the tray on the table: three crystal glasses, already filled with ice, and a pitcher filled with water and lemon slices. Angeline poured a glass and handed it to John Mark's grandfather. She also gave him a small white pill. He grabbed it gruffly and mumbled something under his breath as she walked out of the room.

John Mark poured himself a glass of water. The silence stretched, thick and uncomfortable, punctuated by the faint sounds of Angeline's classical music drifting from the kitchen, mingling with the occasional clatter of pots and pans.

He broke the silence. "I'm going to do the right thing."

"And, if you would enlighten us, John Mark, what exactly is that?" Stan said condescendingly.

"I'm not building condos." His hands were clammy. "And I'm not destroying one more parcel of land or home." He narrowed his eyes as he said it. "It was never what great-grandfather wanted."

"Oh, to hell with him, John Mark. He's dead and gone," Stan spat out dismissively. "We're here now."

"It was never about money for Paul; it was about people," John Mark countered, engaging in the argument with conviction. "For Paul, it was always about community, family, and friends."

"And that's why the old man was a pauper, never had two dimes to rub together," Stan smirked.

"That's not true, and you know it," John Mark retorted sharply.

John Mark squared his shoulders and tightened his fists. He was done with the deception.

"Now you listen here, boy," his dad stood and walked toward him. He put his finger in John Mark's face. "You don't know a thing about business." His voice threatening.

"I may not know much about business," John Mark asserted, "but I know with certainty that Paul Gordon never intended for his land, or Lucy's, to become what you are trying to turn it into."

"What do you know?" His grandfather's voice caught John Mark off guard. He looked at Randall as he nursed his whiskey sour.

"Grandfather, I know that the Belltowns and the Gordons were friends. I know that each family was meant to steward one another's land." His grandfather's brow furrowed. John Mark went on, "when Lucy dies, her land is supposed to be for the community, just as ours was."

"And how do you know all of this?" His grandfather was somehow still relatively calm despite the charged atmosphere in the room.

"It's what Paul wanted." For the first time, a sense of pride swelled within John Mark as he stood before his father and grandfather, a stark contrast to the familiar weight of their disapproval.

"I asked you *how* you came by this information?" A flush of red crept up his grandfather's neck, reminding John Mark of a cooked lobster.

"Lucy told me everything about my great-grandfather; and take it or leave it, I agree with the vision he cast, a long time ago."

Stan shook his head, "It's a stupid dream; it will never happen, John Mark, giving our land to the community."

John Mark's body shook, with rage or fear, he didn't know. *Calm down*, he told himself.

Turning back toward his grandfather, he looked him in the eyes. "Grandfather, admit it, you know about Paul's request. The original will."

John Mark held his gaze, his eyes pleading.

Randall averted his gaze, his eyes dropping to the floor. But not before John Mark caught the faintest flicker of acknowledgment in them.

Stan walked over to the sideboard and poured more amber liquid into his glass. He took a gulp.

"This is absurd." He slammed his glass onto the counter.

John Mark walked over to his grandfather and kneeled in front of him.

"You know exactly what I'm talking about, don't you, Grandfather?"

Randall lifted his gaze to meet John Mark's. Remorse was etched into every line of his aged face. "It's too late."

"What's too late?" John Mark's voice trembled slightly. Randall bit his lip.

"Grandfather, Lucy forgives you."

Stan, still next to the sideboard, nearly choked on his drink. John Mark kept his gaze fixed on his grandfather. He whispered, "I know. Lucy told me everything. You don't have to do this. Grandfather, she's your sister."

"She said that?" A flicker of something akin to hope ignited in Randall's eyes.

"Make amends, Grandfather." He put his hand on his grandfather's shoulder, "you're family."

"Enough of this," Stan Gordon yelled. "Get out of here!" John Mark slowly stood. Stan moved toward him, fast. John Mark positioned himself for a blow. Instead, Stan Gordon grabbed his shoulder and dragged him toward the door.

"We knew you didn't have it in you." He shoved John Mark. "You're weak. Just like your mother."

"Leave her out of this," John Mark growled. His voice low and dangerous.

"We gave you this acquisition to further you," Stan continued. "You could have been rich, John Mark, filthy rich." He turned sharply and began to pace the length of the room.

"And, if you try and battle me on this, I will block you at every angle."

John Mark was enraged.

He looked at his grandfather, who sat there motionless.

His own father seemed unhinged. John Mark watched as Stan raised his glass into the air, a wicked smirk twisting his lips. "It's all ours!" Stan declared. "Lucy is going to be a rich lady. And so are we!"

John Mark felt a wave of shame wash over him. *This* was his family? This man, so devoid of compassion, so consumed by greed? He glanced at his grandfather once last time to see if he agreed. His face remained blank, unreadable. John Mark knew the stakes. If he persisted, if he challenged this, he stood to lose everything. His family. His reputation. His money. Everything.

John Mark's grandfather shook his head side-to-side. "Stand down, son," he said, his voice barely audible. "No good will come of this." A flicker of regret on his face.

Still astride his high horse, John Mark's father seized the moment to put John Mark in his place. "You're a Gordon, and this is what Gordons do," Stan declared vehemently. "We seize the moment! And this is one moment we have been waiting for, for a very long time."

John Mark picked up the photograph of Paul Gordon. A single word resonated within him: *Others*. That was the essence of his great-grandfather's life. For others.

"We're not all bad," he said quietly, a hint of defiance in his voice. "I'm keeping this, by the way." With that, he turned and walked toward the door, pushing it open and stepping through. Pausing on the threshold, he faced the two men who had long held sway over him. A wide grin stretched across his face. "I guess I'll see you in court," he stated, the words a clear and confident challenge. And then, he was gone.

John Mark knew he had to act fast. A plan was forming, and speed was crucial to its success. He accelerated out of the driveway, heading for home. Once there, he ran inside, and grabbed his legal pad and pen, settling at the dining room table with determination; he wouldn't leave the chair until he was finished. Several hours bled into the night, and a slow yawn finally escaped John Mark as the first rays of the morning sun streamed through the window.

His back ached from sitting in the metal chair for hours. He rubbed his hand over his chin, feeling the rough, morning stubble. He had used his home dial-up internet to look up everything he could find on trusts, and land and historical preservation. He was encouraged by what he had found, and used the remainder of the morning to write an official plan for Old Blue and her fifty acres. He looked at the clock. It was 8:15 a.m. Today was the day he would sign the papers, officially transferring the house into the Gordon name. However, we would execute his own plan rather than his father and grandfathers. He anticipated the immediate backlash of his father's and grandfather's first lawsuit. Everything hinged on the specifics of the deed transfer and the speed at which he could enact his plan. If he could successfully designate Old Blue as a preservation, it would become untouchable, effectively blocking any possibility of development. As elated as he was, a significant hurdle remained: funding. Transforming Old Blue into a preservation would require a substantial donation from a deep-pocketed benefactor. Then came step two: ensuring the house itself could generate its own income. As of today, John Mark would be land rich and cash-poor. He may have been broke, but what he did have was a clean conscience and courage to pursue what was right. And that felt good.

His stomach let out a loud rumble. "I need food," he muttered, pushing himself to his feet and opening the refrigerator. Eggs. Cheese. Milk. Yes, he definitely needed to eat. The fridge held the essentials for breakfast; an omelet would be perfect. The picture of Paul that he had taken from his grandfather's house now hung next to his family photo. *If he carried even a shred of Paul's purity and strength, it was enough*, he thought. He scrambled the eggs, greasing the pan with a slab of butter. He shredded cheese over the top, tossing in a few left-over sliced onions. He slid the cooked omelet onto the plate and sat down. An urgency to reach Lucy caused him to quickly fork the omelet into his mouth, leaving the plate on the table as he hurried to get dressed. A swift shave and brush of his teeth completed his morning routine. With a single decision, he had altered the trajectory of his life. Now, it was a matter of whether his actions would prove successful or completely blow up in his face.

The most daunting task ahead was telling Lucy everything. For their plan to succeed, for Old Blue to be saved, she would need to look beyond the secrets he had kept. Just as Old Blue had been a refuge for his great-grandfather, he sent a silent plea that the old house would once again provide sanctuary, now for him, another Gordon seeking its shelter. *Please let her forgive me*, John Mark thought, the weight of his past secrets pressing down. *Everything I'm fighting for depends on it.*

CHAPTER TWENTY

Redemption and Grace

Lucy lay in her four-poster bed staring up at the ceiling. It was still dark out. She curled her fingers to her palm, feeling the tingle in her hands; a new sensation, like tiny needles poking her skin. Another effect of the cancer taking over her body. The day was coming when she would walk away from her family home, leaving the key on the counter. Yet, she wouldn't let that get her down, woven into this day was the potential for hope: Anna. She tried to sit up. All her limbs were stiff. Her body was giving up. She knew it. She laid back down and tried to stretch her legs. Wiggling her toes. She yawned. She had lived every day of her life in this house and now she would be taking up space at Sandy's, stowing away in her spare bedroom until she figured out what she was going to do. Without Jim and Sandy, Lucy knew she wouldn't have coped, not then, the day of Bill's accident, and certainly not now. Once again, they had opened their home to her, enveloping her in their care like a vulnerable child.

Lucy knew it was rare to have a friend who loved loyally, despite a person's flaws. Sandy was that friend. She would tell Lucy the truth, even when she didn't want to hear it, or couldn't see it standing right in front of her.

Lucy lay there, pulling her sheet up to her chin. One memory she could never shake, nor did she want too—the day of Bill's accident. The day her perfect life turned upside down. Lucy remembered Sandy's hot temper flaring up, she chuckled as she recalled her usually calm friend standing inches from her and telling her she was as obstinate as a mule. Although it was forever ago, it seemed like yesterday.

"Go to her, Lucy, make it right," Sandy said, one hand on her hip, pointing toward the back door.

"Sandy, are you asking me to sell everything my daddy worked hard for?" Exasperated, Lucy glared at Sandy. "Bill loved this house. This is the only home I've ever known, and I swear, I will never part with it, as long as I'm living."

Grace would come around. Lucy was not about to chase down a rebellious and disrespectful teenager. She would not get on her knees and beg. Never.

"When I'm gone, Grace gets all of this. And, by then, she will want it. Just wait and see."

Sandy put her hand on Lucy's shoulder, "You have lost much, and I know the last thing you want to do is lose more, but what you don't see, Lucy, is that you're about to."

Lucy waved her away. What did Sandy know about her daughter? Sandy only had sons. Girls are different. Let them go away and lick their wounds for a while and they always come back. Grace needs Lucy. Or was it the other way around?

"It's as though you look at her, but right through her."

"What?" Lucy turned toward Sandy, clenching her teeth. *How dare Sandy. Now she is crossing the line.*

"So now you're an expert on my child?"

"She told us, as much."

The words hit Lucy in the chest. But she wouldn't let it show. Her pride would best her.

"And you're going to listen to a kid?"

"That kid is your daughter. You've got to see it, Lucy. I'm your best friend, and I'm not going anywhere. But you are blind to this."

Sandy stepped forward and looked directly into Lucy's eyes, "Right now, it might seem like this house is everything, but someday, I promise you, you will regret this."

Lucy was obstinate. Unyielding.

"I'm not budging."

Sandy looked away. "And, unfortunately, neither is she."

Sandy had been right that day, as much as Lucy didn't want to admit that now. She closed her eyes against the flood of emotions that swept through her old body and willed herself to get up and get dressed. Lucy slowly and meticulously put on each garment. She checked herself in the mirror. Her skin didn't glow like it used to. Thankfully, she still had all of her hair. She tied a sun hat over her white curls and wrapped a cream, silk, Hermes scarf, around her neck—one extravagance her mother didn't part with when she moved south. It was time. A clock didn't have to tell her that. She knew as she always knew, it was the way the light landed on the hand cut wooden floors of her bedroom. When it reached the end of her bedpost, it was almost 6:00 a.m. She felt cold. The sickness played tricks on her body. She grabbed a shawl from the hook and threw it around her shoulders. She took careful steps down the stairs while holding the handrail. Her hands ran along the smooth wood. Her daddy had built this banister from the live oaks he and Paul Gordon had cleared from the land: two men and a hand saw.

She skipped coffee and breakfast. Her tummy, a bundle of nerves. "Well, here goes."

She stepped out the back door and down the sloping steps into a mowed lawn. Even if Old Blue no longer belonged to her, and perhaps would be torn down within the month, the house would go down in style. Barefoot, Lucy walked away from the house and gingerly stepped down onto the sand. She stopped, spread her arms wide, and breathed deeply. She didn't know how many of those deep breaths she would have left. Smiling, she turned in the direction of the Pier. Her eyes were old, but she could make out the tiniest, little figure, wearing red. Anna was already moving toward her. She wanted to hurry, to time it just right, to show her the Monkey puzzle tree that her mother used to play under. She mustered up her strength and began to walk. Eventually, she was close enough to see Anna wave. Her heartbeat quickened. As she reached Anna, the girl hugged Lucy, and her skin felt balmy against Lucy's cheek.

"Good morning!"

Just looking at Anna's flushed cheeks and windblown hair, so like Grace, made Lucy's heart melt into a puddle. "Good morning, honey. I'm so glad you came."

Lucy linked her arm with Anna's and turned them back toward Old Blue.

"Shall we?"

As they walked, they were silent. The sounds around them chatter enough. Apart from the wildlife, the seagulls, sandpipers, and occasional hermit crab scurrying away, Lucy and Anna were the only two people on the beach. As they neared Old Blue, Lucy thought of the possible outcomes. Anna may turn and walk away. She may be angry. She may have questions. Whatever it was, Lucy felt her chest tighten. She braced herself.

"We're up this way," she pointed to the steps. Anna slowed down. Lucy felt Anna's body turn. She loosened her arm from

Lucy's as she looked behind her and then around. Something was clicking into place.

"Go ahead," Lucy invited, gesturing Anna forward. She wanted Anna to see it first. Anna took the steps slowly, one at a time, until she reached the top. There, she froze. Lucy followed, her heart pounding in her chest. She saw what Anna saw: her Old Blue, standing tall against the sky, a familiar landmark against the horizon. Lucy waited, holding her breath.

"Is this where we are watching the sunrise?" A look of confusion on her face. She turned to face Lucy, clearly perplexed.

Lucy was about to invite Anna to the porch where they could sit up a bit higher when John Mark came running down the yard. *What in heaven's name is that boy doing here*, Lucy thought.

"Lucy, Lucy," he was waving something as he ran toward them.

"John Mark?" Anna looked at Lucy then back at John Mark.

Could this get any worse? Lucy wondered.

"John Mark, I'm surprised to see you," Lucy raised her eyebrows at him.

"Anna!" he grabbed her in a huge bear hug and squeezed her. Her arms stuck to her side; she looked like a fence post. He let her go, then did the same to Lucy. She felt her body squish up like a sponge, then roll back out again, as he let her go.

"I have some good news for you."

Her stomach dropped. He was going to spill the beans. And this is not how she wanted to do it.

She put her hand on his arm, "stop, John Mark," her voice tight "this is not the way."

Anna stepped forward; her brow furrowed. "Wait, who lives here?"

John Mark, ignoring Lucy's appeal, grinned from ear to ear.

Anna's confusion increased, turning into hurt. "John Mark," she asked with concern, "is this your house?"

Before Lucy could intervene, he blurted out, "no, it's Lucy's!"

Anna spun around toward Lucy. She looked like she wanted to say something, but no words came. Lucy reached out a hand toward her, a silent offer of comfort or explanation. Anna did not take it. This was not how Lucy had planned for things to unfold. "Let's all go up on the porch." Her voice was shaking.

"No, I don't want to go on the porch." Anna was glaring at John Mark. "You told me no one lived here."

Now it was Lucy's turn to be confused. So, it was true: John Mark was hiding something. He knew it all along. He knew Anna was her granddaughter—that scoundrel.

"I lied to you," John Mark admitted, his voice flat.

He turned quickly toward Lucy, "she needs to know." He insisted. His eyes pleading.

Anna was shaking her head from side-to-side, like someone trying to shake off a bad dream.

Lucy's heart was beating so fast it sounded like a boom box in her ears. She was speechless.

Oblivious to the train wreck he set in motion, John Mark plunged forward recklessly. "Listen, I've been up all night, and I have a plan for the house. Lucy, I don't care about the land, the money, or the house. This house can still be yours, and yours too," he said, locking eyes with Anna. *What a numbskull*, Lucy thought, anger boiling within. He has no idea the damage he is causing. She turned toward Anna, "I wanted to tell you something," she spoke softly. "That is why I brought you here."

She faced Anna, looking deep into her eyes. The hurt was obvious, written all over Anna's face. Lucy had to recover the situation, and she had to move quickly.

She shot John Mark a look, a silent warning; Close your mouth. Stop talking now. Cease.

Instead, he dropped the bombshell, "I found your grandmother, Anna!"

His exuberance overshadowed his ability to reason or read Lucy's frantic attempts to silence him.

Lucy stared at him utterly astonished. *What is wrong with this man? Did he have no sense at all?*

All Anna could manage was a slow, quiet, "what?"

Lucy had only known Anna for a few days, but she had raised her mother, and Lucy knew that look. It was the same look Grace had worn when her world spun out of control, a look of anguish and panic.

"John Mark, no more!" Lucy shouted, the force of her voice so unexpected that both John Mark and Anna flinched.

Lucy's body was protesting, her strength waning. She wondered how much more she could endure. This morning the tingle in her hands had turned into sharp, stabbing pains, and no longer remained just with her hands but now it had moved down to her legs.

Anna turned toward Lucy; the pain in her eyes was so raw, it almost made Lucy look away.

"Anna," she whispered, her voice barely a whisper.

"I'm sorry, Lucy," Anna replied, as her voice choked with emotion, "but I need to go."

Anna turned and ran down the steps toward the beach. Lucy's knees began to shake, uncontrollably. John Mark stared at Lucy then his gaze darted back to Anna, already a considerable distance away, sprinting down the beach. Then it finally registered on his face: he had just made a complete mess of things.

"Lucy, I'm sorry . . ." he looked devastated.

"Go, son, go after her," Lucy urged, her voice weak and trembling. She was depleted, frightened. She hadn't chased Grace when she should have, and now her own body betrayed her, preventing her from running after Anna. But *someone* could: John Mark.

He nodded, reading her thoughts. He hesitated, she knew he had more to say. Remorse was etched into every line of his face. She shook her head in a quiet no, "just go."

She wanted to reassure him but there was no time. He placed his hand on her shoulder, squeezing it.

Pulling deep from her reserves, Lucy spoke, her voice faint. "When you find her," she pleaded, "tell her I love her. Tell her I was wrong. Her mother . . . "she felt it then, a force like a tide pulling her under. Her body was giving out. She turned once more toward Old Blue, a box overflowing with memories, her heart aching for what was and what could have been. And like an apparition, a wisp of smoke emerging from the past, she saw her Grace standing next to John Mark.

This must be the end, she thought. A strange sense of dread filled her.

Looking at Grace, she whispered, "I want you; I always did." She reached out a hand as if to grasp Grace's, but it was John Mark who met it, closing his own hand around Lucy's. She turned toward him, her eyes pleading,

"Tell her John Mark," she gasped, her voice weakening, "tell Anna, I don't want any of this." She closed her eyes, picturing Grace once more, "I just want her. Tell her." She then collapsed to the ground.

CHAPTER TWENTY-ONE

A Time for Truth

Lucy tried to open her eyes, they felt heavy, weighted. She blinked, trying to focus as best she could. How long had she been asleep? As her eyes adjusted to the room, so did her ears, and her nose. It smelled like rubbing alcohol and overcooked meat. She couldn't hear the waves bouncing off the shore or the sound of seagulls squawking in search of their breakfast. Her throat felt dry. She was disoriented. A cup of coffee would help. She started to inch her legs over to the side of the bed hoping her slippers were just beneath it. It felt cool in the room. She turned on her side and focused her eyes on the beige colored walls.

"Where am I," she said out loud. This wasn't her room. Her eyesight wasn't perfect, but she wasn't a blind bat either. She felt her arm, there was tape holding something down on her wrist. She reached her hand up to her face and felt a rigid plastic device connected to her face. She tilted her head down, trying to see what it was. A clear tube stretched down the length of her body and trailed over the end of the bed. The slow and steady 'beep, beep, beep,' of some machine clued her in.

"Am I in the hospital?" She needed to get out of here. She tried to recall the previous day; it was hazy at best.

"I'll tell her, thank you, Doctor." A familiar voice.

The door opened, and she saw Sandy walk in. She was holding a plastic cup with a straw. She hoped it was water.

"What am I doing here?" She croaked.

"Do you want the long version or the short version?"

"First, I want that water."

She stretched her hand out and Sandy handed her the oversized cup. Lucy drank greedily, propping herself up on her elbow. Small dribbles dripped down her chin.

"Let me set this up."

Sandy pushed a little button on the side and the bed folded into a chair.

Lucy readjusted herself. Although she felt like she could sleep for a month, the exhaustion apparent, the rest of her body felt fine. No aches or pains.

"What do you remember?" Sandy asked, sitting in a blue plastic chair beside Lucy's bed.

"I woke up, it was a beautiful morning. I walked down the beach to meet Anna. The sunrise had been brilliant. Radiant. We walked back to Old Blue."

Lucy paused. She folded her hands in her lap. She felt frail in this hollow room.

"John Mark showed up. And he ruined everything."

The heart monitor hooked up to Lucy began to beep faster.

"Slow down, roadrunner; it's not going to do anyone any good if you get irate."

Lucy took a few deep breaths. The tubes filtering in oxygen to her body, helped her breath.

"The last thing I remember is Anna running toward the beach. Away from me."

Sandy finished the sentence, "And, now you're here."

Lucy turned toward the door. She could hear a man outside her door talking to someone. It sounded like John Mark. Sandy smiled.

"Don't be too upset at him; he is the one who saved your life."

"Oh, nonsense; if it were not for him, my plan would have worked perfectly. John Mark lied to me."

Although Lucy had no way of knowing how it would have turned out, she knew that "perfectly" was not in the cards. There is no such thing. Either way, she would not let this go, easily.

"That all may be good and true, Lucy. But, in his defense when you collapsed, John Mark put you in his truck and drove you to the emergency room. He has been with you this whole time."

Sandy cleared her throat. Lucy knew a lecture was coming.

"We both know Stan and Randall have been hard on that boy. I can't even imagine the pressure and expectation on his young shoulders."

Lucy gave Sandy a half-smile. She was right.

"Before I blacked out, he kept saying something about saving the house. I can't imagine how he would do that."

"There's a chance, if he inherited his grandfather's business sense, and none of his corruption, he might just do it."

Lucy nodded, recalling John Mark's eager certainty, a plan for Old Blue, something beyond demolition. "He wants to break the mold," Sandy said. "To do what's right. A second chance."

Sandy continued, "And correct me if I'm wrong, but I believe someone else here yearns for that very thing," she said looking intently at Lucy.

Lucy sank into the stiff mattress, her muscles loosening. *Forgiveness.* The delightful word lingered on her tongue, like a piece of ripe, sweet watermelon, bringing refreshment.

"Sandy, what's wrong with me?"

"You know what's wrong, Lucy. It's just starting to show itself. And you can't sidestep it any longer."

"I'm dying. I know that, but what did the doctor say?"

"He said you were lucky. You could have broken a bone with the fall you had, or worse, a head injury."

"And?"

"And he said it was time to take you home."

Sandy looked down at her feet and tapped them a few times. Lucy knew what that meant. And she saw that it was crushing Sandy. She wouldn't force her friend to say more.

"Let's get out of here. Take me home." She said gently.

As Sandy began to pack up the few items that belonged to Lucy, a light tapping on the door announced a visitor.

"Come in," Sandy hollered, stuffing Lucy's scarf and other assorted items into a bag.

"Hey," John Mark ducked in. He was holding an enormous bouquet of tulips.

"Where in heaven's name did you find those?"

"Oh, you know, I have my ways," he winked at Lucy.

Before Lucy could say anything else, John Mark was by her bedside. He sat in the remaining blue chair and scooted it next to her.

"I'm sorry, Lucy, I screwed up everything. It seems to be how I operate in life."

He looked like he hadn't slept in a week.

He took off his hat and ran his hands through his hair. "I wasn't thinking."

"Stop, John Mark, you don't need to say more."

He was treating this like a confessional.

"But Lucy, I didn't tell you. I've known for a while about Anna, and I didn't tell you; I lied to you." He hung his head.

"Life has a funny way of giving us clues. I knew she was my granddaughter, John Mark. I, too, could have said something. I had my reasons, and so did you."

He put his hand on her arm.

"Lucy, can you forgive me?"

A mirror. She saw herself reflected in his plea. Those words, the words she should have uttered decades ago to her own child. A shift in time, a heart turned toward another, not away.

She met his gaze, her arms opening wide. "Son, I forgive you."

He leaned in, sliding an arm beneath her back. He held her close, a long, silent moment, before gently laying her down.

Lucy was smiling so big; she could feel the stretch on her face.

"I'm going to need your help, John Mark."

"Anything. Ask it, and it's yours."

Lucy and Sandy laughed, "Be careful what you promise, young man."

Sandy shook her finger at him.

"Well, within reason then," he smiled.

"I need to find Anna before she leaves Naples."

Lucy didn't have much time. She knew Anna deserved to know everything. That the ball would, again, be in her court when she did. Lucy dangled her feet off the side of the bed. The hospital gown was wrinkled over her knees and wedged between her bottom and the mattress, revealing her veined thighs. John Mark blushed and helped pull it down.

"I realize I am being given another chance at all of this," she said.

"I think I am too Lucy."

John Mark grabbed both her hands as she stretched them out toward him and helped her stand. She squeezed his rough work hands.

"Perhaps there are a cloud of witnesses who are watching, cheering us on."

John Mark grinned at her. "After all we've been through, I would say you are probably right, and we will need all of the encouragement we can get if this is going to work!"

Sandy stepped over and put a sweater around Lucy's shoulders, helping her put her arms through the sleeves.

"I'm ready!"

"You don't want to put on any clothes?" John Mark asked.

"No time, son!"

Lucy looped her arm through John Marks, while Sandy gathered Lucy's items. Lucy had cheated death this time, but she knew deep down, there would not be a next time.

"Take me home," she said.

Chapter Twenty-Two

Trust is Broken

Anna felt like she was falling into a tunnel. It was dark and cold. How could it be that Lucy was her grandmother and John Mark knew all along? She didn't want to know. Her body felt flooded. When she pieced together the deception—that John Mark had known Lucy was her grandmother—fury consumed her. The deception closed in, and she did what seemed sensible. She turned away from them and took off running. And she kept running as fast as her legs would carry her. Her feet landing in the sand. She turned around one last time and saw the big blue house standing tall and proud, Lucy and John Mark standing, watching her run away. To say she felt duped was an understatement. This felt like a curve ball, that her bat missed but the ball didn't fly past her, it slammed into her stomach. John Mark knew Lucy was her grandmother, and he just thought he would forget to tell her that bit of information? And Lucy! Lucy, sweet Lucy, in on this charade? Anna wanted to get as far away from this house full of lies, as far as she could from Naples. All the same reasons her own mother left decades ago.

As she neared the Pier, a few people were setting up umbrellas and chairs for a day in the sun. As she walked up the steps onto the pier a sweaty jogger pounded past her, his feet flapping on weather-beaten wood. She found an empty bench, next to a lonely angler. He was casting his line over the side, hoping to catch the big one. She looked at his position in his vinyl beach chair, propping the pole between his legs. She leaned against the bench. It smelled like fish.

She had driven all this way for one thing, and she had to admit, she did find it. The owner of the letter. It was Lucy. If Old Blue belonged to Lucy, she was the mystery woman—Anna's grandmother. This also meant that Lucy was the woman Mom wanted nothing to do with.

Her phone rang. It was Sam.

"Sam!" his call couldn't have come at a better time.

"Hey sis, how's the beach?"

"Better than your ice and snow," she smirked.

Anna listened as he caught her up on his latest find, a type of algae that grew only in subzero temperatures, and she filled him in on her last 24 hours.

"So did you find her?"

"Yes. Sam, I found Lucy."

"Who is Lucy?"

"Have you been listening to a word I have said?"

Sam got silent. "Okay, so Lucy is the one who has the house?"

"Well, it's complicated." Anna breathed out a long sigh.

"Lucy is our grandmother; they are one in the same."

She told him about the last two days. John Mark's elusive answers. Lucy's welcoming nature and the tour of Palm Cottage.

"And the house, Sam. It's incredible."

"It's where Mom grew up?"

"Yeah."

"Wow."

"It makes sense why she loved the ocean so much. The house is so close to the water you can almost touch it."

"So, what are you going to do now?"

"That's what I don't know. Any ideas?"

"Do you need me to fly down?"

"Really, you would do that?"

"I would. And I could use a break and some sun. My skin is so pale, it's opaque."

She hated to admit it, but she knew she couldn't leave yet. Her truck was still in the shop. And Sam would be here in a few days. Whatever secrets were being held, Anna knew that some secrets are best left covered. The angler was reeling in something. She watched the rusted pole bend under the weight. As he brought it up, his prize dangled in mid-air, swinging back and forth. He would be on someone's dinner plate by sunset. Poor fish. Anna could relate to being lured, hooked, then gutted.

Just wait for Sam, she told herself. Then, they'd figure out what to do with the letter and, finally, scatter Mom's ashes. That's what she came to Naples for. Anna sat on the Pier a little longer, feeling better than when she had arrived. At least she still had Sam. And when this whole thing was said and done, they would cut ties with this place, just as their mom had done and never return. "See you soon," she said to Sam before hanging up. The fear of encountering John Mark kept her from wanting to return to his mom's place. Her plan was to remain on the pier as long as the sun allowed, or until she started to feel sun burnt. The stark truth was, she had nowhere else to turn. *Hurry Sam* she thought. The loneliness settling in all around her.

CHAPTER TWENTY-THREE

Her Ocean, Her View

Lucy sat with her hands balled up, clenched in her lap, staring ahead, like she was in a rocket, ready to bolt. The hospital car park had warmed John Mark's truck to a stifling temperature, but it felt good on Lucy's cold toes. Her greatest fear had become her reality. Her worst nightmare had materialized. First Grace, and now Anna, gone.

Hearing John Mark's voice, lifted her from her thoughts.

"Put your seat belt on," John Mark told Lucy as he started his truck.

"Oh yes," she had forgotten.

She pulled the belt across her lap and clicked it. They had rigged Lucy up with a portable breathing machine, and the remainder of the items she would need to go home. Sandy followed behind, in her champagne-colored Buick, as they drove out of the hospital parking lot. Lucy knew where Anna had gone. It was where all Belltown women went when they needed a place to think.

John Mark took the turn a little fast, and Lucy felt her body lean into the door. She pushed against it with her hand.

"Wait, I said the Pier, where are you going?"

"I had clear instructions from Sandy to take you directly home; she is not someone I want to tango with." She saw him glancing up at his rearview mirror where she knew Sandy was barreling behind them, tailing him.

"Oh phooey, she's all bark and no bite."

"Either way, I'm driving, so I'm in charge."

He was trying to be serious with her, but she could see the slight smirk on his lips. She batted her eyes and said in the sweetest voice, "Pretty please, take me with you."

He shook his head back and forth. A solid no.

"I'm taking you home."

"I don't own the house anymore, John Mark; you know that."

"I know you don't. I do, and I get to decide what happens with it."

They turned down the driveway. John Mark parked as close as he could to the back door. He got out and went around to Lucy's side of the truck. He helped her out. The door was already unlocked. He looped her arm inside his and walked her up the back steps. Everything was how it had been since she left. She remembered she had left a few dishes in the sink as they passed the kitchen. The small overhead light was still on above the stove. He wheeled the oxygen machine down the hallway while guiding her toward the front of the house.

"I want to sit outside, John Mark."

"Are you sure that's a good idea?" She knew he quickly regretted that question. Then he quickly corrected himself. "Whatever you want, Lucy."

Even with the tube in her nose, she could smell everything. Her house carried the smell of a thousand memories. "That smell never goes away, does it?" she breathed in.

"What's that?"

"You know, the smell of the ocean. It fills every space."

He stopped and took a deep breath through his nose. "Yeah, I guess you're right. It's ocean all right."

Her house, walls, and furniture held the smell of the sea. Absorbed it really—a centuries worth.

He opened the door for her and saw that one wicker chair awaited her on the porch.

She pointed at it. "That's the ticket, just park me right there."

"Can I bring you anything?" he asked as he helped her sit down. He took the blanket from the back of the chair and laid it over her legs.

"A glass of water would be lovely, honey. Then do hurry. Go and find Anna."

John Mark went inside. And Lucy sat watching the gull's soar. The roar of the waves calmed her.

"Here you are." He placed the glass between her two hands.

"Sandy should be here any minute." He was saying it more to himself than to her, trying to reassure himself. Before they left the hospital, Sandy said she wanted to swing by the store and grab a few things for lunch. Lucy watched John Mark run down the steps and onto the sand. Then, in a flash, he disappeared.

She rocked and rocked in her old chair. Her feet felt itchy, and she realized she was still wearing the fuzzy hospital socks they put on her. She bent over carefully to try and pull them off. After some effort, *viola* her feet were free! She wiggled her toes and felt the sand on the porch. She brushed her feet across the little specks of broken-down seashell. She brought the glass to her lips and her grip loosened. The glass fell onto the porch.

"Oh," she gasped, her eyes falling to the ground. A wave of relief washed over her. The glass cup was intact; only a small puddle pooled on the decking. *This is it, then,* she thought. *This is what losing control feels like.* Leaning back, she waited for Sandy. *Why struggle against the inevitable?* She would no longer fight; she would surrender. Having faced every fear, what else remained but to live?

Chapter Twenty-Four

Rebuilding the Bridge

As John Mark raced down Lucy's broken steps to the beach, he tossed his shoes into a grassy dune and took off like an Olympian. He sprinted down the two-mile stretch of beach, to the Pier. He repeated again and again what he would say to Anna. How he would apologize and explain. He felt confident with each rehearsal, but as he got closer and the Pier was in sight, he felt his body tense up and his practiced lines went out the door. He slowly walked as he reached the Pier. He stopped and bent over, trying to catch his breath. His shirt stuck to his body and sweat dripped off his head into his eyes. He could smell his armpits, a poignant mixture of musky swamp smell and his pine-scented deodorant. He would have to get over it. A worthy result of bolting down a sunny beach in seventy-degree weather. Then, he saw her and heaved a huge sigh of relief. She was right where Lucy thought she would be. His stomach was all twisted up in knots. And it wasn't because he was hungry. Which he was. He was scared. Scared that he had blown it with Anna, but most of all, afraid that he had screwed it all up for Lucy.

She didn't see him, but he could see plainly from the way she looked off into the distance that she was sad. *I'm such a jerk*, he thought. I should have told her at once. John Mark knew he was likely the cause of her suffering. It was on him to make things right. He walked up to the Pier, and she turned. He thought he caught a small smile. Maybe, she was happy to see him. *Oh, let her be happy to see me*, he thought. Then she bit her lip and crossed her arms over her chest.

"Hey," he waved awkwardly as he moved closer.

"You're the last person I want to see right now."

He had to keep his cool and somewhere in this moment, convince her to see Lucy.

"I should say thanks for everything, but I would be lying."

Her voice was void of any emotion.

"That's fair." He replied.

"How did you find me anyway?"

"Lucy."

He moved a few steps closer. She scooted to the far side of the bench, and he took that as an invitation to sit down next to her.

"She said this is where her daughter used to go. When she needed to think, so she figured, 'like mother, like daughter.'" He clasped his hands in front of him. The angler next to them was packing up.

"I need to tell you something." She shook her head no. "I know you don't even need to give me the time of day right now, but if you could just give me five minutes, then I'll be gone."

"And why should I? You lied to me."

John Mark listened. He promised himself he would not interject. That was what got him in trouble in the first place.

Anna went on. She stood, with her hands on her hips and looked at him, standing in front, she blocked the sun and cast a shadow over him.

She pointed a finger at him, "and Lucy, gentle, sweet Lucy, somehow tangled up in all of this."

John Mark squeezed his eyes shut, a wave of guilt washing over him. Anna was right, Lucy was innocent.

He was the one who deserved blame. He stood, facing Anna.

Her lips thinned, a deep scowl etching her forehead. "And the bigger question, John Mark, is why did you keep all this from me? All this time?"

She looked ready to strike. He pressed himself against the pier post, bracing for impact.

At least the wood would cushion the blow. Thankfully, her anger manifested as a glare, daggers of accusation piercing him.

"You're right. It's a lot, and I want to explain."

"How can I trust you? Maybe, you're lying, right now."

She was right. How would he bridge this chasm of mistrust? They both remained silent as the angler walked past them. He probably thought they were having a lover's tiff. John Mark wished that was what was happening.

"I can't convince you. I know that. You have every right not to trust me. I've let you down, and I will never forgive myself for that. But, if you could hear me out, I want to clarify some of this, not for myself, but for Lucy."

He saw tenderness in her eyes. She cared for Lucy. Still, she turned away from him. She walked to where the man had fished and stood, leaning her elbows onto the railing. She closed her eyes. Maybe, she was praying? He would need a big intervention for this one. A God intervention.

"John Mark, I can't. I need to go." She looked like she was about to cry. As she walked past him, without thinking, he reached out for her wrist.

"If you never want to speak to me again. Fine. But hear me out. You need to go to Old Blue. For Lucy. Give her one hour. That's all I'm asking. Then we will leave you alone."

There was so much she didn't know, and it wasn't his to tell.

"John Mark," Anna said, her voice filled with hesitation, "Lucy is my grandmother. I'm still reeling from this." She crossed her arms tightly around her middle, a small consolation for a hug.

"For some reason my Mom chose to withhold that truth, but in her death, she led us here. And so far, it's brought nothing but heartache."

John Mark felt the weight of her words, like his own constant family strife. He longed to tell her about Lucy's illness, to convince her to give Lucy a chance, but he also would honor Lucy and protect her, no matter what the cost. Their lives hinged on it.

"I can't say more Anna, I'm sorry." He reached out a hand toward her and she dismissed it. His shoulders slumped, "This is Lucy's story to tell."

Anna was thinking, her face softening. Maybe, he could reason with her.

"Lucy, she's . . . she's one of the best. I've seen the worst, believe me. You *can* trust her. I know it's hard, but she had her reasons for keeping things from you. Reasons only she can share."

A few tears fell from Anna's cheek as she wiped her nose. She was letting down her guard. Anna looked at the back of her hand, now covered in a mess of mucus.

"Sorry," she smiled.

John Mark scrunched the corner of his shirt sleeve, "here, wipe away."

"That's so gross. Why are boys always so gross?"

He shrugged. He was glad to see her smile.

She breathed out. "Okay, I will go."

"You will?" John Mark clapped his hands and did a small jig.

Anna laughed.

"But first, answer one question for me." She tied her hair into a ponytail then sat on the bench once more.

"Anything." And he meant it.

"Why did you lie to me?"

Cornered. He faced a choice more lies or redemption. *The truth sets you free.*

"Do you have twenty minutes?" he asked, nervously adjusting his watch.

"I have as long as it takes."

John Mark began with a sincere apology, which, to his immense relief, she accepted. His heart pounded as he recounted the story of his family: his great-grandfather's shared vision for the Belltown land, and the ongoing weight of strained relationships.

He unveiled the history of her family, the Belltowns, the origins of the land, and the enduring friendship shared between their great-grandparents. She listened intently, nodding in recognition at certain points.

"So, you're saying that your family, the Gordons, and my family, the Belltowns, used to be friends?"

"Not just friends, more like family."

He had reached a good stopping point.

"Wow. I have never heard any of this before." Anna's shoulders slumped. "My mom gave up all of this, and I still don't know why."

"I haven't told you everything. Lucy will need to finish the rest of this."

Despite the weight of the past few hours—heavy conversation and heartache—a flicker of hope ignited in Anna's eyes. She was ready to seek answers.

Her smile was gentle. "Okay, let's go." She stood up. "Wait, I have one request."

"Your wish is my command."

"What time does Roger's Bakery open?"

"Early! It's open now." Of course John Mark would know that detail.

"Good, can you swing by there? I think some cinnamon rolls and coffee are in order."

He grinned.

"Done."

John Mark suddenly remembered, "I can't drive us; my truck is at Old Blue!"

"Well," she smiled sheepishly, "those two bikes are in the cottage shed."

"I don't mind if you don't."

"Not at all," she smiled as they walked down the pier onto the pavement, back toward the little rose cottage.

Anna held out her hand, "friends?" she looked sideways at him.

"Friends," he grabbed her hand. She shook his hand up and down, then turned to walk, but she held tight to his hand, not letting go. He looked at their intwined fingers, bewildered. Women. So confusing, and yet so wonderful. He followed her forward like a doting puppy.

As they turned onto the side street, Anna gave him a playful grin. "You do know you owe me big time, right?" He raised his eyebrows, a smirk forming. "Me?" he asked, feigning innocence. She looked forward, a glint in her eyes. "A dozen of Roger's cinnamon rolls should just about do it."

"It sounds like an appropriate compensation." They walked together away from the Pier under the gently swaying palm leaves that lined the road. John Mark had lived in Naples his entire life, but he had never seen it as lovely as he was seeing it today.

Chapter Twenty-Five

It's Never Too Late To Forgive

Lucy was glad when Sandy arrived. She needed the help. After cleaning up the spilled water and helping Lucy move into the living room, Sandy prepared a little nibble for them. They sat side-by-side looking at the view munching on their crackers and cheese. Lucy struggled against sleep and Sandy noticed.

"Okay you, lay back." Sandy stood up and fetched a blanket. She laid it over Lucy's legs. Lucy watched Sandy lay on the couch opposite her and close her eyes. Her dear friend was no doubt as tired as she was.

Lucy opened her eyes, startled by the loud knocking. She looked over to where Sandy had been and saw that she was gone. Her ears perked up as she heard Sandy answer the kitchen door. She was talking with someone and by the tone, it wasn't someone Sandy was thrilled to see. Hopefully, it was not John Mark, this would be too soon for his return. Which could only mean one thing. He didn't find Anna.

She braced herself for the hard news as their footsteps came closer. Sandy had her usual small bounce in her step and the other person a slow drag. With determination, she pushed herself up into a sitting position, the weight of the pain making each movement difficult. At least her mind was sharp as ever. Even if her body was failing her.

Sandy arrived and stood in front of her. She looked like she had seen a ghost. Soon, Lucy would know why. She turned slightly to see who was with her. With his head partially bowed, and his fingers laced in front of him, there stood Randall Gordon. Lucy was stunned. This she had not expected.

"I wasn't going to let him in, but he insisted." Sandy's eyebrows shot up and she shrugged.

Lucy wasn't sure how she should greet him. It had been a long time since they had been in the same room. Over the years, she would see Randall around town, but they never spoke. It was better that way. He was a heartless businessman, and most of the local Naples community, including Lucy, tried to avoid him whenever possible.

"Lucy," he said, his voice hoarse, barely a whisper. "I . . . I know this must seem . . ." He trailed off, unable to finish the sentence, wringing his hands anxiously.

Randall looked worn. Evidently, life had not been so kind. His shoulders slumped; his face seemed swollen, and his eyes were watery. Like her, old age had caught up with him, and undoubtedly, he had dragged his burdens from one year to the next.

Being a lady, Lucy would put on a good face and welcome him in.

"Randall, come in, take a seat." She motioned to the last remaining chair—a few feet away which was left uncovered. She suddenly felt embarrassed by her predicament. She was still in the hospital gown they let her wear home. The thin garment hanging loosely off her collarbone.

"Sorry, I would stand and greet you, but, well, you know . . ." her voice trailed off. She hated to admit any form of weakness in front of him. *He had already won, hadn't he? Did he come here to gloat?* If he did come to rub his victory in her face, she would waste no time in kicking him out. Or better yet, maybe she would stand and kick him in the shin. The shin choice was her preference, but she wasn't twelve anymore. He sat down on the chair. His black slacks rose up above his ankles, revealing plaid socks that clashed horribly. He looked pitiful.

"I heard you weren't feeling well." He cleared his throat.

"News travels fast in a small town. Don't we know that?" She said with a twinkle in her eye.

"You haven't changed a bit." He said looking at her.

Sandy watched them. She was standing, holding onto a corner of the bookshelf. Her eyes were darting between Lucy and Randall. She looked ready to intervene, like a referee anticipating a catfight. "Sandy, sit down," Lucy said, a hint of amusement in her voice. "I won't hurt him."

She slowly moved to the chair beside Lucy's, "well," Sandy said a mischievous glint in her eye, "I wouldn't be bothered if you did."

"Why are you here, Randall? Is it because I'm dying?" Lucy said using force on the last word. "Let me guess, you need to get a lifetime of guilt off your chest? Or you want me to know about your future condo venture?"

She decided to jab him where it hurt.

"I know. I have that coming."

He stood up. His joints creaked.

"I don't know why I thought this would be a good idea," he muttered, turning to leave.

"Wait," Lucy said. *Hear him out*, she told herself. *It must have taken a small bit of courage to show up here today*, she thought.

He stopped, his back to her, and stood still.

A memory surfaced that Lucy had tucked away decades ago: Paul's last words to her. "When you see my son, tell him I forgive him." Lucy had never had the chance. Perhaps now was the time.

"Your dad loved you," she said softly. "He was proud of you. Things could have been different, Randall." He was frozen to the spot.

"Do you know he used to brag about you?" she added.

"He once told my Daddy," Lucy continued, her voice gaining strength, 'Randall threw that ball twenty yards further than a kid five years older. My boy has a strong arm.'" Lucy remembered when Randall left for the city job, his parents hanging their heads for days, a silent acknowledgment that he was now lost to them. Paul had pulled Lucy aside, his voice a low murmur, "My boy, he just needs some time to figure things out, that's all. He'll be back. He's a good boy."

Paul, she thought, had been one of those rare people who could find the diamond in the rough. He saw through a man, believed there was always a thread of good, even in the worst of situations. "His favorite line, if you remember," she said to Randall, "'The sweetest water is in the deepest well; it just takes time for it to surface.'"

"He believed that about you," she said resolutely, her gaze fixed on Randall's back. "That eventually you would come around, that there was good in you."

She watched his body twitch. She felt emboldened. She pressed on. He needed to hear these words, she felt it in her gut, as if his very life depended on it. "You could have come back," she said, her voice firm. "Your dad would have taken you back. No questions asked. We both know it was his way."

Randall turned around and faced Lucy.

His guilt, unmistakable.

Lucy felt compassion towards her childhood playmate. Her friend. Her brother. He hadn't always been so shrewd and uncaring.

"Remember when that garter snake found its way into my garage?" she laughed. "Oh, how I screamed until you came, rushing in with a shovel. My hero," she smiled at him. "You were so brave. You scooped it up and threw it out."

"You always did hate snakes." He smiled at her, a softness in his voice.

"We had a lot of fun, didn't we?" She looked at Sandy, who shook her head in agreement. "You were my best friend, Randy."

"And you mine, Lucy."

He moved closer to her bed. Tears pooling in his eyes.

"I came to say goodbye, Lucy," he hesitated, "and I'm sorry."

Calling him by his childhood name, she gave him her biggest grin. "Randy, I forgave you a long time ago." I think it was you who didn't forgive yourself."

Lucy tried to stand, but her arms didn't have enough strength. "Sandy, can you help?"

Sandy bent down and wrapped her arms around Lucy's waist. "One, two, three, go!" they counted, and Lucy, with Sandy's help, was back on her feet.

"I can't walk very far," Lucy said, "so you'll have to come to me." She held her arms wide open, and Randy walked toward her. As he approached, Lucy saw the freckled face of her friend, ten years old, a cowlick sticking out from the back of his head. As he walked toward her, he had a massive grin on his face. She hugged his heavy frame tightly, patting his back. When they finally let go of one another, there wasn't a dry eye in the room. Sandy held a tissue out to Lucy. Randall pulled a linen handkerchief from his front pocket and wiped his eyes.

"Lucy," he said, his voice thick with regret, "if there was any way I could give you back this house, I would. My son—he's smart. Smarter than me. And sadly," he paused, a shadow crossing his face, "even more of a black heart. He has it all tied up, John Mark won't know what hit him, when it all comes out." He shook his head, bewildered. "I still don't know how he did it, behind my back like that, but he did."

The betrayer betrayed. Lucy felt a pang of remorse for him.

"It's too late for all of that, Randall," she said softly.

Too late for so many things.

"I'm dying," she confessed, her voice barely a whisper. "I don't *want* this house."

She felt her leg muscles spasm and moved back toward the couch.

"When I'm gone, I'm gone. The same fate awaits you. Make things right with your family." Lucy lowered herself onto the velvet couch with a groan.

Randall went to help but she put up her hand, "I'm okay, now you listen to me, you've taken a step toward me, now go even further. You have a spectacular man for a grandson, make things right," she said again.

"I will, Lucy," he said, his blue eyes taking in her frail state. "I better go."

"Thanks for stopping by," she replied, a hint of wry amusement in her voice. "It's been a wild ride, hasn't it, Randall Gordon?"

He gave her a reassuring look, his smile genuine. A storehouse of memories shared, flickered across his face. For a fleeting moment, she saw her old friend again, the cheeky grin of his youth.

He waved his hand, then turned toward Sandy and nodded, acknowledging her presence.

"Randall," Sandy responded.

He turned and walked toward the door.

"Randy," Lucy called out.

He stopped, turned, and faced her. Time seemed to hang suspended. So much could have been avoided: the wasted years, the harsh words, the regrets. But here they were, today. Here *he* was.

And they weren't too far gone to admit their mistakes. That had to count for something.

"Oh," she added, a touch of finality in her voice, "and if I wasn't clear . . . I forgive you." She knew she needed to say it one more time. To make sure the words went deep.

She watched his shoulders loosen, the tension visibly draining away. He fidgeted with his blazer sleeves, pulling them down over his wrist, clearly unsure what to say. He uncomfortably looked down at his feet, then looked back up at her. With a catch in his voice, he replied, "That means more to me than you could ever know."

Lucy had lived a lifetime under the crushing weight of unforgiveness—both from her daughter and, even more heavily, from herself. Now, finally, it was different. Forgiveness means letting go. Now she was extending that hard-won forgiveness to another, freely given as it had been freely received. *Freely given, freely give away,* she thought, a lightness spreading through her chest.

"Bye, my friend," she whispered, as he walked away. She thought she saw him standing a bit taller as he departed through the doorway.

CHAPTER TWENTY-SIX

A Gift from the Sea

Anna watched from the cottage steps as John Mark wheeled out the bike—his mom's pink bike. He put the kickstand down and closed the shed door. She walked down the steps and chuckled as he struggled with the seat.

"It just needs to be a little higher." She saw the sweat on his brow. He was determined.

"Seriously, take the silver one; I can ride the pink one." And she meant it.

"No way, the pink bike has a bent front rim, and I can't guarantee the brakes will work."

"They don't work at all?" she questioned.

"I guess we will find out." he patted the bike seat making sure it wouldn't move before he sat on it.

"Perfect, ready to go?"

She grabbed the silver bike, hesitant with the arrangement, "okay, but just take it slow. We don't want any accidents." John Mark did one more check to ensure the rim and brakes were the only issue. After manipulating the greasy bike chain, he stood up and wiped his hands his pants.

"Well, pink is supposed to be the new black, I'm told," he smirked.

Anna put her hand in her pocket to make sure the letter was still there. She knew it belonged to Lucy, and she fully intended to give it to her when she saw her.

"Okay, you ready, Casanova?" Anna teased. "Lucy is probably wondering where we are." John Mark's hair was windblown, and he was still barefoot. He looked like a true surfer boy. She had to admit, she was starting to like this arrangement. John Mark was becoming a fixture in her life.

"Ready!" He said pushing the rusty bike pedal forward.

Gus' leash was tied around Anna's waist, long enough to give him room but short enough that he wouldn't get too far into the road.

They cycled away from the shed, the promise of sweet pastries pulling them down the road. Outside Roger's bakery, Anna lingered while John Mark emerged, his arms full of cinnamon rolls, steaming bread, and a generous bag full of chocolate chip cookies. With a bit of strategic wiggling, they managed to wedge everything into their front baskets.

"That should do it!" He climbed back on his bike.

As they turned onto Gordon Drive, the road stretched straight ahead. Anna, however, was still wrestling with what she was learning about Old Blue's imminent destruction. John Mark had filled her in on a few things, leaving her with questions.

"I'm still struggling to comprehend how our family's original plan went so wrong, and that you ended up with our land," she said, taking a deep breath. "And your grandfather wants to tear it all down. Honestly, it's confusing and sad." They rode side-by-side as Gus did a fast trot next to her, an expert by now.

"I know, and it's not something I'm proud of, Anna."

Anna saw the shame in his eyes. "I know John Mark, so what do we do now?"

"Well, I want to give it to the community. I've done some analysis on what that would mean. I need to inquire more, but I think it can happen."

They were almost to Lucy's driveway. Gus was slowing down. A Great Pyrenees could only run so far before pooping out.

She stopped and hopped off, willing to push the bike the rest of the way up the driveway.

"The house will be placed in trust. I will turn it into a nature preserve, coupled with a historic home preservation clause. It was what our great-grandparents would have wanted."

He turned toward her, "And I think it is what Lucy would want."

"I will do whatever Lucy wants." They walked on, their bikes crunching over shells. She wasn't about to lose the only family she had left.

"One question: if we put the house into a trust, what happens to Lucy?"

"That's the beauty of it! She can live in Old Blue until she . . ." He trailed off.

"Until what?"

Emerging from the shaded tunnel of shrubs, they leaned their bikes against the small blue shed.

John Mark's expression turned somber.

"Lucy can stay here for as long as she wishes." He avoided her gaze, instead focusing on an overgrown path that led from the pond towards the wooded grove, ultimately reaching his family's condos on the other side.

She glanced to where his eyes had settled. "Is that a path?" Anna wondered aloud.

"Looks like it."

They walked towards it, noticing the crushed shells pressed into the soil, and the small stones outlining its edges.

"This was their way of staying close. They never let it become overgrown." He crouched down, pulling at a few stubborn weeds, uncovering a fresh layer of shells. "Not anymore, though."

Anna placed her hands on her hips and looked up, then slowly turned, letting the landscape sink in, once again she had that feeling. A deep sense of belonging washed over her: this was her legacy. These people, this land, this place. An unspoken truth echoed within her: she was meant to safeguard this home, the stories, her family's treasures. It was all clear.

She spun around and faced John Mark. With determination she asked, "John Mark, how are we going to do this?"

His whole face lit up.

"Really? Because if you wanted to help, I mean I would love that, of course. I mean, it is your house."

"I'm all in!" She didn't know what 'all in' meant yet, but she knew she would do whatever it would take.

"Wow, okay, I wasn't sure what you would say or what your future plans would be." He ran his hand through his hair.

"Tell me in five minutes, the condensed version!" She said excitedly.

He held out his palms in front of him, like an unfolded book, "So, I did a bunch of research, and the house would be placed in a trust. The trust would pay for the house now and into the future," he went on, watching her response. "And, it would keep it from demolition."

"Kind of like a historic monument?" she asked.

"Yes, sort of," John Mark explained, "If I understand the stipulation of a home turned into a National Preserve, it will remain protected from here on out." He looked at the house, smiling, "It's such a special place, I think we could even rent it out for events, with the hope that it would generate a small income."

"How much money do you need?" She asked cautiously. "Like, don't we need something to get it up and running?" Her wheels were spinning now. She pictured weddings, garden parties and home tours. That is, if Lucy would permit it. John Mark shook her out of her daydream.

"Yeah, about that." He scrunched his nose.

"With more analysis and crunching some numbers with an accountant, I'm guessing somewhere in the high millions."

"Excuse me?" she gasped.

"Where are we going to get that kind of money?" She questioned.

She cupped her hand over her eyes as she squinted toward the house. The repairs alone wouldn't be cheap. She didn't know much about house repairs, but from the little she had already seen, the house would need a fresh coat of paint, outdoor maintenance, and who knows what was needed inside.

"I don't know." He squirmed and rubbed his arms like he was cold. Maybe, this was a pipe dream idea.

"Okay, so as of right now, you just have a good idea but no traction?"

He put his hands out in front of him, like he was trying to duck a punch, "Geez, give me a break. I only produced this plan twenty-four hours ago."

Anna sighed. Naples was proving to be more complicated than she had anticipated. *Wait until Sam got here. He was the brains. Maybe, he would know how to move this plan forward?*

She had about a hundred questions to ask him but thought it better to wait until she could give him her full attention. Right now, she needed to focus all her attention on Lucy.

They walked up to the back door. Anna paused at the door before knocking.

"Do we tell Lucy all of this now or when we have details on implementing it?"

"Probably best to wait." John Mark's initial exuberance trickled out like a turned off hose nozzle. Anna pushed aside the conversation about Old Blue. She needed to step back about twenty steps and ask Lucy the question that loomed in her mind since she found the letter: *Lucy, what happened between you and mom?*

Anna knocked.

"Oh, and one more thing. Someone would need to manage the estate, or trust rather." John Mark said at a rapid speed. Trying to fit in one more sentence.

The door opened, "hi, Sandy," John Mark greeted, going in for a hug.

"Hello, John Mark," she said, her eyes never leaving Anna.

She grasped Anna's hands, her touch surprisingly warm. "You look just like her, you know."

"Thanks, I've heard that before." Assuming this woman was referring to Anna's mom.

Sandy moved aside and motioned them in. "She's waiting for you. Walk just that way," she said, pointing toward the front of the house.

Anna removed her shoes, leaving them by the doorway. "And just so you know, I'm Sandy," she said formally introducing herself. "Your mama and me, we're old friends."

"Pleased to meet you," Anna said as Sandy led the way through the hallway.

The floor's gentle creak drew her attention. Worn, knotty pine floors stretched out before her. Anna ran her hand over the green and gold vine wallpaper, covering the hallway walls. As she walked barefoot to the next room the quiet was almost tangible. The mingled scents of furniture polish and an unfamiliar, yet familiar, fragrance enveloped her, and she let the house settle around her. John Mark and Sandy were speaking to Lucy in the next room, giving Anna space to explore. She walked towards their voices, entering a room with floor-to-ceiling windows draped in rich blue velvet. She paused, a wave of belonging washing over her, a missing piece found. She wished Sam were there, to share this deeply personal moment. As she stepped further into the room, she breathed, "this is our home."

Although the room was almost empty apart from a few chairs, two couches, a table, and sealed boxes, it was something to behold. John Mark was sitting across from Lucy. Anna saw a small tuft of white hair, barely visible, above the back of the couch.

"Lucy?"

Lucy made to stand. "Sit!" Sandy snapped, rushing to her side.

"Stand me up, Sandy," Lucy insisted, her tone unwavering. Sandy didn't budge.

Lucy's voice, though low, was laced with steel. "John Mark, if you know what's good for you, you will stand me up."

John Mark knelt, carefully adjusting Lucy's legs, then helped her to her feet. He offered his arm, and Anna watched as Lucy leaned heavily into him. Lucy, who had seemed robust just yesterday, now appeared as delicate as porcelain. Anna hesitated, unsure whether to approach or remain still. Then Lucy smiled, and Anna, in that instant, saw it clearly—her mother was there in that smile. She rushed forward, embracing Lucy tightly. The scent of Dove soap filled her senses, and she felt Lucy's fragile frame through her robe. Lucy's body began to tremble. Anna stepped back, her gaze meeting Lucy's. Tears welled in Lucy's eyes, then spilled over, tracing delicate paths down her cheeks.

Anna wanted to remember this. The house, the woman, the town—they shaped her mother, and her. This was what Grace had kept from her and Sam. She couldn't understand why.

Lucy reached for John Mark's arm to steady herself.

"Lucy, let's sit down," he whispered to her. She smiled and nodded.

John Mark helped her back to the couch. Lucy patted the spot next to her, "please sit," she motioned to Anna.

Sandy handed Lucy a tissue which she used to blow her nose.

As Anna sat next to her, she picked up a few scattered pictures that had been lying next to Lucy.

"I can't get over how much you look like Grace," Lucy reached for Anna's hand; she gave it effortlessly. No one knew where to begin. So much needed to be said, yet words seemed amiss. Finally, Anna broke the silence.

"I can't believe you, are you," she laughed. She felt embarrassed. "Sorry, that sounds funny, what I mean is . . ."

Lucy interjected, "No, need to explain, honey. I also cannot believe I am me, too." Lucy had always been Sam and Anna's grandmother by blood, but not in heart. Grace hadn't let her.

"You have a grandmother." Lucy patted Anna's knee. Anna still found it surreal, as if she had stepped into a dream and was being carried along on an unfolding adventure.

"I bet you're wondering why your mother left." Lucy asked the question Anna wanted to answer more than any other. Lucy held her hand out and nodded toward the pictures Anna had seen earlier. Anna handed them over and as she did, she looked closer at the top one, a bit faded in color, "is that mom?"

"She's beautiful, isn't she?" Lucy looked at the picture and ran a finger over Grace's face. She handed the picture to Anna. She laced her hands together and laid them in her lap.

"You didn't know about me, did you honey?"

Anna shook her head, "No, we were told you and grandpa had died." Anna was ashamed her mom had told her this lie. John Mark gave her a half-smile. Like her, his past wasn't a clean bill of sale either.

Lucy took a deep breath. Anna felt the letter burning a hole in her pocket and wondered if she should give it to Lucy now.

"I'm glad you came," Lucy whispered. She started to cough, and John Mark beat Sandy into the kitchen to get a glass of water.

"Lucy, are you okay?" Anna was worried.

"Honey, I'm fine." She said between gasps.

John Mark came back in and handed Lucy the water. After taking a long sip, she held the glass. Her breathing was labored. Sandy stood up and began to fiddle with something on the other side of the couch. After a few moments, Sandy handed Lucy a clear tube and helped her lace it over her nose. Obviously, Lucy was not fine.

"Ah, better. Now, to address your question about your mother."

Lucy's shoulders rose and fell with each breath.

"We all make choices that, in retrospect, we either celebrate or deeply regret. There's rarely any middle ground."

They each settled in as Lucy began to recount some of the family history: "Grace's birth," she paused a smile played on her lips, "my miracle child and purest joy." Lucy said proudly. "I loved her fiercely." Lucy shared a few funny stories about Grace when she was in elementary school. Anna listened as Lucy led the story along, then transitioned to Old Blue, detailing its construction and the tidbits of her own childhood. Anna did not interject, just listened. Lucy paused. She adjusted herself into the couch. "Then there was the moment that changed so many things . . ." she trailed off.

She turned toward Anna, "your mom was telling the truth when she said her parents died when she was young."

"What?" Anna asked, her brow furrowed in confusion. She had hoped for clarity, but instead a fresh wave of bewilderment washed over her.

"Her daddy died, and I all but died with him the day Grace left." Lucy's face dropped, as she looked at her hands in her lap. Anna reached out her hand and grabbed Lucy's. Offering her strength to go on.

Lucy looked up a small smile on her face, "your grandfather," she looked at Sandy for help. Sandy nodded reassuringly. Lucy went on, "Your grandfather, he was the salt of the earth, he loved this house, he loved me, and he adored your mom." Lucy looked out toward the sea through the bank of windows. "The day he died, like I said, it nearly killed me too."

Anna recalled the day her own father never returned. And then her mom. The weight of the grief had consumed her.

"And that was the day I committed the greatest error of my life." Lucy nearly choked on the words, trying to catch her breath.

"She can't breathe," Anna looked urgently at Sandy and John Mark. Sandy was already at Lucy's side. She wheeled the small canister, the same one hooked to the clear tubes, to the front of the couch now. Anna got a good look at it. It was a hospital breathing machine. Sandy fiddled with the knob and Anna heard more oxygen release from the valve.

Lucy winked at Anna. Everyone knew something Anna did not. Why did Lucy have a breathing machine?

"That's better, thank you, Sandy."

"As I was saying," Lucy resumed, her voice laced with sorrow. "That decision altered the course of everything. I missed a lifetime with Grace, my most precious Grace."

The story unraveled, a tale of heartache, and Anna absorbed it all, the highs, and lows of their conflict. Grace's plea. Lucy's unwavering resolve. Teenage angst, maternal pride. Painful choices, forgiveness withheld. *Could it have been different?* Anna wondered, unsure whether to judge her mother or Lucy. But perhaps the past was beyond judgment. They had this day, this present moment. There were two sides to every story, and tragedy belonged to both.

It was as though Lucy had read her mind. "Don't hold your mother's actions against her. She did what she believed was right, in that moment." Lucy blinked her eyes closed. "And so did I."

Lucy reached her hand to Anna's arm, "and in her own way, by withholding things from you, it was her way of protecting you. That's a mother's instinct."

"I couldn't just give this place up. Whether that was right or wrong, I guess I'll never know."

Looking around the room at the other faces, Lucy slowly spoke, "But I've learned, perhaps too late, that I should have paused, allowed her to express herself, listened to her . . ." her voice trailed off.

Anna took out the letter.

"This is what brought me here. This is how I knew where to find you."

Anna handed it to Lucy. Lucy looked closely and her eyes widened.

"Grace's handwriting!"

Lucy hugged Anna.

"It belongs to you Lucy," Anna said smiling, "I mean Grandma."

Lucy closed her eyes, letting the word linger. It fit perfectly. Like a delightful breakfast, dark coffee, fruit, and hot croissants with melting butter. She could savor that word all day.

Of course, Lucy was itching to read it, but she would wait. Grace's words were meant for her and her alone. She wanted to sit with them. Wrap herself inside of them.

"Thank you for bringing this to me, honey." She rested her palm on Anna's cheek. As she sat back the plastic tubing tangled behind her back.

"This stuff is such a nuisance," she tried to sit up and reach behind her. Anna helped and laughed as she straightened it all out.

"What is all this stuff anyway?"

"I thought that rascal over there would have already told you." She eyed John Mark, who shrugged.

"I gave her the details about the house, and confessed my blundering mistakes, but I didn't tell her everything, Lucy." He looked down at his feet.

Lucy nodded.

Anna saw bleak expressions all around. Sandy's initial cheerful disposition had turned gloomy.

Lucy put her hands on her knees and stared forward. As she did, she looked as though she was trying to muster up something from deep within herself.

"Honey, I'm sick."

Anna quickly ran through her mental checklist. Of course, she's sick. She's older. She has a cold, people get sick all the time, then they get better. Not everyone dies. Panic set in. Here she goes, zero to sixty. Why? Because everyone else she has loved, died.

"Okay, how sick?"

Lucy looked at Sandy. John Mark looked toward the bank of windows. No one would look directly at Anna. All gazes were averted.

"The kind of sick that doesn't get better." Lucy gave a sad smile, then looked at her hands.

"Let's just say the timing stinks."

Anna's chest felt tight, a band of grief constricting her. *This can't be happening.* She had just found her grandmother, and now she was losing her; their lives intersecting at this impossibly brief moment. It felt like a cruel trick of fate. John Mark stood up, catching eyes with Anna before he walked to the windows.

So, this is it, Anna realized. This was the truth he wouldn't share, the reason he'd said, "it is Lucy's to tell."

"I can't imagine what you're feeling right now," Lucy said, her hand a gentle weight on Anna's. Anna exhaled, squeezing her eyes shut, then opened them, her voice barely a whisper.

"This can't be."

The room fell silent.

Grabbing Lucy's hands in her own, she looked down at them. Incidentally, she noticed they looked like her hands: the same nail beds and long, thin fingers. The only difference was the addition of sixty years of life worked into them.

Sam will be here soon, Anna thought, a wave of relief washing over her. They'd faced these kinds of situations before. The Belltown family's future was on them. Looking at Lucy's smile, Anna felt strong. She wouldn't leave. She'd take care of Lucy. Again, Lucy read her mind.

"I'm going to hold on for as long as possible," she reached her finger to the tip of Anna's nose. "I want to get to know you and Sam. I have so many stories to tell you," she winked. "But there is one thing you need to know, honey." Anna wasn't prepared for more bad news. She braced herself.

"This place," Lucy said, looking around with sadness, "it's not ours anymore. I just couldn't keep up."

Anna looked at John Mark.

"Go ahead, Anna," he nodded.

"Lucy, we've got a plan. You get to stay in your house."

Lucy's brow furrowed. She looked questioningly toward John Mark, the new owner of Old Blue.

"What is this all about?"

"I think I've figured out a way to keep the house from being torn down, Lucy, and it would mean everything to me if you would stay here," he said with confidence. "We will make sure you are comfortable."

Lucy was taking it all in, still confused.

"I know this is a lot, we can explain more details later, if this is too much right now."

Anna's doubts about John Mark evaporated like droplets of water on a sweltering day. And, it seemed Lucy's had too.

"Sandy, isn't he the spitting image of Paul Gordon?" Lucy asked.

"I see that." Sandy agreed.

"Yes," Lucy said gently, "Just like Paul. It's that heart of gold. The deep down, goodness."

"Thanks, Lucy." John Mark blushed.

Lucy turned toward Anna, "you know this guy right here, he may just save your life one day."

John Mark chuckled, "you saved mine, Lucy."

Not wanting to waste one more minute, as of late, Lucy's time clock was ticking quickly.

"I'm ready to hear how we're going to save Old Blue," Lucy said. "I'm all ears."

John Mark almost tripped as he rushed to the couch where Lucy and Anna sat. He caught himself, embarrassed, he stood up and reached into his back pocket and pulled out a folded stack of papers. It was a wonder that it had fit there in the first place. He sat himself right between Lucy and Anna, without noticing he sat on Anna's hand. "Ouch," she said pulling from underneath him. "Oh sorry!" He smirked. He placed the sheets on Lucy's lap. Like a small child, holding up their prized artwork, he was almost giddy. Lucy looked down. She saw a bunch of scrawled numbers and phone numbers.

"Honey, you will need to break this down for me."

"Yeah, yeah, I will totally."

He stopped and put his hand up. Anna wondered if John Mark lived on caffeine. He had so much energy. They watched him jump up from the couch.

"But first, let me call some friends and see about getting your house back in order." He looked around the living room. "Where is all your other furniture, Lucy?"

She chuckled, watching him, he was a whirlwind. The perfect person to save Old Blue. Lucy tried to remember what had gone where.

Sandy answered for her. "Some went to the Preservation Society already, the rest has been boxed up and is in storage."

"Let's bring it all back!" John Mark exclaimed.

"Oh my," Sandy said, putting her hand up to her heart. Anna felt like a bystander watching everything take place.

Tears flowed down Lucy's cheeks. She was speechless. "But how?" she questioned.

"I can explain everything in a minute." He clapped his hands together.

Anna turned toward Lucy, "Grandma, when Sam get's here, we can tell you our plan."

Lucy looked up and met Anna's eyes, "Sam?"

"Yes, Grandma, he will be here tonight."

She hugged Anna, holding her tightly.

John Mark took that as his cue to get started.

"Daniel, yeah, it's me. What are you doing right now? I need your help. And bring your brothers too." John Mark said from the next room.

An immediate sense of kinship settled over Anna, as if she had known this woman her entire life. *It must be the connection of family,* she thought. Their shared loss was a bond in itself. As Anna gazed at the wrinkles etched around Lucy's eyes, she saw decades of life and history, *her* history, *her* stories, all held within this woman. In Lucy, the pieces of the mystery were falling into place. A silent "thank you" escaped Anna's lips, directed towards her mother: *thank you for bringing me here.* Even in her departure, her mother had steered her children towards safety, towards what was inherently theirs. She had pointed them to home.

CHAPTER TWENTY-SEVEN

Lucy's Legacy

Lucy lay in her bed. Her muscles ached and her feet were giving her trouble. She decided to sleep in a bit longer. It had been a busy week. She felt exhausted, even if all she had done was watch everyone move furniture, clean, and start some of the repairs Old Blue had sorely needed. John Mark had rallied friends and community members to unpack boxes, reshelve dishes and cups, and bring Old Blue slowly back to life. The furniture already gifted to the Naples Preservation Society was reclaimed, and the President of the NPS was pleased to hear about the preservation of Old Blue. She pledged to help raise support for the endeavor and was their biggest cheerleader.

Finally, Lucy propped herself up in bed. She slowly surveyed her surroundings, a lifetime of cherished possessions gathered around her. Her mother's vanity, the rose-colored settee, framed photographs, and the familiar touch of the lace duvet she had slept under throughout her marriage—all were present. She sighed, a wave of relief washing over her. From below, she heard sounds of life, there were bodies bumping around in the kitchen. Sam or

Anna, she guessed. It was music to her ears. Both had promptly moved in with Lucy that night, Anna sleeping in Grace's old room and Sam in Bill's old study. Sam reminded her of her daddy— smart, hardworking, and uniquely himself. He wasn't afraid to venture into the unknown, just like her father. In her eyes, both men were pioneers, one drawn to swamps and heat, the other to ice and frigid cold. She still couldn't believe how her life had taken this turn. Like a roller coaster turn, it came on her swiftly and left her with nothing but pure joy. She reached over and opened the drawer of her nightstand. It was where she had left it. The letter from Grace, still unopened. Amidst all the hustle and bustle she left it untouched. But this morning, she knew it was time. Anything could be inside. Rebuke. Regret. Or, what Lucy hoped for most, an explanation. She held it in her hand and ran her fingertip over her name, "Mama," tracing it.

She slid her finger under the flap breaking the seal. Inside, tucked in the envelope were two thick, creamy, white pages, folded together. A sense of anticipation settled over her as she carefully unfolded the sheets.

She heard Grace's voice.

> *Mama,*
>
> *It's been too long. I know it has, and I'm so sorry. I barely know where to start; I have so much to tell you, but I'll save most of it for when we see each other. I'm hoping to plan a trip next year, maybe in the fall. Would that work for you?*
>
> *I want Sam and Anna to meet you. They deserve to know the truth I've kept from them. When I left, I was angry and grieving. I saw your decision about the house as you choosing it over me. I was young and foolish.*

I know I hurt you, but I was hurting too. I moved to California, got married to a wonderful man, and built a life. I thought of you every single day. I didn't know how to ask for forgiveness, nor did I know how to give it. I was at a loss on how to fix what was broken.

It was too hard to talk about you, so I lied to the kids when they asked. I regret that so much. I loved my new life, but there was always a hole. I missed you.

Lucy stopped reading, squeezing her eyes together she felt the salty tears trail down her cheeks. *I've never cried this much in my life,* she thought.

She wondered if her daddy had cried this much when he was walking this same road, illness softening a heart. She looked down at the page and continued to read:

Mama, when my husband passed away, although it's been some time, our hearts still weigh heavy. My children are strong, but they grieve his loss as deeply as I do. It took me time to realize that I abandoned you during a time of darkness. I did not stand by you as you buried daddy, a regret I carry heavily. I didn't know how to face you, so I turned away. I want to rectify that. Mom, I long to come home. Will you find it in your heart to forgive me? You were a good mother, and I was blind to it then, but I see it clearly now.

I love you, Mom. Talk to you soon.

Love, Grace

She used her palm to wipe away the wetness on her cheeks. Then Lucy pressed the letter to her lips. Soon, she would see Grace. "I forgive you, I forgive you . . ." she held the letter up, closing her eyes, "I was so stubborn, my girl." She set the letter on her lap. "Forgive me, too," she said out loud.

An immeasurable sense of peace washed over Lucy. Leaning back into her pillows, she felt a wave of love for her daughter flood her heart. She heard the banging pots and pans in the kitchen, *maybe they were making breakfast*, she wondered. More than anything, right now, she wanted to be with them. She looked at the picture she had put in a frame yesterday, ten-year-old Grace sitting next to her dad in the sand, their backs to Lucy, the two looking at the ocean. Lucy traced the edge of the frame. "Wait for me," she whispered, "I'll be there soon." A crash echoed from the floor below. She kissed the photo. "I still have things to do."

Lucy turned toward the gentle tapping at the door. "Grandma, are you awake?" Grandma, the name she knew she would never tire of. "Yes, honey, come in," she replied warmly. The door opened, and Anna entered, Sam following close behind, a tray held carefully in his hands and a bright smile on his face.

She sat up straight, as Sam gently placed the assortment of goodies on her lap.

"Oh, what a surprise, you two!"

She looked down at the steaming cup of coffee atop a linen napkin. Beside it on a porcelain plate were two pieces of buttered toast with a little dollop of jam, on top.

"We thought you could use a little something before we dive into numbers this morning."

Her appetite hadn't been much lately, but Lucy would devour all of this, as though it were her last meal.

Sam hugged her, "good morning, Grandma."

"Yes, it is."

Sam sat down in a chair opposite her and Anna sat on the end of the bed.

She took a bite of her toast, "delicious!"

Lucy saw Anna fingering the lace on the quilt.

"That," she said pointing at the lace covering, "belonged to your great-grandmother," she said between mouthfuls of toast.

"It's so detailed."

"She was a detail woman. An artist."

Lucy felt more vital now that the kids were around. Her breathing was stronger, and she didn't need the oxygen machine, as much. *Maybe, this disease wouldn't take her so soon*, she thought. She could only hope.

Lucy wasted no time catching up on Sam and Anna's lives, eager to bridge the years.

"Now, tell me something, anything at all." She licked a stray bit of jam from her finger.

"Like what, Grandma?" Anna asked, her curiosity peaked.

"You go first, Sam," she looked at him. "When you were a boy, did you always know you would live amongst polar bears and glaciers?"

"No way, never!"

"Sam would beg our mom to take him to the coast to surf, any chance we could get away," Anna added. "Mom loved the beach too, so it was a trip we took often."

"I should think not," Lucy laughed. "So why the Arctic?"

"I think it was the unknown of the place, that drew me. Only a few had gone that far and stayed," he said matter of factly. "It has grown on me, even if it is always below zero."

"I know your mother would be so proud of you, Sam, as I am."

Lucy finished her toast and wiped her mouth with the linen napkin.

Anna looked at her watch.

"Grandma, if you're up for it, John Mark is coming by with an accountant, this morning. They want to crunch numbers on the costs of putting Old Blue into a trust fund."

Lucy hadn't yet disclosed to the kids that she intended to give all the money she had gained from the sale of the house which, if her records were correct after taxes, landed somewhere around fifteen million. Indeed, a large amount like that would cover everything. She wanted to wait until the accountant gave them the round number and then surprise the kids with it.

"Yes, of course. How much time do I have?"

"We don't want to rush you, but he will be here in twenty minutes."

"Oh!" She lifted the tray from her lap and set it on the bed next to her.

Sam rose and walked to the upstairs bay windows, his gaze drawn to the breathtaking view. "Mom used to tell me about Naples," he said softly, "about this grand blue house where she played as a child, the golden sand, and the warm water. She'd share stories of the games she played, especially hide-and-seek, and all the secret nooks and crannies she would discover. Honestly, it sounded like pure magic to me. It must have taken incredible strength not to return."

He turned to Lucy and Anna, a sense of awe in his voice. "Because now, I don't know if I'll ever be able to leave."

"Your Mama did love this place." Lucy nodded knowingly, "even if she ran away from it, it was part of her, "and when you truly love something, you feel compelled to share it."

"Hey, where is everyone?" They could hear John Mark yelling from downstairs.

"He doesn't know how to do things quietly, does he?" Lucy said, smirking.

"It's something he's working on." They all laughed.

Anna hopped off the bed and went to the landing, yelling, "We're up here; give us ten minutes or so!"

"You got it!"

Anna went back into Lucy's room, she reached for the tray, "here, I got it."

"Thank you, honey," Lucy used her arm to maneuver herself to the edge of the bed.

"Now, if you could just help me up, I can do the rest."

Sam was already by her side.

"Lovely," Lucy smiled up at Sam.

Sam grabbed Lucy's arm, and from a sitting position, they both stood, Sam bearing the weight, as he pulled her to her feet.

"Anna, please go down and make that man some coffee." Lucy turned to Anna, "on it!" She was already out the door.

"And you," she said placing both of her hands on Sam's shoulders, "go to the shed and dig out my daddy's old surfboard. He made it with his bare hands from a felled tree on this property. It has your name written all over it."

"Cool!" Sam didn't waste any time; she could hear him skipping steps on his way down the staircase.

Lucy turned toward her closet, "Now, what to wear?"

When Lucy entered the living room, she saw three heads huddled around an oversized calculator and several papers. They had set up a card table and looked engrossed in whatever was in front of them. She cleared her throat as she entered.

"Lucy!" John Mark rose. He walked over and wrapped his long arm around her waist. They walked to the table together. Anna pulled the chair out as Lucy sat next to her.

"Lucy, this is my friend, Newman," John Mark said. "He will be able to help us with this mess."

"Pleased to meet you," he stood and bowed partially.

"So, what have you three cooked up?"

Should she disclose information now? Or let them sweat a little? The money she had would be more than enough.

Newman slid a piece of paper in front of Lucy; it had calculations scribbled all over it. He pointed his finger at a few amounts, "I haven't added up everything, but you can see some of the expenses we will incur." He shuffled some more papers, looking at Lucy and Anna, "and that's without the necessary repairs, after the inspector combs through this old place."

She didn't look down at the number.

Instead, she asked, "what inspection? This house might look shabby, but it was built by the best builder on this side of the Mississippi. Not one board will be out of place."

Newman took the paper back, then looked at John Mark for backup.

John Mark turned toward Lucy, he scratched his head, and a few pieces of dandruff fell to the table.

"I received a letter yesterday from the agency in charge of certifying Old Blues' preservation status. This place must be up to code, Lucy. And, as it stands, I'm already aware of several violations, just from walking through the place."

Protective, Lucy crossed her arms, "it's an old house. It has been a lot to take care of on my own. I know I've let some things go."

"It's nothing to apologize for, ma'am." It was Newman again. "The agency has rigorous standards. Standards most personal homes would never have to abide by."

Anna rested her hand on Lucy's shoulder, "you've done a good job."

So, this is what it felt like to hand over the reins, Lucy thought. She looked around the table at the three young people. If this house was going to survive, she would have to trust them.

She uncrossed her arms and slowly leaned forward, her face relaxing. *Let go*, she told herself. "Okay, so back to the amount?"

"And give it to us straight, Newman, no funny business, we want the final number." John Mark folded his arms in front of him. Newman wrote a few things down. The scratching of his pen was the only sound in the room.

"If my calculations are correct, you will need a starting point of forty million to form the trust. He circled the number a few times in red ink. That will be the seed money. Think of it as an investment that will keep growing. It would supply the resources needed to maintain any future renovations and the upkeep of the home and allow the public to enjoy the property.

"Wow," Lucy breathed out a discouraging sigh.

"Yikes." Anna's head hung. "It's a ginormous amount."

"Nearly impossible," Newman added.

It far exceeded what she had to offer. How is that possible? She currently had access to more money than her family would ever accrue in a century, and it didn't even cover half of the amount Newman had produced. She scrunched up her nose. How disappointing.

"I didn't see that coming," Lucy shook her head side-to-side.

"Me either." John Mark's eyebrows rose, almost touching his hairline.

She could still help. But now was also a time to let her grandchildren make the choice she never gave to Grace. To let the house go. She felt the knot in her stomach. She looked at Anna, who seemed sad.

"Anna, I want you and Sam to think about something." Anna looked intently into Lucy's eyes. "Yes, Grandma?"

"Suppose you two want nothing more to do with this home, . . ." her voice trailed off. Anna was taken aback. "What do you mean?"

"You know, what if you just take the money I got from the sale and run, so to speak?" Lucy neither wanted them to be tied to it, nor have it destroy her relationship with them.

"Grandmother!" Anna laughed.

"I am not joking, honey. It is your inheritance. I will do whatever you both choose with it, and I hope you can agree."

Sam had told them to fill him in when he came back from catching the waves. Lucy knew he trusted Anna.

"Well, I already have my answer and so does Sam."

"You didn't even think about it."

"We don't need to. We want to keep this house! It's home!"

"Anna, are you sure? This will be a heavy burden," Lucy cautioned, a weight she herself had carried for a lifetime. Yet, even in its difficulty, that burden had also held immense joy.

"Honestly, Grandma, Sam and I knew you were going to ask this, so we discussed it, and we are all in. We're not letting this house go!"

Lucy had to admit she was overjoyed and relieved. She swallowed the lump in her throat. She felt undeserving of such profound love, yet it continued to flow freely towards her.

"Well," Newman interrupted. "Now that the house issue is settled."

John Mark looked at Newman, and Newman shot him a sideways glance.

"Lucy, I think Newman is itching to ask you what your contribution might be."

"Yes, if my grandchildren don't want the money then I want all of it to go towards this endeavor," she stated confidently.

She calculated in her head the amount, "I think after taxes, it was somewhere around fifteen million, give or take. And that includes some of my personal savings and pensions, things Bill invested in."

Anna's eyes shot up, "Wow, Grandma, that is a lot."

And then Lucy remembered Grace's will and her final request, the stock bonds.

She looked at Anna, "the money your mother left, she requested it to go toward Old Blue . . ." she stated, "but you kids need to do with it, whatever you see fit."

Anna didn't hesitate, "Mom would have wanted it to stay right here. This was her home too."

"Okay, then that is all I have for you, Mr. Newman," Lucy said with a nod. She and Anna exchanged a warm smile. The business meeting was over, and Lucy wasn't about to let him bring everyone down.

Newman's expression remained neutral, a stark contrast to the cheerful atmosphere. "So, perhaps a final figure closer to seventeen million then?"

John Mark nodded, "that sounds about right."

What about John Mark, Lucy wondered. This would affect him more than any of them.

Lucy turned to John Mark; her brow furrowed with concern. "Are you sure this is what you want?"

The proposed arrangement meant John Mark would receive an annual stipend and a management fee from the property, an amount that would barely cover his monthly expenses for food and gas. If he proceeded with this deal, he would be financially depleted and excluded from any future transactions with Gordon Developers. This decision would be the nail in the coffin.

"Sometimes one has to sacrifice, to do the right thing." He said it so quietly that Lucy was sure the others hadn't heard. Anna put her hand on John Mark's arm.

"Grandma's right, John Mark, you don't have to do this."

"But I do, Anna."

A knowing look passed between Lucy and John Mark. She understood the "why" behind his actions. While his bank account might soon be empty, he was clearly investing in something he valued more than money. "Okay, that settles it then," Anna stood with a determined look on her face.

Lucy had to be the sensible one in the group, "so now I have to ask, how do we get the remaining money?"

"Donors, we are going to try to gain donors, Grandma."

She had to give them credit. Youth, such vitality, and optimism.

She couldn't be much help; she didn't have much in the way of strength to offer. But she could offer her encouragement, her support, and her fight.

"Okay, I'm ready," Lucy placed her palms on the table. Her smile taking over her entire face.

Newman looked down at his papers, shaking his head from side to side. He probably thought the three of them were utterly crazy.

John Mark wrapped an arm over Anna's shoulder and pulled her close.

"Let's give this everything we've got," John Mark said, the initial excitement now shifting into practical planning. He and Anna stood up, and John Mark began outlining the extensive repairs needed, his words painting a grand vision for Old Blue. A pang of emotion, a blend of excitement, and a gentle melancholy, resonated within Lucy as she listened. *My turn is done,* she mused. *The torch passes to my grandchildren. This is as it should be. Time to let go.*

Chapter Twenty-Eight

An Ocean of Memories

Anna led the way up the ladder into Old Blue's attic, a stuffy smell filling her nostrils. Sam followed closely. They stood side by side, gazing at the expansive, dust-filled space.

"Ach-hoo." Sam didn't cover his mouth and Anna felt wet droplets land on her arm.

"Gross, Sam, cover your mouth next time. You just spit all over me." Brothers.

"Sorry," Sam said quietly, then walked to the center of the room and pulled the string. The light flickered on. "Wow, it works," he said, a note of surprise in his voice. Anna noticed the spiderwebs stretched across the corners, creating a slightly creepy atmosphere.

"There it is," Sam said, pointing to a circular window. They walked across the aged floorboards, and Sam gently pushed the window open, inhaling the fresh air. He stuck his head through the window, just large enough for him to climb out.

He paused, his eyes narrowing at something etched on the frame.

"Paul Gordon, 1947," he read aloud, his voice puzzled.

"And this," he said, his face close to the peeling white paint of the window frame.

"Howard Belltown, 1947."

Anna peered at the frame. "And here's Deborah Belltown, 1947, and Nancy Belltown, 1947."

"It's the founders," Anna said. "Just like grandma said, the originals."

She traced the names with her finger, picturing the four of them leaving their mark.

"Oh gosh, we got sidetracked, John Mark needs those measurements."

"Hey, what's taking you two so long, did you get eaten by a monster mouse or something?" John Mark's head peeked through the opening.

"This house is full of endless surprises, we just found your great-grandpa's name written over there," Anna pointed toward the window.

"Nice!" he climbed the rest of the way up.

She saw him look around, his eyes landing on the large webs hanging from the rafters.

"I'll just wait here. Give me the numbers, and I can write them down." He pulled a small note pad from his pocket.

"Wait, you're not afraid of spiders, are you?"

He smiled hesitantly, "nah." He looked around, then made a motion to step forward, and as he did, he walked right into an invisible web. "Son of a Jed!" He clawed it off.

Yeah, she thought. *He's afraid of spiders.*

Sam was laughing as John Mark tried to sidestep the remaining spider obstacles and finally made his way over to them.

"Wow, this space is enormous."

"Yeah, we were thinking the same thing. It could have been an entire floor."

She pulled out the tape measure and walked to the far eastern corner.

"Here, I'll hold, and you pull."

Sam took the tape out of her hand and began to walk the length. As she called out the measurement, John Mark wrote them down. They did the same with the remaining walls.

"Hey, what's this." She ducked under a small truss and used her foot to push out a hidden box. The rest of the attic was empty, so they assumed nothing would be up there.

"Hey, look, it says Grace," Sam announced, dusting off the box. "This has to be mom's." Anna and Sam lifted the lid. "Wow . . ."

Anna covered her mouth, her eyes wide as she peeled back layers of tissue paper. She knew what it was; her fingers gently touching the pearl embellishments.

It was Lucy's wedding gown, a cascade of lace with a sweeping train. A true vintage treasure. She held it up, amazed it was still in such good condition after being stored in a simple cardboard box. She turned, "What do you think?" She asked, her voice filled with amusement.

Sam, his attention already elsewhere, was busy searching for more hidden boxes. But John Mark was transfixed. He stumbled over his words, "it's, uh, nice. Really pretty."

Anna chuckled, a warm, genuine sound. She carefully folded the dress and returned it to its tissue-lined box. Before carefully placing the gown inside, she noticed a large envelope at the bottom of the box. Picking it up, she peered inside and saw a drawing.

"What's that?" Sam asked, joining her.

"I don't know, I was just about to find out," she replied, gently pulling it out. It was a detailed, hand-drawn picture of Old Blue. "It says 'DB' in the corner."

"Deborah Belltown!" Anna exclaimed, recognizing the initials.

"Wait, that is *the* drawing!" John Mark exclaimed, moving quickly to Anna's side. "This is it, the one Lucy told me about." John Mark's finger traced the outline of the other house in the drawing, the one that would have belonged to his great-grandfather. "That's it," he whispered. Anna heard the emotion catch in his throat. "We need to show this to Lucy."

Anna laid the picture on top of the folded wedding dress.

"Can one of you carry this down?"

She knew Lucy would love to see both the drawing and the dress.

She switched off the light while Sam picked up the box. Together, the three of them maneuvered it down the ladder, setting it on the floor.

"I'll take this down to grandma," Sam hoisted the box onto his shoulder. She loved having her brother around. He walked down the hall, whistling. John Mark started to follow.

"Wait, John Mark, I have to tell you something."

"Sam and I talked it over, and we want to invest what our parents left us into the house," Anna explained. "Sam said it's where the money needs to be, and since you've made us equal owners, it is a worthy investment."

"Anna, you don't have to do that."

"I know, but we want to, and we think it will help."

"And what will you two do for money?"

"Sam and I are young. We can work, just like anyone else. Sam will eventually go back to his research, and I . . ." she looked at the floor, "I plan on staying here, indefinitely."

John Mark raised his eyebrows, "I like this plan." He grinned. She felt her face warm.

"Sam crunched some numbers, and he said we were rich!"

"My parents prepared well in life, in the event of their deaths; their life insurance left Sam and me with around five million."

Wowed, John Mark whistled.

"So that leaves us, if my math is correct, with a total of twenty million!"

They were halfway there.

Maybe they would make this plan work after all, Anna thought.

Anna eased open the screen door and stepped onto the porch. Lucy sat in her wicker rocker, a blanket draped across her lap. *Her breathing is labored,* Anna thought, listening to the rhythmic whoosh of the breathing machine, forcing oxygen into Lucy's lungs.

"Hey, sweetie pie," Lucy said, reaching for Anna's hand, her voice soft.

"Hey, how are you feeling?"

"Oh, you know, same old, same old." Lucy smiled up at her.

"Give me some updates on the house, you three have been working so hard."

Anna sat down next to Lucy, "Well if we keep at this pace, Old Blue will be a historic home before the year is out!" She tried to mask the discouragement. Earlier, they had all agreed, give Lucy only good news.

A few days ago, Stan Gordon had his lawyer deliver a stack of paperwork. After reading the first few lines, they knew what it was for. He was suing them. They had a small grace period before it would be enacted. Thirty days. One month, to get their state and national registrations approved. Anna shivered as she thought about it. What they were hoping to achieve seemed impossible.

Even with John Mark expediting everything, they were still short a lot of money.

After seeing Lucy get flustered yesterday, regarding anything other than positive news, they would keep to themselves.

Anna squeezed Lucy's hand before letting it go.

"Hey, I found something fun in the attic." She would show her the dress first.

"Oh, you did? We must have missed a box," Lucy looked curious.

Anna turned over her shoulder and hollered, "Sam, we're ready."

Sam walked out, holding up the wedding dress, humming a slightly off-key bridal tune. "Oh my goodness," Lucy gasped, her face filled with joy. She clapped her hands together. "It's just as beautiful as I remember."

"We found it hidden in a dark corner of the attic. Must have been overlooked during the move," Sam said.

"Oh, the memories this brings back," Lucy murmured, reaching out to touch the delicate fabric, a tear glistening in her eye.

"Silk and lace. So costly. We couldn't afford such things. My father had a rich friend, who traveled between Naples and China for work. My father would look after his house, refusing payment. So, the man gifted him this ivory silk." She held the train of the dress with reverence.

"And my mother, a talented seamstress, spent many nights sewing this by lamplight." She pressed the fabric to her cheek.

"It still smells of roses," Anna said, leaning in.

Lucy winked, "It's rosewater. It was very popular when I was young."

"It's so lovely, Grandma; you had exquisite taste."

She turned to Sam. "I'm so happy you found this. I'd completely forgotten about it."

Lucy let the fabric fall, her voice tinged with sadness. "I kept it, hoping Grace might want it someday." Anna and Sam exchanged sad smiles. Hearing their mother's name never got easier, but the pain did soften with each mention.

"What do you kids think? Should we donate it to the historical society? Do you think they'd want it?" Lucy asked.

"Grandma, it's a classic! Of course, they would," Anna replied, then hesitated. "But . . . do you think I could keep it?"

"Oh, honey, nothing would please me more," Lucy said, a mischievous twinkle in her eye. Anna could only guess what Lucy was thinking.

"We have something else to show you," Anna gently laid the drawing on Lucy's lap. Lucy gasped. "Oh, wherever did you find this?" she gently touched the edge of the paper. "My mother drew this."

"It's the drawing, Grandma, the dream Paul had." Lucy leaned closer, pointing. "See that?" she asked, indicating the path between the two houses. "That was Paul's hope that the path between the two families would always remain intact." She looked up at Anna, a hint of wonder in her eyes. "Somehow, it seems his wish has come true."

Anna squeezed Lucy's shoulder, acknowledging the moment.

"Oh, I completely forgot," Anna continued, a sudden burst of excitement in her voice. "The Historical Society called this morning, and they've agreed to host the gala! It's on the calendar, a week from tomorrow!"

"How wonderful, I'm so pleased."

"When I approached Ms. Woodburn, she rearranged a few commitments and wholeheartedly agreed to provide the space, food, and drinks. It will be a night to remember."

"I can't wait." Lucy looked at the picture on her lap once again. A look of contentment on her face. Remembering the day it had been created, she let the memory rest with her a few moments. Anna interrupted her.

"Grandma, we must find some dresses! They are pulling out all the stops. Sam, we need to find you a tuxedo."

"Do I have to?"

Lucy eyed him.

"I mean, yes, I can't wait."

"That's the spirit, Sam."

The next day, Sam went downtown and was fitted for his penguin suit. When he got back Anna had made sandwiches, stacking them high on a platter in the kitchen.

"Whoa, I'm starving," he reached for the sandwich, and she swatted his hand.

"Wait."

"Oh, is Grandma eating with us?"

"No, she's resting."

"What gives then?" he said trying to grab another sandwich.

"I want to talk to you about something."

"Okay, go." He grinned.

"Well, tonight might be a good night to let mom's ashes go to the sea."

Saying it was almost as hard as doing it.

Sam cleared his throat and heaved a sigh. "Yeah, I suppose so. Have you talked to Grandma about it?"

"Not yet. I wanted to hear your thoughts first."

Lucy stepped into the kitchen, her eyes resting on the plate of sandwiches. "Well, it looks like I came at the right time."

"You're like a little mouse, Grandma, we didn't hear you coming down the stairs."

Anna wasn't sure how much of the conversation her grandmother had been present for. "Are you hungry?" she asked.

Lucy stood behind Sam and placed her hands on his shoulders. Sam reached up and cupped his hand around hers.

"No thank you, honey." Lucy's eyes were moist. "Yes, I think tonight would be a fine night, to lay your mom to rest." Lucy choked up, as she leaned into Sam, wrapping one arm around the front of his chest. She seemed strong. Like nothing was amiss. Like her body wasn't dying. But Anna wasn't fooled.

"I was thinking sunset," Anna offered.

Looking up, Lucy moved toward the small Formica table. Anna joining her. "Your mom always loved the golden hour," Lucy replied softly.

"She and your grandpa, bathed in the sun's warm glow, would don their swimsuits and go for sunset swims in the sea." Lucy's heart swelled. She opened the door to her private gallery of the past. *Perfect*, she breathed. *Grace's final swim, with the sky a canvas of fire, a brilliant crown of light.*

"Sunset it is," Sam murmured, his hands reaching for Lucy and Anna's. Three hands, a three-strand cord, bound together and not easily broken.

CHAPTER TWENTY-NINE

A Mother's Wish

Lucy clung onto Sam's arm as they slowly, descended the uneven, water-warped steps toward the sand. The cancer kept her in a balancing act of pushing herself too hard or giving into her limitations. Her strength was a fickle thing, arriving in unpredictable waves. Some days, her lungs felt tight, each breath a struggle, and she couldn't manage without assistance. Other days, a strange sense of normalcy would settle over her, and she'd wonder if she had any cancer at all. Thankfully, today was one of the good days, a rare reprieve.

"I keep meaning to get these steps fixed." She adjusted her weight as she felt them slant and lean with the added weight of a second person.

"I've got you." Sam was now clutching her hand in his own, not hurrying her, but also wanting to get off as soon as possible.

"Ah here we are." Lucy looked down at her feet. Her toes were slightly curled. The sun- spots, from decades of sunshine, were now almost hidden under all the wrinkles. She let her feet sink into the soft sand, like a pair of slippers. She hadn't been down to her beach in weeks.

She relished the sights and sounds as they walked to Grace's favorite monkey puzzle tree, where it stood towering over the sand. It had been a precious marker for her family, and she hoped it would remain so.

"Let's go," she tugged Sam's arm. She was determined. She wanted to do this for Anna and Sam. But, mostly for Grace.

"Are you okay, Grandma?" Sam stopped; Anna was following from behind carrying the box with Grace's ashes.

"I'm fine, just a little tired."

Anna fell in step with them. Lucy caught her gaze and gave her a half smile. She wanted to be the steady one, able to help her grandkids say goodbye to their mother. They needed her.

A few more minutes and the golden hour would begin. Lucy knew this part of the day like her own name. She had sipped from its chalice for almost a century. Anna cradled the small box as three generations of Belltown's walked into the tide. Lucy, Grace, Anna, and Sam. Lucy felt the warm water run over her ankles. Anna stood tall. Next to her, she felt Sam's chest rise and fall.

The water had now reached the hem of Lucy's white, linen dress. As the tide went out, she felt it stick to her legs. Sam's rolled up Docker's were soaked through. They stood staring out, three arms linked, Lucy sandwiched between her two grandchildren.

"It feels good, doesn't it?" She looked up at Sam, grinning. His sandy blond hair, that he had let grow since he had been home, had streaks of sun bleached yellow, the same color she once had.

"Yeah, it does."

"Are you ready, Grandma?" Anna asked, meeting Lucy's gaze.

Lucy nodded and reached out her hands.

Anna gently handed her the urn, treating it with care, like a fragile crystal figurine. Lucy gripped it tightly between her hands. She wanted to go deeper, further out. The waves continued to roll in, but they seemed to have softened, their usual strength subdued. It was as though they, too, recognized the sacredness of the moment and were joining in quiet reverence.

Lucy felt a profound sense of release. Forgiveness had left its indelible mark on her life. Sam and Anna stood beside her as she lifted the box to her lips and placed a kiss on its side. "My baby," she murmured.

She lifted the lid off the box, and as she slowly bent over, she dipped it under the tide. The contents mixed with the sea and washed away. Lucy couldn't tell where the sand met the ashes as they collided. All around them, the yellow hues were blending with the orange, lighting up the sky in a brilliant display of color unlike anything Lucy had ever seen. She felt an arm wrap around her waist. It was Anna. Then another one, on her right side, there was Sam. Lucy's heart ached anew for their loss, for her own. But deep within, a quiet knowing settled. Though grief would always be a part of them, so too would joy. It was a profound concept, one that, even at her age, she was still learning to grasp: a cup overflowing with both joy and suffering, neither possible without the other. She rested in their embrace, knowing this gift—this reunion, this love—had been given to her, freely. It was a gift of Grace.

CHAPTER THIRTY

One More Miracle

"John Mark, can you believe this?" Anna asked, amazed by the turnout.

From all appearances the fundraising gala was a tremendous success.

"There are over three hundred people in attendance!" John Mark counted the last ticket, putting it into the wicker basket next to the money box.

"And I've already emptied this twice, we ran out of room, and I had to stash some of the cash in the office filing cabinet, where I could lock it up."

He was so excited; she thought his head might explode. The Naples Preservation Society donated the venue, champagne, and hors d' oeuvres, which allowed all remaining donations to go directly to the preservation of Old Blue. With her hands on her hips, Anna again surveyed the crowd. Many of the people were foreign to her. But, not to Lucy. She loved seeing Lucy surrounded by a crowd, Sam sitting next to her.

"I'm going to go and check on Grandma, can you hold down the fort?"

John Mark nodded, "only if you bring me back a piece of that chocolate torte."

"Easy."

She heard peals of laughter as she got closer to the small circle of people, squeezing in under a large banyan tree. One of the many shaded spots in the garden.

"And then I said, oh no you don't, and if you do, I'll chain myself to that tree." Lucy was retelling a story Anna had heard before.

"And you almost did." Someone piped in.

"Thankfully, I didn't have to. They decided not to tear down the theatre but instead raise the funds to improve it, and so it stands today, on Main Street."

"I hate to interrupt, but I wanted to see if the guest of honor was interested in any dessert?" It was a half-truth. Anna was worried about Lucy. This morning, she took a bad fall. Lucy would not let Sam take her to the emergency room. She acted like everything was normal, but Anna had learned Lucy's tics. Lucy was in pain.

"I won't let a silly thing like this keep me from tonight." She had scolded them.

They couldn't argue with her. And once they had arrived at the gala, she had made sure they hid her breathing machine behind her chair, covering it with a small scarf. Even if the tubes ran through her nose, Lucy would act like everything was completely normal. It was her way.

"Oooo, did I see a banana cream pie over there?" Lucy raised her head slightly, looking toward the dessert table.

"You did!" An older gentlemen stood up. "I made it this morning. I remembered it was your favorite. Remember at Deacon's

Creamery, when Mrs. Deacon made those banana creams, fresh every afternoon?"

"How could I ever forget," Lucy licked her lips.

"There's also a marionberry pie, Lucy." Sandy, who sat dutifully to Lucy's left, smiled.

"Oh, how does one choose?"

"How about a little bit of everything, Grandma?"

That was just like Sam, with his sweet tooth, to indulge.

"I will take one order of 'a little bit of everything' like my grandson suggests," Lucy chimed in.

All this activity gave Lucy a radiant glow. As Anna walked to the dessert table she turned around and glanced at Lucy again; it was as though she was soaking up the sweetness of friends, saying her small goodbyes in her own way. Anna didn't want to think about it. Tonight was supposed to be fun.

As she piled thin slices of pie, torte, and cookies onto a plate, she looked at John Mark. He looked so handsome. He cleaned up nicely when he had a shave and a haircut. And the tuxedo was an attractive addition to his polished look. He was helping a woman fill out paperwork to become a "friend of Old Blue." Anna knew, if not for John Mark's tireless dedication to her family home, it would have received the same fate as many other historic homes in Naples—which is a pile of rubble. He looked up and caught her staring at him. He waved and grinned. Her face turned the same shade of pink as the roses climbing the lattice behind him. She quickly waved and hurried back to Lucy and the group.

"Dessert's incoming," Sam declared, grateful the spotlight was now on Anna and no longer on him. He seized the moment to get up, and Anna watched him make his way to the dessert table.

Anna handed the plate to Lucy, and her eyes lit up. "I think I may devour each morsel on this plate."

Anna hoped she would. She was far too thin.

Anna listened as the women chatted, and watched Lucy bask in the warm glow of her old friends. She loved being Lucy's granddaughter. Lucy's desire for a send-off for Old Blue had materialized, though not as she had thought. It was no longer a farewell party, but a rescue mission. Anna had spared no effort, bringing out the Belltown china and a wealth of linens. "Great-Grandma Sundry's candlesticks, from Poland!" Lucy had exclaimed, her voice tinged with gratitude, when she noticed them displayed at the check-in table, flanking a framed black-and-white photo of Lucy and her parents, waving from the steps of Old Blue.

"Anna is responsible for all of this." Lucy waved her arm like she was scooping up a cloud.

"Grandma is being a little too generous; it was the work of many people."

Lucy dipped her fork into the cream atop the banana pie. She moved it around in her mouth and closed her eyes.

"This is delicious. I will never forget this taste."

Anna relaxed in the white plastic chair as the lively conversation resumed. Just that morning, Anna had discovered an elegant black evening dress tucked away in Lucy's closet, a full-length gown with fitted sleeves and pearl-studded wrists. Tonight was an occasion to shine. Sandy had even taken Lucy to the salon for a wash and set, resulting in a perfectly coiffed style with delicate strands framing her face. Lucy radiated energy, utterly stunning. Anna committed Lucy's features to memory; her grandmother the bell of the ball tonight. Her earlobes sparkled with her mother's diamond earrings as she turned her head and laughed. Anna found herself wishing for the one thing everyone desired: more time.

"Excuse me, Anna, I have something I want to show you," Julie Woodburn said, leaning over, her hand gently pressing on Anna's shoulder.

This must be important, Anna thought, *if the head of the Naples Preservation Society needs me.*

"Excuse me," she said, smiling as she stood. A few people glanced her way, but most were deep in conversation. Everyone, except Lucy. She gave Anna a knowing wink and blew her a small, affectionate kiss.

Anna followed Julie into the cottage.

"I know time is of the essence, so I had my accountant begin to tally some of the donations."

At the start of the evening, once the guests had arrived, Julie passionately described the plight of Old Blue to all in attendance, then made a bold request for generous donations. "You can write a check or fill out a pledge card at the table over there," she said, pointing to a small, folding table, draped in a crisp white tablecloth, on the cottage porch. Anna noticed people steadily approaching the table throughout the evening, assisted by John Mark or an NPS volunteer.

"Right through here," Julie said, leading Anna to a door, which appeared to be her office. "This is my sanctuary," Julie quipped with a knowing smile.

Julie sat behind her desk, pulling out a basket overflowing with cash and placing it before Anna.

Incredible, Anna thought. "Oh my gosh," Anna exclaimed, leaning forward and grabbing handfuls of hundreds and twenties.

Julie was beaming. "As of right now, we've surpassed $500,000!"

Anna gasped. A huge amount to raise in one evening. Yet, her heart sank. It wasn't enough.

She forced a smile, "Oh, that's wonderful, Julie," she would not rob Julie of the joy.

"And that's not all; I wanted to save the best for last."

Just maybe, Anna's wish had come true, and they had gotten the full amount.

Julie's face lit up like a full moon.

"Not only does the NPS want to match your total donation, but we have had an anonymous donor pledge an additional match to the night's total donation."

Anna was terrible with numbers. Where was Sam? He needed to compute this for her.

Julie was waiting for Anna's reaction.

"Yes, that is wonderful!" she exclaimed, still calculating the amount in her head.

Julie grabbed Anna's hands and began bouncing up and down in her chair, "Anna, that is two million dollars!"

Her shoulders sank again, it was a considerable amount, but still not the amount she needed.

Another let down.

"Wow, I can't wait to tell my grandmother. Julie, this is incredible." Julie stood and hugged Anna.

"Julie, you and your team have done so much, we are indebted to you!"

"Anna, what you are trying to do is admirable. And we will continue to do what we can to help you. Preserving the past has its place; don't let anyone tell you differently."

They heard the front door close. Sandy rushed in. "Honey, your grandma isn't looking so hot. I think it's time to take her home."

Anna thanked Julie again and ran out the door. Sandy followed close behind. John Mark and Sam were already beside Lucy, helping her stand.

"Hey, is everything okay?"

"Oh yes, I just had trouble catching my breath. Nothing new," Lucy said. Sam shook his head mouthing "she almost blacked out." They walked her to Sandy's sedan and practically lifted her in. As Anna buckled her, Lucy patted her hand, "But, as you can see, I am well-cared for. My knights in shining armor, rescued me again."

"Okay, let's get you home, party animal." Anna closed the door and waved at Jim, behind the steering wheel and Sandy in the back seat.

"We will follow shortly."

Anna watched them drive away. Lucy didn't have much time left, even if she wouldn't admit it. Anna knew. As Sam and John Mark broke tables down, Anna returned to the gala. Most guests were gone, a few danced under the stars. Anna resolved to keep the failure a secret from Lucy. The heartache might hasten her decline. She'd make Sam and John Mark promise. As far as anyone knew, Old Blue would live forever, a comfort for Lucy in her final days.

CHAPTER THIRTY-ONE

The Last Guest

At home, Lucy sat up in bed, a mound of pillows keeping her upright. The rented hospital bed had proved useful, and allowed her to be in the living room, so she could see the ocean. Sam and Anna had made sure it was as close as possible to the windows, if Lucy stretched her toes out, she could almost touch the wall.

Lucy's cancer came alive inside of her body, biting like a rabid dog. The constant fatigue was a heavy burden, but the loss of her mobility was a cruel blow. Her legs, once so strong, were now lifeless. She couldn't stand without assistance.

The sounds of her family filled the other room: Sandy, Jim, John Mark, Sam, and Anna.

They were doing what they believed was best for her, and she chose not to argue with their care decisions. She wanted to ease their worries, so she complied with everything, even the distasteful bedpan.

"Grandma, are you awake?" Anna asked, standing nervously beside Lucy, her hands twisting together.

"Yes, dear," Lucy answered.

Anna sat down on the edge of the bed. The girl was a ball of nerves. The past few days taking a toll on her. She had faced death before, and here she was facing it yet again, and so soon. It broke Lucy's heart.

"Let me look at you." Lucy reached out her hand to grasp Anna's.

Lucy loved looking at the girl, so much like Grace, yet distinctly different too.

The doctor left a few minutes ago, and by the look on Anna's face, delivering the news fell to the one who drew the last straw. Lucy hated that she had brought more grief upon her grandchildren. They had been through too much already. She had thought backwards and forwards, how to make her passing easier on them. She had already enlisted Jim and Sandy to be stand-in grandparents, and over the last few months, she had seen them both graciously rise to the occasion.

"Come here," Lucy opened her arms to hold her granddaughter. Even if she was a young woman, she was still able to be held. Especially now. Anna curled up next to Lucy and let her stroke her hair.

She began to sob. "Grandma, I'm sorry, I don't know how to do this."

Lucy shifted, turning as much as her position allowed, to face Anna. In Anna's eyes, Lucy saw only sorrow, a profound sense of defeat.

"You don't have to say a thing. I know." Her time was through. Her lungs were collapsing quickly.

Lucy held Anna. Sam was there. He laid his hand on Lucy's shoulder and Sandy stood on the other side of the bed. Her eyes were moist, holding a lifetime of shared history.

Anna sat up and looked into Lucy's eyes. "I just found you." Looking up at Sam, "we just found you." She laid her head on Lucy's chest. "You can't go yet."

Lucy's heart ached. She felt helpless. She wanted to fix this.

"Look at me, . . ." she lifted Anna's head up, and locked eyes with her. "Sam," she grabbed his hand.

"You two are strong, and I believe in you both." She pushed herself up in bed. "You come from strong people." She knew it deep down in her bones. "It's called Belltown grit. You come from a long line of strength and courage. As you keep that balanced with temperance and humility, things will work out, you will see."

Anna's eyes pleaded, "How are we going to manage without you? You're the pillar holding everything together." Lucy gently cupped Anna's face and smiled. "Don't sell yourself short, dear." She pointed to Anna's chest. "This," she tapped the place where her heart was, "is good, and you are more capable than you know." Lucy knew this from personal experience. "And never forget, you have a community around you, always."

"You have me." John Mark stood and placed his hands on Anna's shoulders.

"And me." Sam smiled.

"And us." Jim and Sandy spoke together.

"Well, it looks like you're covered." Lucy winked. The stab on her side caught her breath.

The pain had, at times, become unbearable. Everyone turned when a loud knock echoed from the back door.

"I'll get it," John Mark said, already heading toward the kitchen.

Anna was pulling the sheet up over Lucy as John Mark returned.

"Uh, Lucy, I think you need to take this," John Mark said hesitantly.

"Who is it, dear?" Lucy asked.

"Well, it's not a who, it's a lot of who's . . ." his voice trailed off as footsteps approached.

Lucy felt a flush of embarrassment, lying in bed in her pajamas with unwashed hair. She tried to smooth her hair with her fingers as the first person approached her bedside, followed by a second, and then a third.

"Shari!" Lucy said overjoyed. "Linda!"

They kept coming, filling the space before her bed. Some held vibrant flowers, others brought comforting baked goods and heartfelt cards. *What a beautiful sight,* Lucy thought.

"My goodness," Lucy exclaimed, her voice filled with delight. "What is all of this?"

She felt a surge of energy, the prior pain momentarily fading into the background of overwhelming love. Sandy leaned down and whispered gently in Lucy's ear, "News travels fast in a small town," her own voice choking up, "I believe they've all come to say goodbye."

Lucy understood.

"Lucy, thank you for all your contributions to this community," a man said, placing a bouquet of roses at the end of her bed.

"We'll carry on your legacy, Lucy," a woman, holding a small boy's hand, smiled warmly as she touched the edge of the blanket.

This poignant procession continued for almost an hour. It appeared as though the entire town had turned out. Anna and Sam watched in disbelief as a steady stream of people filed through the door.

Tears flowed down Lucy's face, creating warm droplets on her chin. Her life's work on display, in each person, all filling the room. It was why, when asked by Grace, Lucy couldn't bear to part with her home, because it was deeply intertwined with this place and its people. As the final visitor left, Sam handed Lucy a glass of water with a straw. Her heart was bursting, this was her final gift.

"Thank you for that, Grandma."

"Whatever do you mean, honey?"

"I understand more than I did. I can see why you couldn't leave. In fact, I think I am having that same problem." he chuckled.

Lucy sipped the water. It hurt to drink; she winced.

"Is there time for one more?"

Lucy knew that voice. She had always known that voice.

"Only if he brought me a banana cream pie." She croaked.

"Grandpa?" John Mark seemed surprised.

Lucy wasn't. When he left last time, she saw a changed man. She knew he would be back.

"John Mark." He nodded as he came around to the foot of the bed.

"Randall, I would like you to meet Grace's children. This is Sam, and this is Anna."

Both extended their hands toward the man who had made it his life's work to destroy anything related to the Belltown name. They nodded but nothing more.

Randall cleared his throat and faced Lucy.

"I couldn't live with myself if I didn't come by and see you. Just one more time."

"I've wasted a lot of time chasing smoke, and I've hurt a lot of people in the process."

He turned around and looked at John Mark.

"This house and land were never meant to belong to me or to any other person for that matter. And it has taken me a lifetime to see that."

He reached into his pocket and pulled out a small, folded piece of paper. He opened it and handed it to Lucy. It was a check. Lucy squinted her eyes, but she couldn't quite make it out.

"Anna, honey, please tell me what this says." Anna scooted next to Lucy and looked at the check.

"Oh my gosh," she almost fell off the bed, but Sam caught her in time.

He leaned in and looked at the check. He looked at Mr. Gordon, his eyes the size of saucers.

"Grandma!" Sam yelled.

Lucy didn't need to ask. Somehow, she knew it was the money. It was the remaining amount required to secure the house.

Anna sat frozen on the bed next to Lucy.

Out of the depths of Lucy's soul came an earth-shattering laugh. Then Randall began to laugh. John Mark stood unaware of what was transpiring. He probably had never heard his grandfather laugh before. He stood over Anna and turned his head sideways to read the check. "What?" He asked, confusion on his face.

He looked at his grandfather, "this is a check for thirty million dollars."

"I'm glad you have finally taken to the numbers, my boy." Randall stood with his arms crossed, he winked at Lucy, the two sharing an understanding.

"This is crazy!" Sam had grabbed Anna and was spinning around in circles, a sort of ring-a-round the rosy. John Mark stood dumbfounded and speechless. Sandy and Jim stood arm-in-arm, Sandy with tears streaming down her face.

While the room buzzed with elation and rejoicing, Lucy reached a hand out toward Randall.

"Thank you," she whispered.

"I'm gonna miss you," he replied, his voice thick with emotion.

"Take care of the kids," she said, her gaze locking with his. A silent understanding, and deep-rooted appreciation, passed between them.

"You have my word," Randall promised.

John Mark walked over to his grandfather and extended his hand. His grandfather grabbed it and shook it, then pulled him into a hug.

Releasing him, he put his hand on John Mark's shoulder, "if you need more than that amount, ask."

"I can't believe this." John Mark laughed, shaking his head in bewilderment.

"Your dad tied up the paperwork. I couldn't change the deed. But that doesn't mean I can't give you the money," he said with a sly grin on his face.

Lucy watched the two of them, from her post, propped on pillows in her hospital bed and as she did her vision began to blur. She looked at Randall, but it was Paul she saw. She knew her eyes were deceiving her, playing tricks in these final moments. Randall had just shed fifty years, his face morphing into the baby-faced Paul of her youth. *Her* Paul stood there, framed by the light streaming through the windows, smiling at her.

As she smiled back, a tingling sensation spread through her hand. The pain taking her breath away. She heard Anna and John Mark laughing over something, their joy contagious.

"It's a miracle!" Sandy's voice caused Lucy to turn. The pain slowly moved up her arm, now unbearable. She remained silent. Sandy looked at her, a wide grin.

"We did it!" Sandy's voice, brimming with triumph, rang out as she joined John Mark and Randall. They all chattered excitedly, their words a jumble to Lucy's ears. But she didn't need to hear the specifics; their body language spoke volumes. They were at ease with each other, comfortable, like old friends once again reunited.

Then as if connected by an invisible thread, Anna, Sam, Sandy, Jim, John Mark, and Randall, her family, turned toward her. She met each of their gazes, a wave of love washing over her. Her eyelids felt heavy, so heavy. *A lady never overstays her welcome,* Mama's voice echoed in her memory. *One last look.* Yes, it was time. Time for her to take her leave.

CHAPTER THIRTY-TWO

Together Again

EPILOGUE

Anna couldn't believe it. Old Blue had been open for only a few short months, and it was a hit! People were coming from everywhere—across the country, even from Canada and Ireland! They decided to begin the renovations a few weeks after Lucy's passing. It was what she would have wanted. The restoration had begun, and with Randall's help, the house had breezed through the inspection and historic preservation process. Stan Gordon's lawsuit fell to the ground, leaving him empty handed.

Sam and Anna maintained the property alongside John Mark. Sandy, Jim and Randall, along with a handful of devoted volunteers, could be seen milling about the grounds daily. Sandy graciously gave bi-weekly tours of the gardens and house. And Randall had become one of the most resolute board members and advocates for preserving the home and grounds.

"Okay, are you ready?"

Anna turned to her steadfast companions, her family: Sam, Jim, Sandy, John Mark, and Randall.

"After you," John Mark said, placing a gentle hand on Anna's back, guiding her through the door.

Stepping onto the porch, Anna saw the assembled crowd. The lawn was filled with people, both familiar and new, gathered closely together. They had come to honor Lucy's memory. After Lucy passed, Randall had wisely suggested, "I think she'd want the house ready before the town arrives, to show it at its best." He was right. And so they had waited, worked tirelessly, and prepared with care. Now, the moment had arrived.

Anna gazed out at the lawn, where hundreds of people had gathered. She stood on the top step and smiled warmly. "Welcome, everyone. We are so grateful you are here. Today, we celebrate the remarkable woman we all knew and loved, Lucy Belltown Wright." She swallowed the lump in her throat.

"If you would please follow me, as we make our way to the sea."

Anna took a deep breath and cradled the small wooden box as she walked down the steps. The crowds stepped back, making a path, some nodded their heads as she passed. Men removed their hats. She reached the steps, she hoped her grandma was watching as she confidently walked down each one. Thankfully, John Mark took it upon himself to fix the broken-down stairs the day after Old Blue was approved for the National Historic Home status.

Barefoot, she felt the cool sand under her feet. The crowd followed and filed in behind her.

She handed Sam the carved wooden box, as she reached into her jean pocket for the words she had to share. She was not a public speaker. But she owed this to her grandmother.

Even if her stomach was tied in knots.

She was a Belltown and Belltown's were brave. She looked up at the smiling faces, young and old, standing barefoot on the sand. These were Lucy's people.

"Thank you for coming today. Grandma would have loved this."

She held the hastily scribbled paper, scrunched up in her hand in case she needed a cheat sheet. "My brother and I want to thank you for coming," she repeated. *I don't know how I'm going to get through this*, she thought.

She looked at Sam, her eyes pleading.

"You got this, sis," he whispered.

Looking around, she met the gazes of her community, the people she now considered her own. Her chosen family. A deep sense of peace settled over her as they smiled back.

"Home," she continued, "this is where Grandma felt most alive, at peace, and content. It's also, a place that held grief, pain, and sadness. Home isn't just a house. It's people. It's stories. It's where you come from. Home can be complicated, but it belongs to all of us. I think the message my Grandmother would want us to share today is this: don't run away from home, let it be the place you run to. And when home hurts you, learn to forgive it. Forgiveness is what brought Sam and me home. And when you're lost, or don't know where to begin, start here: Home."

A few "amens" and "yeses" drifted from the crowd, a sense of quiet affirmation washing over her as she tucked the paper into her pocket. *It's over*, she thought, turning to face the ocean.

As they had done with Grace, Anna and Sam lowered the box toward the water, but before it could touch the surface, a sudden wind swept in, lifting the cinders in a dance, a fleeting spiral before they drifted into the sea.

Anna glanced at Sam, a hint of amusement in her eyes.

"I guess she wanted to do it her own way."

They stood side-by-side, sharing a peaceful silence, simply being present in the moment. She squeezed her brother's hand. *I'm so glad he stayed*, Anna thought. Despite his dedication to his research, Sam's love for surfing was undeniable and what better place to be then right on the beach. And, she had to admit, it was a fortunate coincidence that he could continue his studies of sea currents and ocean creatures at the aquatic base in nearby Fort Myers. She heard the crowd slowly making their way back to the house for the light refreshments. Eventually the beach was empty.

"Hey, you, okay?"

It was John Mark. He came back down the steps. She was glad to see him. He hugged her and rested his chin on top of her head.

"I'll see you guys up there," Sam grinned at her as he walked away.

"You know, somehow I think my mom knew." Anna said, looking at John Mark.

"Knew what?"

"That we would need this."

She looked up from below where she stood and saw Old Blue, standing tall. This was her home. These were her people.

Taking John Mark's hand, Anna started toward the steps. She paused, turning. Two women in white sundresses and straw sun hats walked down the beach toward the pier, their backs to her. She watched them, noticing how they occasionally bent to pick something up.

"Huh," she murmured, shaking her head.

Just then, they turned, smiling and waving. Anna's heart leaped. She knew them.

"What do you see?" John Mark asked.

"This is going to sound crazy, but . . ." A wave crashed, enveloping the women in mist. When it cleared, they were gone.

Anna laughed. He'd never believe her. But she knew.

He nudged her, puzzled. She smiled at him as she clutched his hand and started walking toward Old Blue.

One last look at the beach. She knew they were home.

Author's Note

The breathtaking beauty of Naples, Florida, first struck me with its azure Gulf waters meeting the dazzling white sands. During one long walk down the beach with my mother and sister, we encountered a massive blue house set on expansive grounds. Unlike the numerous new constructions and comparatively large and imposing mansions nearby, this house exuded a sense of history and welcome. Even then, nearly ten years ago, I felt its story. That house, named White Sands, had belonged to the same family for almost a century, a fact I later discovered. This book draws heavily from the true evolution of Naples, a town that has undergone notable change. Yet, a determined group has consistently strived to safeguard its historical heart. It is a magical place with tales waiting to be heard. When you visit, I hope you'll see beyond the contemporary grandeur and remember the generations who lived and toiled here. May its charm resonate with you as deeply as it does with me.

Acknowledgments

It truly takes a village to bring a book to life, and my gratitude runs deep. First, thank you to Jeff Schlesinger and the incredible team at Barringer Publishing, who championed my manuscript and skillfully guided me to delve deeper.

To my cherished "first readers"—my dear friends Emily Jooste, Sarah Sanderson, Hillary Gaines, Mrs. Orletta Evoniuk and Benjamin Norens—thank you for embracing my vulnerable early drafts with such kindness and unwavering encouragement. Your belief fueled my persistence.

Amanda Claire, you were a creative comrade from the very beginning. Holding babies in arms, we dared to dream of bringing our visions to life. Thank you for that early spark and continued support. Lauren Shea, thank you for seeing potential in my initial blog posts, planting the seed that I could indeed write something substantial.

To my steadfast tribe—the friends and family who continually push, love, and listen to my endless updates and ideas: Katie Dickey, Emily Hall, Kat Hussain, Jenny Hernandez, Aunt Pat, Jessica Eggen, and my wonderful siblings, Benji, Kandice, and Desi—your unwavering support has been my bedrock.

And to my mom, who declared me a writer long ago and explained after my first rejection—"not everyone will see your potential right away, don't stop, keep going." Those words have kept me going.

A heartfelt 'thank you' to my remarkable writing group. Your camaraderie, insightful feedback, and the way you inspire me to refine my craft have meant the world. Thank you again for embracing me and my humble words.

To the dedicated individuals on the ground in Naples who generously shared their knowledge: a special thank you to the amazing Elaine Reed, former President of the Naples Historical Society, for her tireless work preserving the area's rich history. Anne Slade, thank you for providing the invaluable missing photograph of the original "Old Blue." And to everyone at The Historic Palm Cottage, your commitment to safeguarding the past for future generations is deeply appreciated. Thank you to the wonderful docent who patiently answered countless questions during my first visit.

To my dear readers, thank you for opening your hearts to my story. This book is a piece of my soul, and it is my sincere hope that you find goodness and truth within its pages.

And to my extraordinary husband, thank you for being my first reader, navigating its messy beginnings with such love. And after reading the first draft that I reluctantly handed you, replying with, "So, when are we publishing it?" will forever be etched in my heart. You are my greatest champion, and I love sharing this life with you. What's next?

Colossions 3:17

www.ingramcontent.com/pod-product-compliance
Lightning Source LLC
Chambersburg PA
CBHW030645020726
47493CB00006B/1885